A CRY IN THE NIGHT

JESSICA DANIEL 15

KERRY WILKINSON

ALSO BY KERRY WILKINSON

The Andrew Hunter series

SOMETHING WICKED | SOMETHING HIDDEN |
SOMETHING BURIED

Standalone novels

TEN BIRTHDAYS | TWO SISTERS

THE GIRL WHO CAME BACK | LAST NIGHT

THE DEATH AND LIFE OF ELEANOR PARKER

THE WIFE'S SECRET | A FACE IN THE CROWD | CLOSE
TO YOU

The Jessica Daniel series

LOCKED IN | VIGILANTE

THE WOMAN IN BLACK | THINK OF THE CHILDREN

PLAYING WITH FIRE | THICKER THAN WATER

BEHIND CLOSED DOORS | CROSSING THE LINE

SCARRED FOR LIFE | FOR RICHER, FOR POORER

NOTHING BUT TROUBLE | EYE FOR AN EYE

SILENT SUSPECT | THE UNLUCKY ONES

Silver Blackthorn

RECKONING | RENEGADE | RESURGENCE

Other

DOWN AMONG THE DEAD MEN

NO PLACE LIKE HOME

ONE

Samuel strained for the alarm clock and tapped the button on top. There was the familiar plasticky clunk and then the emotionless male voice cut through the silence.

'It is twelve ten a.m. and forty-one seconds.'

A little after midnight? Was that it? He'd barely been asleep.

Samuel reached for the alarm one more time, slightly misjudging the distance from the bed to his nightstand and fumbling across the glossy front. He slid his finger over the familiar groove on the side and then pressed the button once more.

'It is twelve ten a.m. and fifty-two seconds.'

Why was he awake?

Samuel tucked his arm back underneath the warmth of the covers and then he heard it.

Footsteps outside his room.

Not his mother's.

He knew the delicacy of how she walked around the apartment, especially when it was late at night. She'd been in her slippers when he went to bed anyway – and this person was wearing something with harder soles. The mystery person was heavier, too.

Samuel pressed his tongue to the top of his mouth and then clucked it down into place. He did it four times in quick succession.

Click-click-click-click.

Four more, a little quicker this time, turning from side to side. His room was as it should be: the nightstand by the bed, the bookshelf in the corner, the pair of wardrobes on the opposite side and the clothes hamper by the door. That was it. He didn't want any extra furniture because that would mean more things to process.

Click-click-click-click-click-click.

Definitely nothing else in the room. No*body* else.

And yet the footsteps were still moving around in the hallway outside his door. More than one set. More than one person. Neither were his mother's.

Samuel spun his legs out of the bed, losing concentration for a moment and clipping his knee on the corner of the nightstand. He winced but gritted his teeth and hauled himself out of the bed. He moved towards the door one step at a time, an arm outstretched, still clicking with his tongue.

He could hear a man's voice, the words muffled by the wall but the harsh, hard tone clear. Samuel pressed his head against the door, ear resting on the smooth wood. It sounded as if the man had moved away from the hall and was now in the kitchen. His shoes squeaked against the floor.

'...Where's the money?'

A tingle rippled up Samuel's spine, tickling his neck. Money? What money? Why did the man want money?

He heard his mother trying to reply, but there was a gasp in the middle of her sentence.

A sob.

Samuel fumbled the door handle and faltered into the hall,

one arm still outstretched, turning towards the voices. His cane was in his bedroom and he couldn't go back for it now. It was silent in the hall, except for his rapid rat-a-tat of tongue clicks.

His mother was pressed against the fridge and there was someone tall standing close to her. The figure shifted slightly, shoes squeaking.

'Who's that?' the squeaky-shoe man hissed. It was the same man who'd asked about money.

'My son.'

Samuel's knees wobbled at the sound of his mother's crumbling voice. He straightened himself and stepped towards her, feet cold on the wooden floor, trying to be as imposing as he could.

Click-click-click-click-click-click-click.

He turned from side to side, firing off another barrage of tongue clucks. There was someone else standing next to the kitchen counter by the toaster. The second figure was shorter and moved towards Samuel.

'Stop clicking,' he said harshly.

'It's how he sees,' Samuel's mother replied.

Click-click-click.

Samuel turned to face the second man. He was only a little taller than Samuel and stank of something Samuel hadn't smelt before. He never forgot smells.

'He's blind,' Samuel's mother added. She was pleading. Terrified.

Samuel lunged forward, trying to get to his mum, but the man by the counter snagged him around the neck, wrenching him backwards and strangling him with the collar of his pyjama top. Samuel flailed, lashing out with both hands, kicking with his feet and screaming for all he was worth.

Which wasn't much.

The man clamped a hand across his mouth and yanked Samuel towards the countertop, pinning his arms to his sides.

The smell, whatever it was, was all over the man's hands. It burned Samuel's throat, made him cough. He tried to click, to get a sense of where everyone now was in the kitchen, but the hand was too tight across his mouth.

'What d'you mean it's how he sees?'

The man closest to the fridge was talking. He had a slight accent that Samuel couldn't place. Sort of like the people who lived around them, but with a suggestion of something more. Samuel had lost all sense of what was going on. His breathing was becoming shorter and shallower, that once-familiar feeling of knowing a panic attack was near.

'He clicks with his tongue,' Samuel's mother said. 'He sees with the soundwaves. It's complicated.'

She spoke calmly but Samuel knew every tiny intonation of her voice. He could tell when she was happy or sad, angry, tired, or trying to do too many things at once.

He knew when she lied – or at least he thought he did. Sometimes he'd let on, other times not.

He definitely knew when she was scared – and, right now, she was as frightened as he'd ever heard her.

The man holding Samuel loosened his grasp ever so slightly, enough to let him breathe more comfortably. Samuel wanted to fight but his arms were still clamped tight to his sides and he now had little idea of where everyone was. He was trying to remember the picture his mind had painted; his mother by the fridge, the man with the squeaky shoes standing close by – but the image was already fading.

'We know you stole it,' the man holding Samuel said.

'Stole what?' his mother replied.

'You know what we're talking about.'

'I promise I don't.' She gasped, trying to keep her voice level, thinking of Samuel. 'Take anything you want – but please let Samuel go. He can't see. You're scaring him.'

The man's grip loosened even further and Samuel couldn't

resist the urge. He spewed a stream of clicks into the room, but the man's fingers were too close to his top lip for him to build up a proper image of where everyone was. The hand quickly clamped around him once more.

The man with the squeaky shoes spoke next: 'We know you've got money. Where is it?'

'I'll—'

Something skidded across the tiled floor and then there was a clang. It sounded like one body colliding with another but Samuel's senses were so clouded that he couldn't process it all.

Whump!

From nowhere, there was a bone-gnarling crunch. The type of noise that Samuel had never heard before, even though he knew impulsively that it was the thud of a human skull on something solid.

He suddenly realised the man had released him – but it made no difference because his body wasn't obeying. Samuel was on his knees, feeling the cold of the floor through the thin material of his pyjama bottoms. The reflex was to cluck his tongue, to find out where everybody was, and yet he couldn't, because he already knew.

There was silence except for the breathing of the man nearby, perhaps his own as well.

'Shit.' The squeaky-shoe man had backed towards the hallway.

The other man was moving away as well. 'What did you do that for?'

'I thought she was going for the knife.'

'What knife?'

'The one by the fridge!'

The two voices were edging further into the hallway, closer to the door. Samuel could hear them moving, sense their nerves and panic. Everything had changed.

Click-click-click.

The image swarmed into Samuel's head. He didn't want to believe it.

Click-click-click.

Samuel crawled across the floor, tracing the slim grooves of the tile pattern with his fingers. Errant flecks of grit scratched at his palms.

And then he reached her.

Gloopy liquid was pooling on the floor, sticking to Samuel's fingers as he stretched.

Click-click-click.

'Mum?'

The word caught in Samuel's throat. His mother's skin was greasy with sweat, her hair matted to her forehead. She didn't try to speak, didn't roll towards him or groan under her breath. She didn't move at all. The liquid was oozing through her hair.

The *blood* was oozing through her hair.

'What do we do with the kid?'

Samuel froze as the man with the squeaky shoes spoke.

'What d'you mean?'

'Well—'

'Let's go. It's not like he's seen us, is it?'

TWO

Despite the seriousness of the situation, Detective Inspector Jessica Daniel was finding it hard to look anywhere other than at the teenager's school tie. The fat part was nestled inside the kid's shirt, with the thin flap of stripy yellow and blue poking out the front. The knot was a marvel of human strength, wrenched tight to the size of a small walnut, hanging low below his collar. It had been the same at her school all those years ago: if the great oppressors were to insist upon a uniform, then the least teenagers could do was to undermine it by turning the school tie into something ridiculous.

'I thought he was just some homeless bloke,' Kareem said, half turning to where the ambulance was easing out into traffic.

The spinning lights doused the roadside in a gloomy blue glow as the ambulance weaved ahead of a builder's van and accelerated into the distance.

Jessica turned back to face the boy. 'Where was he?' she asked.

Kareem pointed to the hedge that lined the golf course. There was a shallow ditch underneath filled with fast-food wrappers and various other scraps of rubbish. A pair of uniformed officers were dutifully standing guard. Dutifully in the sense that one of them was checking his phone while the other blathered on about something he'd watched on television the previous night.

'I'm going to be late for school,' Kareem said. He shuffled from one foot to the other, edging towards the other side of the road while he scratched at his patka. He had wispy bits of bumfluff stuck to his chin, like someone had drawn it on.

'I'll deal with your school,' Jessica replied, thinking it was one more thing she'd have to remember to do. She wasn't even supposed to be here on the side of the road. She'd been merrily driving to the station, definitely *not* singing along to eighties classics, and then spotted the ambulance. She could have driven on, *should* have, but then she'd have spent the rest of the day wondering what was going on.

Kareem was shuffling towards the crossing. 'I'm already on a warning for being late,' he added. 'One more and Parkes will put me in detention. Then my dad will find out and he'll—'

Jessica placed a hand on Kareem's shoulder and he stopped talking. It felt like the instinctive thing to do. 'You've done a really kind thing,' she said. 'Not many people would stop to help, let alone hang around and wait for an ambulance. I'll make sure I tell your teacher what a credit you are. Your dad, too, if you want.'

Kareem bit his lip and forced back a flattered smile. 'Right...'

Jessica nodded towards the cut-through next to the hedge. 'So, you were walking along the alley to school and you saw what you thought was a homeless bloke...?'

He nodded. 'Right. I saw him lying by the hedge. He was sort of hidden because of the long grass. I'd walked past him and then thought I should probably check he was, y'know... all right.'

'Then what happened?'

Kareem gulped. 'I thought it was mud or oil or something on the grass, then when I got closer, I realised it was blood. He was facing the hedge and I touched his shoulder, tried to roll him. I asked if he was okay, but he just sort of… flopped back. His eyes were closed. That's when I called 999.'

Jessica turned to the verge once more. A paramedic's car was parked a little down the road and the driver was chatting to the uniformed officer who wasn't on his phone. She could see the darkened smear on the trampled grass.

'Did you move anything?' she asked.

'Only him. I just waited – then the ambulance showed up, then the police car, then you. I thought he was… y'know… I didn't want to touch the body. They said he was still breathing.'

Jessica made sure one of the uniformed officers had the kid's details and then dug into her pocket for a business card. She scribbled her mobile number on the back and handed it over, telling Kareem to call her directly if he had any trouble with the school.

'Who is he?' Kareem asked, nodding towards the ditch.

A shake of the head. 'I have no idea.'

'Do you get a lot of men in hedges?'

Jessica took a moment, thinking about it. 'Too many,' she said.

Kareem bit his bottom lip, considering whether to ask something and then spitting it out: 'The blood was around the back of his head. It looked like he'd been whacked with a bat or something. Did someone try to kill him?'

Jessica turned from the verge to Kareem and back again. 'I don't know that either, I'm afraid.'

He nodded and then heaved his schoolbag higher on his shoulder. 'Can I go, then?'

'Yeah, sorry… you head off. Someone might need to take a

proper statement from you later today or tomorrow, but you did a good thing this morning.'

Kareem shrugged modestly, half turned before Jessica spoke again.

'You probably saved his life,' she added.

His lips were tight but he nodded once more, bobbed on the spot, unsure of how to reply. What was there to say? He mumbled a 'right' and then his phone was out of his pocket and he was away. He jabbed the button on the nearby pelican crossing and then walked across the road, not waiting for the flashing green man.

Jessica waited until Kareem was out of sight and then shuffled over to the uniformed officers and the paramedic.

'Late one or early?' she asked, weary smile and all.

The paramedic laughed and then yawned as if to emphasise the point. He flapped a hand in front of his mouth. 'Late. Gotta get the car back, then I'm done for the night.'

She nodded at the patch of blood. 'What d'you reckon?'

A long intake of breath. 'Someone's given the poor bastard a right kicking. Left him for dead. Good job it wasn't a cold one last night.'

The Scene of Crime team would be along in the coming hours to see if they could find anything – perhaps establish when he'd been left in the ditch – but whatever they found would be limited because the scene had been tainted. The mystery man's health was the first priority and Kareem and the paramedics had already trodden across the patch of grass.

One of the uniformed officers handed across an evidence bag. 'He did have this in his pocket. No wallet or anything.'

Jessica took it, peering through the transparent plastic to the driving licence within. She scanned the front and then flipped it around to check the back.

'Wasn't it a white guy they took away?'

The paramedic and both uniformed officers nodded.

She held up the driving licence. 'This is for a thirty-five-year-old Asian bloke.'

Three shrugs and a yawn from the paramedic.

'Was there anything else?' she asked.

'Not that we found,' the officer replied.

'He had a tattoo on his arm,' the paramedic added. 'A lizard or something like that.'

Jessica eyed the licence one more time and then tucked it away. A battered body carrying someone else's ID was a really good way to start the day.

She took a step away, ready to head back to her car, when her curiosity got the better of her.

'Do you think he'll live?' she asked.

The paramedic clasped his lips tightly, fought back another yawn. 'Honestly? With the kicking he's taken, I'm surprised he was still alive to begin with. Someone's battered him in the back of the head, there are bruises all over his back and arms, defensive marks on his hands. Face was swollen up like a balloon.'

Jessica sighed. She didn't get a chance to reply because her hip started to buzz. More precisely, the radio on her hip. She checked her watch and sighed once more – it wasn't even half eight.

THREE

It was a porcelain cat that nearly sent Jessica tumbling for the first time that day. She headed into Deborah Wareing's hallway and then immediately clipped her foot on the metre-high monstrosity, almost toppling both it and her to the floor. Jessica just caught herself on the post at the base of the stairs, steadying the cat with her knees and regaining her balance in time so that the homeowner didn't notice anything was wrong.

Deborah closed the front door, clinking the bolt into place and then turned. 'Sorry about the mess,' she said, not sounding that sorry. 'I really need to get it all cleaned up, especially with Samuel here now. I don't know where it all comes from.'

She held up her hands to indicate the cluttered hallway and Jessica couldn't disagree. As well as the cat, there was a rack of shoes, mirrors on opposite walls reflecting each other, two welcome mats, a pair of recycling boxes and a hat stand.

A hat stand? Who had so may hats they actually needed a stand?

'I'll take you on through,' Deborah added. She tucked a greasy thread of dark hair behind her ear and then pressed a hand to the door opposite the stairs. She didn't push, but stepped away, biting her lip.

'Do you know about Samuel?' she asked.

'What about him?'

'He's blind.'

Jessica blinked, cocked her head.

They stared at each other until Deborah added: 'I assumed someone would've told you...?'

Jessica would have assumed the same thing – but then she wasn't entirely surprised. She'd been sent off to talk to a witness, so why would it be of any use to tell her that the witness couldn't actually see?

As Jessica considered who would be first in line for a bollocking, Deborah continued speaking: 'It's just... he's not like any blind kid you might have met before. He does this thing with his tongue. I'm not sure I understand it myself, but he clicks.'

Jessica took a moment, unsure if she'd misheard. 'He clicks?'

Deborah clucked her tongue a couple of times. 'Like that,' she said. 'Evie, his mum, said it's how he sees. Something to do with soundwaves. I guess I'm used to it now, but it can be a bit, well...' she licked her lips, searching for the word, lowering her voice to a whisper, '...unnerving.'

Jessica found herself scratching her head, not entirely sure what to make of it all. She'd been told a woman had died in her own home and that her son had been there. Nobody mentioned anything about blindness, clicking, soundwaves, or anything else that might have been sodding important.

Deborah nodded towards the door, picking up on Jessica's confusion. She continued in a whisper. 'I can't explain it properly, but Evie said he was born with a cloudy cornea. His eyes are all white. You'll see. He had two different operations when he was younger...' Deborah spun a finger close to her forehead, trying to weave out the words, '"corneal trans-plants", I think – something like that. I guess it didn't work.' She leant an elbow on the banister and started to play with her hair. 'Have you been to Evie's place? They wouldn't let me in.'

'Not yet,' Jessica replied. 'People are there now trying to get information.'

'Shouldn't take them long – she lives in a block of four, but the other three flats are empty.'

Jessica figured she'd find out for herself soon enough. 'A family liaison officer will be here very soon to help with Samuel,' she said. 'I was hoping I could talk to him first.'

'They told me hours ago that a support officer would be coming...?'

Jessica tried not to wince but her face must've told the story because Deborah started to nod.

'Oh, right... cuts and all that. Can't get the staff. Same everywhere. I do some work for the council here and there.'

Jessica smiled weakly, neither confirming nor denying. 'How is he?' she asked.

'Samuel? Quiet. He's not been crying, or anything like that. Poor kid. How are you supposed to react when you find your mum's body?' Deborah gulped. 'Do you know what happened?'

Jessica shook her head. 'Not yet. It's still really early. How well did you know Evie?'

'We worked together and I did the odd bit of babysitting when she had a shift she didn't want to turn down.'

'Is that at the council?'

'We do agency stuff – whatever we can get. Mainly it's cleaning.' She shifted her weight from one foot to the other and then nodded towards the door. 'C'mon – I'll introduce you to Samuel.'

Deborah pushed it open and led Jessica into what turned

out to be the living room. As soon as the door was open, Jessica heard the clicking; a quickfire drumbeat that made her jump.

The boy in the armchair had short dark hair and was wearing a Teenage Mutant Ninja Turtles T-shirt. His milky white eyes beamed across the room, snaring her on the spot. There was the merest hint of blue behind the cream, but Jessica shivered nonetheless. She couldn't stop herself. She'd not seen anything like it in person.

Samuel's mouth was partially open, baring his front teeth as he fired a series of tongue clicks in her direction.

'Samuel, this is Detective Inspector Daniel,' Deborah said.

Jessica stepped forward, hand outstretched instinctively before she caught herself, realising how stupid it was to offer her hand to a blind kid. Before she could retract it, Samuel took her palm in his, clicking twice more and then shaking her hand.

'Hello, I'm Samuel,' he said. He was perfectly calm, although far more polite than many of the teenagers Jessica came across.

'Jessica,' she replied as he released her.

From what she'd been told, Jessica knew Samuel was fourteen. He somehow managed to look both older and younger at the same time. There was the hint of acne around the corner of his mouth and the awkward, elbowy gait of the way he was sitting. That was coupled with the intrinsic vulnerability of a boy who was sitting with a white cane at his side.

'The inspector wants to ask you a few questions,' Deborah added.

'Okay.'

'I'll be in the kitchen – but you can call for me at any time.'

There was a laptop on Samuel's thighs and he snapped the lid closed, removing a pair of earphones and curling them up before tucking them into the side of the seat next to him. 'Thank you.'

Deborah hung in the doorway, apparently unsure what to say. When she realised Jessica was watching her, she spun and disappeared, closing the door behind them. Jessica was hovering nervously in the middle of the room.

'You can sit down,' Samuel said.

'Right… sorry. Is there anywhere that's easier for you?'

'My ears work.'

Jessica apologised again, but there was a curious smile on Samuel's face. She couldn't quite read it – but then the poor kid's mother had died mere hours before. It didn't feel like he was angry at her.

She perched on the edge of the sofa and Samuel clicked four or five times in rapid succession.

'You don't like my clicks, do you?' he said.

'It's not that… I'm not used to it – that's all.'

'It's called echolocation,' he said. 'The click bounces back and I know how far away things are.' The smile grew slightly. 'You can google it if you don't believe me.'

'I believe you.'

There was a moment or two of silence before Jessica realised that she was the adult here; Samuel had an unerring confidence about him.

'I know it might be hard,' Jessica started, 'but can you tell me what happened last night?'

Samuel turned slightly, staring her down with the endless white eyes. 'I didn't see much,' he said, before haw-hawing to himself.

At first Jessica wasn't sure what to make of it. She squinted to take him in. It was only then she realised the problem was all hers. She'd spoken to witnesses and victims in the past who behaved in the same way after being involved in something traumatic. Some fell to pieces; others were blank and said little; occasionally people joked because the alternative was a deep descent of darkness. It was a perfectly normal coping mechanism. If Samuel hadn't been blind, Jessica wouldn't have thought twice at his behaviour.

He breathed through his nose, firing off a quick trio of clicks that were there and gone so quickly that Jessica barely registered them before he started to speak. 'There were two men,' he said.

'I'm so sorry at having to ask this – but how do you know there were two?'

'I heard them,' Samuel said. 'Saw them, too, if you like. Not like *you* see them but...' He held both arms out, palms up. Seeing for him was something different to the way Jessica could see. There was little point in trying to force him to explain.

'Were there definitely only two?' she added.

'Definitely. They were asking about money.'

'They asked your mother about money?' Jessica clarified.

'They woke me up. One had squeaky shoes. He said, "Where's the money?"'

'What did your mum say?'

'Not much because I went into the hallway and they saw me. They said they didn't know I'd be there, then one of them grabbed me.'

'Can you, er... describe him?'

Jessica wasn't sure whether it was a stupid question but Samuel didn't hesitate. 'He was a bit taller than me and smelt of something I didn't know. Like smoke but different. Sort of spicier.'

It took Jessica a moment or two to clock it. She almost blurted out 'marijuana', before realising that, if Samuel didn't know what it was, saying the word wouldn't change things.

'Was there anything else about him?'

'The man by the fridge was tall, like the height of the fridge. He had squeaky shoes but was too far away. The one who grabbed me though... he had a limp when he walked away.'

'You can recognise a limp?'

'It sounds different. If you had your eyes closed, you'd probably hear that someone was dragging their leg a bit, wouldn't you?'

Jessica closed her eyes involuntarily and then opened them again. She wasn't convinced she would.

'What were their accents like?' she asked.

'Normal. Like the people around here.'

So they were looking for a Manc with a limp and another the height of a fridge who had squeaky shoes. All on the word of a blind kid. The guv was going to love this...

Click-click-click-click.

Samuel had a hand stretched in Jessica's direction, as if summoning her.

'You're wearing a necklace,' he said. 'Not too chunky... there's something dangling in the middle. It might be a circle.'

Jessica cupped the necklace in her palm and looked at the disc of silver.

'Also,' he added, 'you hurt one of your knees at some point. Probably recently.'

'How do you know that?'

A smile and a shrug. 'There was a delay between your steps when you walked in. You put one foot ahead of the other a little quicker.'

Jessica had banged her knee on the way to the car that morning.

'That's impressive,' she said.

'I'm not making it up.'

'I never thought you were.'

Samuel clicked towards her a few more times and then, with prompting, told her how he'd heard the terrible *thunk* before he found his mother on the kitchen floor. How the men had run out of the flat, leaving him to find his mum's phone to call 999. He spoke as clearly as any witness she'd ever interviewed. There was usually some sort of doubt about what had happened and when, but Samuel's memory seemed near photographic. He described smells and sounds until Jessica could picture the scene herself. The fact he couldn't see made little difference.

When he was finished, Samuel pressed back into the chair. He turned away and sat staring into nothingness. He wasn't clicking but he was rubbing at his eyes.

'Are you okay?' Jessica asked, realising he was crying. It had crept up from nowhere.

Samuel nodded, but his cheeks were puffy, the rims of his eyes red. Before she knew it, Jessica was across the room and Samuel was reaching out. He gripped her hand, squeezing it hard.

'You're Jessica?' he said.

She shivered at the mention of her name.

'Yes,' she replied.

'You're going to find the men, aren't you?' he asked.

Jessica had to gulp away the lump in her throat. 'I'm going to do my absolute best.'

FOUR

Deborah was sitting on a stool in her kitchen, staring out the window to the garden beyond. A radio was on quietly in the corner, some cheesy-voiced DJ carping on about some pregnant celebrity. She turned as Jessica approached, smiling sadly.

'How is he?' she asked.

'He's all right – said he was going to get back to his game.'

'He's better on a computer than I am – and he can't even see the screen.'

'He's quite some kid.'

Deborah nodded in agreement and then turned back to the garden. Her fingers were looped through a mug and she took a sip of whatever was inside.

'Evie doesn't have any family,' she said quietly. 'Her parents died years ago. No brothers or sisters, so who knows what happens now. I brought Samuel back here when I got the call last night, but it's not like this place is set up for him...' She tailed off, sipping at her mug once more.

'Samuel said the men who broke into the flat were asking about money,' Jessica said.

Deborah twisted, blinked, turned back. 'Money?'

'Did Evie have savings or anything like that?'

'I doubt it. You don't do agency cleaning work through choice.'

'Could her parents have left her anything?'

'If they did then she never said. She works around Samuel's school hours. If he's on a half-day, then she'll do a half-day and then be around to pick him up. Every now and then, she'll be offered a shift and won't want to turn down the money. I'll help out then – pick him up and cook him tea, that sort of thing – but it's rare. She looks after him full-time and then goes out to work as well.'

'Could she have borrowed money?'

Deborah shrugged. 'I don't know. Maybe.'

'But she never mentioned it?'

'We never really talked about money like that.'

They both went silent for a moment, listening to the DJ introducing the next song. Nineties pop.

'She might have had another job,' Deborah said.

'Like what?'

'I'm not sure. She asked me to sit in with Samuel on a couple of evenings. I thought she might have a bloke on the go but she said it wasn't that. She said she was doing a bit of work more suited.'

'Suited to what?'

'I didn't ask. None of my business, really. It wasn't very often. It didn't seem like she wanted to talk about it. We did favours for each other but didn't really hang around outside of our shifts – she was too busy with Samuel.'

'If the people who broke in were asking about money, they must've thought she had some tucked away...?' Jessica paused for a moment, wondering if Deborah might fill the gap. When she didn't, Jessica spoke again: 'Was there anything unusual going on?'

'Like what?'

'I'm not sure.'

Deborah took a moment to think and then replied: 'Someone broke her window a few weeks ago. She was having problems with people knocking on the door and running away, too. Y'know what kids are like.'

'Any specific kids?'

Deborah pushed up from her stool and put the mug in the sink. She shook her head and fought back a yawn – someone else who looked like they'd pulled an all-nighter. 'I don't think so. I know she reported it.'

'Do you know if anyone was arrested?'

'You'd know better than me.'

Jessica nodded shortly. It wasn't true – she didn't have a handle on every single crime reported in the entire Greater Manchester region – but she took the point.

'Did you spend much time at Deborah's flat?' Jessica asked.

'Sometimes – it was easier to look after Samuel there than here.'

'Why?'

'In her words, the flat is "Samuel-proof". He still has the odd accident – walks into the corner of something, stubs his toe, or whatever. She's got soft edges on everything, plus there's no clutter... not like here.'

She sighed and tugged at her hair, glancing past Jessica towards the hallway. The kitchen was mucky, too – the sink filled with dishes and pans, the bin overflowing. Some irony, considering she was a cleaner.

'Do you think your support officer thingamalarkey will help me clean up?' Deborah asked.

Jessica felt the weight of stitching up a colleague as she answered. 'If you ask nicely...'

FIVE

Detective Chief Inspector Lewis Topper was on the phone as he waved Jessica into his office. He pointed to the seat on the opposite side of his desk and then rolled his eyes as he trawled out the usual plaudits into the receiver.

'Absolutely', 'I completely agree, sir', 'Tell him I said that's an ideal course of action' and 'I couldn't agree more. No, seriously, I couldn't agree more' were among the snippets Jessica earwigged before he finally hung up.

'That's some world-class arse-licking, guv,' Jessica said.

'Watch and learn,' he replied. He might have winked, but there was every chance it was a stress-related tic. He cleared his throat and then added: 'So the kid saw the whole thing...?'

'I wouldn't say, "saw" – he's blind.'

One of Topper's eyebrows twitched as if he was trying to figure out what the joke was. *The witness is a blind kid – ha ha, you're hilarious – now get on with it.*

When he realised she wasn't joking, he pressed back into his seat.

'Blind? As in... he can't see?'

Whenever he was tense, angry or confused, Topper's

accent grew a distinctly sandpapery glass-some-bloke-in-a-pub vibe about it.

'That's where it gets complicated,' Jessica replied. 'He's blind but he does this clicking thing. He says it helps him see.'

'I don't get it.'

Topper's eyes narrowed, once again wondering why she was choosing to wind him up at such an early hour of the day.

'My knees click – but it doesn't mean I can see any better.'

Jessica clucked her tongue. 'Like that. Something to do with soundwaves.'

'How much are you making off this?'

It was Jessica's turn to be confused. 'Sorry?'

'What is it, "wind-up-an-old-man-on-his-birthday"? They've clubbed in downstairs to get you to come up here and feed me all this? See if I fall for it?'

'It's your birthday?'

'Right, you've had your fun. Tell 'em all to piss off. So, what did he actually see?'

They stared at each other for a few moments, but Jessica blinked first.

'I'm not winding you up, guv. The son really is blind – and he really does do this clicking thing. Also... it's your birthday?'

Topper nodded to his empty desk. 'Aye, well... it's not like I expected balloons or owt but a cake would've been nice.'

'How many candles?'

'Never you mind. Now, tell me again about the blind kid who's not blind...'

Jessica did her best, but the more she spoke, the unlikelier it sounded. She finished with a shrug as they eyed each other.

'The blind boy says one of the killers drags his leg...?' Topper asked.

'I know,' Jessica replied.

'I'd love to hear that identification in court. Imagine the

defence getting stuck into that. Are you sure there's nothing else?'

Jessica shook her head. 'Scene of Crime are there now. I'm heading out for door-to-doors and the usual. It sounds like a burglary gone wrong, so we'll check the lists for anyone with a known limp in case there's someone obvious.'

'What about the father?'

'Evie's friend says he left and moved abroad years ago. She didn't seem to know an awful lot about it. We'll see if the register office has anything – but the blokes who broke in weren't asking about family, they wanted money.'

Topper grabbed a pen from a mug on his desk and started drumming it on the edge as he pursed his lips in thought. He smirked slightly.

'Things are never easy with you, are they?'

Detective Constable Archie Davey was scowling from the passenger seat. He adjusted his tie and then crooked his neck to the side, peering around a parked car as Jessica waited at a set of traffic lights.

'What's wrong now?' Jessica asked.

'Bit blue round here, innit? Gets me a bit itchy.'

'What are you on about?'

He nodded towards a side street. 'Sheikh 'n' Vac stadium down that way.'

It took Jessica a moment to realise he was talking about Manchester City's football ground. She rolled her eyes and ignored his grumblings, as she did much of his football talk. At times, he'd blather on for five or ten minutes, either whingeing about some result from the night before, or banging on about how a recent victory meant his beloved United were the greatest football team the world had ever seen. Jessica nodded along because it was easier. A tactical 'right' or 'yeah' every now and then was enough to make him think she had the slimmest iota of interest in whatever he was saying.

He was busy talking about 'oil money ruining the game' when the lights turned green. Jessica took the turn and eased the car in behind a battered Mazda.

'If you've quite finished having your little strop,' she began, 'you can read me that list now.'

Archie thumbed through a few pages of A4, mumbling to himself.

Jessica was never quite sure if he deliberately set out to wind her up, or if it was all natural ability.

'There was a window smashed at Evie's apartment two weeks ago last night,' he said. 'Someone threw a brick that went straight through and landed in the kitchen sink.'

'Did anyone visit her?'

'Nope. Gave her a reference number, that's all.'

Jessica bit her tongue. Typical.

'Before that, she'd called us for someone setting a fire in her front yard,' Archie added. 'She also asked us to log that someone had smashed bottles on her front path. There's a note that she has a blind son who could've stepped on the broken glass...' He hummed once more, flicking to another page. 'On that same call, there's something about someone playing music at three in the morning, a series of knock-and-runs... I think that's it.'

'But no officers visited her?'

Archie didn't say anything; he didn't have to. There was only a finite number of officers and only so many hours in the day. Perhaps the only surprise was that Evie hadn't been to the papers – or kicked up a social-media storm. The police not attending when broken glass had been left on a path where her blind kid walked had tabloid written all over it.

It occurred to Jessica that with Samuel to care for and the agency work, Evie was likely far too busy for all that.

Jessica and Archie got out of the car and headed along the pavement until they reached the line of police tape and the single officer who'd been left behind. Behind the line was a scuffed moss-ridden giant breeze block of a building.

The crime scene protection officer blew into his hands and asked if they knew where the closest public toilets were, before dropping the really bad news. Whatever Jessica had been told earlier, the Scene of Crime team hadn't arrived yet. There was some sort of staff shortage and a backup of jobs around the city. They were 'on their way', but, until then, he'd been instructed to stop anyone from entering the apartment complex.

Oh, and he was 'bursting like a snake who'd just eaten an alligator' – so if they could cover for him for ten minutes, it'd be much appreciated. Archie pointed him towards a nearby supermarket, Jessica told him to get on with it, and then they stood around waiting.

'Typical,' Jessica muttered as they passed under the tape. There was no gate at the front and then a dirty courtyard beyond that was surrounded by a dozen windows over two floors. The muck-soaked, pebble-dashed exterior made it look like the sort of place that could do with a friendly introduction to a bulldozer or five. In the centre of the yard was a blackened circular scorch mark imprinted onto the concrete.

Archie nudged Jessica with his elbow, pointing towards the other side of the road. 'Not going to get many eyewitnesses, are we?'

He wasn't wrong. There below a pair of abandoned shops and a boarded-up house that had been graffitied with a series of squiggly tags.

Jessica indicated the windows above. 'Evie's friend said three of the four flats are empty.'

Archie peered up. 'Christ, I wouldn't want to live in this place on my own. It's like a scaled-down Strangeways.'

Jessica couldn't disagree.

When Officer Needapoo returned, Jessica and Archie headed back the way they'd come, knocking on the door of each house. There was no answer from a grubby number thirty-seven, but a raggedy chain-smoking woman with a face like a pickaxe yanked open number thirty-five and glared at them with all the warmth of an ice cube tray.

She'd apparently not noticed any commotion the night before, nor the fact that an officer was standing guard a few doors down. She was stroking Archie's arm, though, which was enough to keep Jessica talking if only because she was enjoying the terrified look on her colleague's face.

'Do you get many problems round here?' Jessica asked.

A shake of the head. 'I'm out on my feet by ten o'clock,' she replied, before nodding across the road. 'Everyone's moving out anyway. Like living in a morgue.' She winked at Archie, as if she'd suggested something he could get on board with.

'Have you had any issues with noise at night?' Jessica asked.

'I sleep like a log. You could have Oasis out here and I'd doze through it.'

'Do you know anyone who lives in the block at the end of the road?'

Jessica indicated the flats where Evie lived and the woman poked her head further out the door to check.

'Nah, I don't really talk to anyone round 'ere. More hassle than it's worth, ain't it? One minute you're saying hello, the next they're asking for a lift to the airport, or whatever. I keep myself to myself.' She winked at Archie once more. 'Well, *almost* myself.'

Archie shivered and Jessica bit back a laugh before thanking the woman for her time.

They continued weaving back and forth across the road, knocking on doors. Around half the houses seemed to be unoccupied and, of the ones that had someone living there, nobody seemed to know much. No one knew Evie or had any knowledge of the antisocial behaviour that had been going on outside her flat. Hardly anyone had noticed the police tape – and even fewer were willing to have much of a conversation. The police were as popular as that person who keeps sticking inspirational quote memes on Facebook.

There was a general bewilderment that anything exciting should be happening on the street at all.

By the time they were back at the car, Jessica and Archie had spoken to a dozen people. Jessica rested her with back on the vehicle, peering along the street towards Evie's flat.

'Bit of a waste of time, wasn't it?' Archie asked.

'When you checked the calls from Evie, did you look to see if anyone else had phoned to report trouble?'

'Aye – nothing. Just her.'

'No other complaints about the fire?'

'Not one – though, if it happened at night, it's quite likely nobody else saw. It's not like the place is crawling with activity.'

'True – but if some kids were causing trouble around here, why go for Evie's flat specifically? There are abandoned shops across the road, boarded-up houses – empty homes, too. If you're going to chuck some bricks about, play some music and set a fire, wouldn't you go for any of those places first?'

'Perhaps they thought her building was empty?'

'Maybe – but it's a bit of bad luck they threw a brick through *her* window instead of any of the other three flats on her block, let alone any of the other houses on this road.'

It took Archie a couple of seconds. 'You reckon she was targeted?'

Jessica thought about it for a few more seconds and then puffed out a long breath. 'I really don't know.'

SIX

Jessica was driving steadily through the city, trying to focus on the road as Archie rambled on once more. The good news was that he'd moved away from football, the bad that Jessica was beginning to question his mental health. Or perhaps her own.

'So you have a man and you have Superman,' Archie said, predominantly to himself. 'A man's just a man – but Superman can fly, leap buildings, all that. Same for a girl and Supergirl.'

'Is there a point to all this, Arch?'

'Then you've got a moon and a supermoon. The moon's just the normal moon – but a supermoon is closer, brighter and bigger, right?'

Jessica eyed the bridge in front. It stretched high across the road, with huge concrete pillars on either side and in the central reservation between lanes.

'If I accelerate into that bridge post as fast as I can, do you reckon you might get to the point a bit quicker?' she said. 'I know I'd probably break a few ribs, perhaps puncture a lung, maybe sustain permanent internal injuries – but it'd be much better than listening to all this.'

Archie was unmoved. 'Anyway, so then you have a model

and a supermodel. But what's the difference between the two? They're both just women, aren't they?'

'Why are you asking me?'

'I wanted a woman's perspective.'

'It's hardly one of the great unanswered questions, is it? Not quite up there with the meaning of life, or how the universe began.'

'What do you reckon?'

Jessica accelerated steadily *underneath* the bridge. 'Honestly? I reckon a model and supermodel are identical in as much as neither would look at you twice.'

Archie took a moment and then sniggered to himself. He straightened his tie, pumped his shoulders upwards, chest out. 'I'd fancy my chances. Those surveys all say women want a sense of humour in a bloke.'

'How are you going to make them laugh? Take your pants off?'

Archie sniggered once more. 'I have my ways.'

'You know supermodels are six foot tall, don't you? You're five-foot-nothing. You'd be a little handbag dog yapping away at some poor woman's feet.'

'I'd bloody love that.'

Archie continued mithering on about some book he'd read full of dating advice specifically for men, but Jessica zoned out once more. He hadn't mentioned his girlfriend once, which didn't bode well. For the merest moment, she thought about asking – but then sense quickly gripped her and she figured she really didn't want to know.

With his chirping as the soundtrack, it wasn't long before they reached a smart cul-de-sac of detached houses to the south of the city. It was a far cry from the murk of Evie's flat, with manicured lawns and hanging baskets dotted smartly among the houses.

Shaun Viceroy was almost a cartoon caricature of a Scotsman. Barely comprehensible and with a shock of ginger hair, he was a kilt and set of bagpipes away from featuring on a box of porridge oats. When he spoke, it felt like they were on an international phone call with a short delay as Jessica took a moment to work out what he'd said.

He welcomed Jessica and Archie into his house with something that might have been a 'come in' and then led them into a living room.

A manicured woman in a smart business suit was sitting at a computer desk and he introduced her as his wife, Julie. The rest of the room was decorated with an array of photographs showing the pair of them on various exotic holidays.

Julie fussed around, offering tea and biscuits and then disappearing into the kitchen as Shaun took a seat on one side of a circular dining table, leaving Jessica and Archie on the other.

'I gather you're a bit of a housing mogul?' Jessica said when they were settled.

'Aye, well I dunno about that, like,' Shaun replied.

'But you own a bunch of houses around the area…?'

Shaun nodded.

'How many?'

'Fifteen or sixteen. Jules'll know – she does the paperwork.'

'I know someone contacted you earlier to say there'd been an incident at the flat you're renting to Evie Briers.'

He grunted. 'Aye – poor wee girl. You dunno what to say, do ya?' He paused and then added: 'They said I can't get round there yet…'

'It's going to be at least a couple of days, I'm afraid.' Jessica waited, before adding: 'Is it right that of the three flats in Evie's block, hers was the only one occupied?'

'Aye.'

'Why?'

He shrugged, glancing from Jessica to Archie and back again. 'People moved out.'

'How long ago?'

'A few months. Not long.'

'They all moved out together?'

'Not together – but within a few weeks of each other. One of those things, I guess.'

'Didn't anyone want to move in?'

He pouted out a lip and nodded towards his wife, who was carrying in a tray of teacups. 'I suppose not,' he replied.

Julie fussed around some more, finding some coasters and then placing cups in front of everyone before taking a seat herself.

'Is that normal?' Jessica asked.

'Is *what* normal?'

'Leaving your flats empty? Isn't that money being wasted?'

Shaun looked to Julie who, despite not hearing the first part of the conversation, picked things up anyway.

'We needed to do a few repairs but it was a busy summer, what with holidays and the like. We do everything ourselves with the listings and the vetting, so there was no point in putting up a lot of adverts and then not being around to ask for references, request credit checks and so on.'

She fiddled with a gold heart necklace that hung high, close to her neck, and Jessica remembered her own smaller piece of jewellery that Samuel had identified so successfully. She wondered if he'd know Julie's was in the shape of heart – if he even knew what a heart shape was.

Jessica turned to Archie, who started going through the complaints Evie had made to the police about the brick being put through her window, the fire, the broken glass and the other smaller things.

'Did she mention any of this to you?' he asked.

Shaun answered before his wife could. 'Only the window.'

He paused and exchanged a worried look with Julie. 'There was a fire?' he added.

'I don't think it was serious,' Archie replied. 'She said someone set fire to rubbish on the courtyard.'

'Probably just kids. She didn't mention it when she called about the window.'

'Did you visit her?'

Shaun nodded towards Julie. 'I was up in Edinburgh. You sorted a glazier, didn't you?'

Julie was in the middle of sipping her tea and answered when she put it down. 'We have some contractors on retainers.'

Jessica took her moment to chip in: 'Did you know her well?'

'Only as landlord and tenant, so not really,' Shaun replied. 'She always paid on time.'

'And how long had she lived there?'

Shaun looked to Julie, who answered almost immediately: 'She's one of our oldest tenants, so a little over seven years.'

Jessica turned back to Shaun. 'And are you sure she never mentioned any harassment?'

'Should she have?' he replied.

'As well as the broken window and the fire, she says someone scattered glass by her front door, she had people knocking and running, occasional loud music in the early hours... Didn't she bring up any of that?'

'Not to me.' He turned to his wife: 'Jules?'

'I don't know what to tell you.'

Jessica let it stand for a few moments. 'Do you own any other properties on that road?' she asked.

'No,' Julie replied.

A phone on the computer desk started to ring and Julie popped up to check the screen. She passed it to her husband, who then headed into the kitchen.

When they were alone, Julie took another sip of her tea. She uncrossed and recrossed her legs, glancing towards the kitchen. 'Is there anything else we can help with?'

'The names of the other tenants,' Jessica replied.

'Which other tenants?'

'The ones who used to live in the block with Evie. Your husband said they moved out a few months ago.'

'Oh...' She reached towards the computer and then stopped herself. 'Isn't there confidentiality or something like that? We get these leaflets about data protection and how we could be fined if we're not careful.'

'We're only asking for names and contact details of the three tenants who moved out.'

'Why?'

'Because I think Evie and her son were targeted by a person or a group who wanted to make their lives difficult.' Jessica paused and then added stingingly: 'You realise she's dead, don't you?'

There was a moment in which Jessica thought Julie would dig her heels in, make them get a warrant and waste more time. Then the other woman slid her chair back.

'Of course,' Julie said.

By the time Jessica and Archie were back at the car with the list of previous tenants, there was a pair of missed calls on Jessica's phone.

She pressed to call back and Detective Sergeant Isobel Diamond answered on the first ring.

'Are you on your way back to the station?' she asked, sounding busy.

'Not yet. Arch was sidetracked by some mad neighbour stroking his arm. I had to give them twenty minutes of alone time.'

Archie was on the other side of the car, about to clamber in when his head popped up, meerkat-style, over the passenger's side door. 'Who's that?' he called.

Jessica turned her back on him and returned to the pavement.

'What are you after?' she added.

'The vending machine in the canteen hasn't been refilled and it's all kicking off,' Izzy said. 'Could you nip into Tesco Express and get me a Double Decker or something? Big bag of Maltesers as well. I'd go myself, but Ruth's in court this morning, Dave's skiving and Franks can't be arsed doing his own work, so he's nicked a constable to go and look at some school break-in last night. I'm snowed under.'

Jessica glanced back to where Archie was leaning on the car, eyeing her carefully. 'I'll smuggle something back especially for you.'

'Ta. Also, I was thinking about the whole leg-drag thing you mentioned earlier.'

It took Jessica a moment to realise Izzy was talking about Samuel's description of the man who'd broken in. 'What about it?' she said.

'Could it be that one of the men had one leg shorter than the other?'

That hadn't crossed Jessica's mind. 'Any specific reason?' she asked.

'I remember seeing the memo a month or so back that Carl Brompton was up for release.'

'Who's Carl Brompton?'

'Serial shoplifter.'

Jessica's brain was grinding slowly. 'He nicks cornflakes?'

Izzy didn't miss a beat: 'Serial with an "S". He's got a hundred offences or something stupid like that. Probably more. I was in court when they put him away the last time and I remember him dragging his leg. It came up in the trial that he's got one leg shorter than the other. The defence were trying to argue he couldn't run because of it. Stuck in my mind.'

'Bit of a step up from shoplifting to killing a single mum.'

'I know – just thinking out loud.'

'It's fine – good thinking. Probably worth checking out. See if you can find out where he's been living since leaving prison and we'll go knocking on a few doors. Kick one down if we're lucky.' Jessica turned back to the car and then added: 'Anyway – I've got one more job to do and then I'm off on your chocolate dash.'

SEVEN

It was a little after lunchtime and Izzy's devil-on-the-shoulder talk about chocolate was making Jessica hungry. She parked the car outside the butty shop a few streets over from the station and then treated Archie to a bacon and sausage doorstop special. The Iranian bloke behind the counter seemingly had an endless supply of butter, given the amount he slavered on the thick bread – and he left the brown sauce bottle on the counter for customers to use at will. It was one of the city's best-kept secrets and, if nothing else, the sandwich shut Archie up for a few minutes.

After lunch, it was a short walk to the red-brick row of semi-detached houses that marked the border of Rusholme, Levenshulme and Longsight.

Chatresh Lodi was a familiar face when he answered his door, despite the fact Jessica had never met him. He had slick black hair below his ears and the hectic, darting-eyed look of a man who was in the middle of a busy day. He was wearing a smart open-necked suit with a sharp-collared white shirt. Not really the kind of outfit for lounging around the house. His dark brown eyes flickered between Jessica and Archie.

'Can I help you?' he asked.

Jessica pulled the driving licence from her pocket and held it up. It was still in the see-through evidence bag. 'I think this is yours,' she said.

Chatresh squinted towards the plastic rectangle. He reached towards it, but Jessica pulled it away, muttering an apology.

Chatresh frowned, but remained polite. His accent had a hint of the local – but without the sometimes brutal twang Archie's could have.

'Sorry, who are you?' he asked.

Jessica and Archie reached for their warrant cards in regimented order. Even though he'd asked, Chatresh barely gave the IDs a glance.

'Why have you got my driving licence?' he asked.

'Can we come in?' Jessica replied, repocketing both her own ID and Chatresh's licence.

He glanced over his shoulder, winced slightly. It didn't seem like he wanted them there – but then he shrugged. 'Fine – but the house is a mess, I'm afraid.'

He wasn't wrong. The hall was lined with cardboard boxes, as was one end of the living room. There were two photographs of planes on the wall and a handful of model airplanes on the shelf opposite the door. A pile of plastic and silicone phone cases of varying shapes and sizes were scattered across the sofa and Chatresh shuffled them to the side as he nodded Jessica and Archie towards it.

'Can I have my licence back?' he asked.

'Not yet,' Jessica answered. 'It needs to be tested for fingerprints.'

He blinked and then reeled back slightly. 'Why?'

'Because it was found in the pocket of a man who'd been left for dead on the side of the road in Swinton last night.'

He stared at her, waiting for a punchline that didn't come. 'Sorry, what?'

'A man was beaten half to death overnight. His body was left in a ditch and the only piece of ID on him was your driving licence.'

They stared at each other, Chatresh's eyes widening slightly and then narrowing. 'I don't understand what you're saying. He had my driving licence?'

'Exactly.'

'Who is he?'

'That's what we're here to ask you.'

Chatresh's mouth was half-open. He looked between the officers, still waiting for the punchline. 'Do you think I beat him up or something?'

Jessica gave it a couple of seconds, not too long, just enough to see how he'd react. He didn't flinch, sitting tall, gaze unwavering from her. 'Did you?'

'No! Of course not.'

'Where were you last night?'

'In bed, like most other people?'

'Can anyone confirm that?'

Chatresh turned to Archie as if wanting support. He smiled, chuckled humourlessly to himself, then rocked back in his seat. 'You think I beat some bloke up and, because I'm single, I can't prove I didn't? That's ridiculous.'

'I never said I thought you did anything – I merely asked if you had.' Jessica nodded towards Archie, who started fumbling with the cardboard folder he'd brought into the house. 'I was more hoping you could help us identify the man we found.'

Archie offered a photograph towards Chatresh, who took it and gulped when he turned it over.

'Bloody hell...' he whispered.

'I know the poor guy's a bit of a mess,' Jessica said, 'but if there's anything you could identify...?'

Chatresh stared at the picture and then shook his head. 'I have no idea who it is.'

'There's a tattoo on his arm – a lizard or something like that. Sound familiar?'

Another shake of the head, slower this time.

Chatresh passed the photo back to Archie and then pressed back into his chair. He seemed genuinely shocked, which wasn't a surprise given how graphic the photo was. Aside from the fact that the mystery man was white with brown hair, there wasn't an awful lot more by which to identify him. His cheeks were a swollen, shattered mess; lips cracked with blood, eyebrows leaking the red stuff, too.

'Why would someone have your driving licence?' Jessica asked.

Chatresh was in a daze. He stared towards the window, blinking rapidly. He stuttered that he didn't know without looking towards either Jessica or Archie.

'Did you know that you'd lost it?' Jessica pressed.

'No... I mean, well, sort of.' He coughed. 'I had my wallet stolen on a Friday night a week or so ago. I guess it was inside. I thought I'd just lost a bit of cash, so no real harm done. I didn't think my licence was inside. I don't always have it on me.'

'Did you report the wallet stolen?'

Chatresh blinked and then he was facing her. 'No.'

'Why not?'

'I thought I'd only lost fifty or sixty quid. Didn't think it was worth it. I phoned round the pubs I'd been in just in case someone had handed it in – but no one had. I had work the next morning so didn't have much time.'

Jessica asked him to give the names of the bars to Archie and then asked what he did for a living.

Chatresh indicated towards the boxes. 'I run a market stall in Wythenshawe.'

'Not working today?'

'My brother Rajiv is covering.'

Jessica remained sitting for a few moments, wondering if he'd add anything. Not that it meant too much, but Chatresh didn't seem like the violent type. He had no criminal record, no matches at all on their system. He wasn't particularly tall or well-built, he was a regular bloke running a market stall.

When he didn't add anything, she got to her feet with Archie following. 'That's all for now,' Jessica said.

Chatresh stood quickly, surprised. 'Oh, right... I thought...' he tailed off.

'What's with the planes?' Jessica asked, nodding towards the shelf with the models.

'My dad got me into flying when I was young. I part-own a Cessna up in Lancashire. Started learning to fly when I was seventeen.'

Jessica stepped towards the models and eyed them closely. One had been made with matchsticks, using the sort of precision and patience she knew she didn't possess. If she'd tried, she'd have glued herself to the carpet before an hour had passed.

Archie led the way back to the front door, Jessica trailing behind. She stopped in the kitchen door frame and turned back to Chatresh.

She handed him a business card. 'If you have any other thoughts, you've got my number there. You can call 101 if you prefer.' She waited for him to place the card on the counter. 'You said your brother was covering the market stall – do you have many other family members nearby?'

'Raj has a wife and three kids, but that's it. Our parents are in Bangladesh.'

'Could you ask your brother about the man? We'll leave you a photograph. Don't forget to mention the lizard tattoo.'

Chatresh took the picture of the battered man from

Archie. He folded it, not looking at the contents. 'I'm seeing him later,' he said.

'Can I take your number?' Jessica asked. 'Just in case. Someone will be in touch about returning your licence. It might be quicker to contact the DVLA and cancel it to request a new one.'

Chatresh agreed, scribbling down his number on a Post-it note and passing it over.

Jessica thanked him for his time and then headed outside, leading Archie past a house that was marked 'For Auction', through the estate back towards the butty shop and the car.

She waited until they were a good street away before she spoke next. 'Reckon he's our bloke?' she asked.

'No chance,' Archie replied. 'I've seen fighters and he ain't one.'

'Only takes a few Stellas to turn anyone into a moron.'

'True – but d'you reckon he had it in him? That poor sod you found in the ditch hadn't just taken a few punches – someone had kept kicking the shite out of him even when he was unconscious.'

'I know. When you get back, check in with those pubs Chatresh says he was in when he got robbed. See if you can find either Chatresh or the robber on the CCTV.'

'We heading back now?'

'Soon – first I've got chocolate and a birthday balloon to buy.'

EIGHT

As she got through her front door, Jessica kicked off her shoes and then dumped her bag over the banister. The kitchen smelled of something she wasn't used to.

Food.

Hot food that didn't come in a takeaway box, or a pre-packed microwavable plastic tub. Jessica breezed into the kitchen and inhaled the tomatoey flavour.

Caroline was standing at the cooker, apron wrapped around her waist, greasy dark hair stuck to her scalp. 'Ten minutes,' she said, looking over her shoulder.

'What is it?'

'Vegetarian spag-bol.'

Jessica pulled a face, didn't even bother trying to disguise it. Caroline's recent lose-the-baby-weight health kick apparently involved not eating any meat. She'd been trying a new diet roughly every two or three weeks, each based upon some sort of bullshit science found in various magazines. There was the 1-2-3-4 diet, whatever that was; something else about water; another one which seemed to consist of eating ninety per cent asparagus. The list went on.

'What's in it?' Jessica asked.

'Vegetables.'

'I gathered that much.'

Jessica crossed to the crib at the back of the kitchen that hadn't been there in the morning. She stared down at the child inside. Russell was a little over six months old and wide awake. He strained up towards the dangly, luminous plastic zoo animals that were hanging from a mobile over the top of his cot. He gurgled when he saw Jessica and reached higher towards her.

She thought about picking him up, but then remembered he was seemingly never more than a burp away from projectile vomiting over either his mother, his father, Jessica, himself, the floor, the sofa, or anything else within chucking-up distance.

'You can pick him up,' Caroline said over her shoulder.

There was no getting out of it now. Jessica unclipped the straps that were holding Russell in his crib, gave him her best 'don't-even-think-about-it' look and then lifted him onto her shoulder.

He gurgled ominously. Either that or laughed. Jessica feared the worst.

'Did Hugo get off okay?' she asked.

Caroline was busy stirring a big pot of pasta sauce. 'I checked his flight online and it was on time, so I guess so. He texted to say he was boarding and that was the last I heard.'

She didn't add anything, but Jessica saw her friend's shoulders slump slightly. Caroline was Jessica's oldest mate and, at least for now, they were back living together like the old days. Hugo, her boyfriend and father of her child, was a semifamous magician – but that meant he made his living through touring. He'd taken six months off after the birth of Russell, but it couldn't last forever and he'd headed out to north America that morning.

Jessica rocked Russell on her shoulder. 'You don't have to cook every night, you know.'

'I enjoy it.'

'I know – but don't feel you have to pick up after me, or cook. You don't have to do all the housework.'

'It's no problem. If I wasn't here, I'd be living in a flat above a bookies' and anything's better than that.'

That was probably true. Caroline had endured a car-crash a few years ago which, although Jessica wouldn't mention it, was largely down to her own poor choices. She'd nearly been killed by an ex-boyfriend and then rebounded into a marriage and divorce. That had left her with all sorts of financial issues as she tried to sell the place in which she'd been living and then carve up what belonged to her and what was her ex-husband's. She'd fallen into a relationship with Hugo and then had his child, not realising she was pregnant. Hugo had never moved out of the flat in which he'd spent the past decade. They were talking about buying a house but an offer had fallen through on one place and then... blah, blah, blah.

At one point, Jessica had been living in Caroline's flat – now things had switched around completely. As Caroline waited for the paperwork to go through on a different house she and Hugo were buying, she'd asked to move into Jessica's place.

Caroline was pretty much the living embodiment of the real-life trash stories that were featured in her weekly magazines. Jessica had never thought that, of her and Caroline, *she'd* end up being the grown-up with a house and regular job.

'As long as you're happy,' Jessica said.

Caroline switched off the hob and then started scooping their grim-looking veggie special into a pair of bowls. Perhaps because he didn't fancy it either, Russell burped loudly. Jessica rocked him once more, patting his back and then taking him off her shoulder and cradling him close to her belly so they could see one another.

'All right, kid. Let's make a pact here and now. You, your mother and I will all keep our bodily fluids to ourselves, yeah?'

He stared at her, boggly-eyed, not answering – which she took as a 'no'.

Jessica carried their food into the other room as Caroline put Russell back into his crib and carried him through. He rested on one of the dining chairs, staring up at them as they ate.

'How is it?' Caroline asked a little after Jessica forced down a mouthful.

'Good,' Jessica lied, trying her best not to grimace. It was like eating a marinated old shoe. She wasn't quite sure what had gone into it as, aside from the pasta, onions and peppers, it was hard to identify anything that might be real food. There were chunks of green and something that looked like potato but tasted like a dishcloth.

'Are you busy tomorrow?' Caroline asked.

'What do you need?'

'Can you take me to the clinic? I don't like driving with Russell in the passenger seat and have you ever been on a bus in this city? It's not that I hate the general public, but I do actually *hate* the general public. It's all nose-pickers and bum-scratchers out there. It's germ warfare every time you sit down.'

Jessica laughed. She'd not had the best experiences with public transport over the years.

'What's going on at the clinic?' she asked.

'Russell's monthly check-up.'

'What do they check for?'

'To make sure he's growing at the right rate, that sort of thing.'

'Not to see if he's growing a tail?'

Jessica laughed but Caroline didn't. She frowned.

'Sorry,' Jessica added. 'Long day, shit joke.'

'Can you not talk about my only child having a tail, please?'

Jessica took a mouthful of the disgusting meal and forced herself to swallow. She planted the fork back into the bowl. 'This is nice,' she said, thinking it would be a lot nicer if it wasn't for all the vegetables.

NINE

The receptionist on the ground floor of the Manchester Metropolitan University building had no idea who Jessica was. She looked from Jessica to her computer, to a pad on the desk, to the phone, to a piece of paper that was pinned to a board at her side. All the while, she spoke about Jessica 'not being on the list' and 'usually being notified about this sort of thing'. Jessica offered her warrant card and said that someone *had* called the previous day to set things up. That was, unfortunately, news to the sour-faced receptionist. She said she'd 'see what I can do' with such grudging annoyance that it was as if she'd been asked to donate a kidney to an alcoholic, drug-addled relative.

Jessica smiled awkwardly as the receptionist spoke firmly into a phone and then told her that someone would be down shortly.

It took another ten minutes until some studenty showed up to lead Jessica through a bewildering array of corridors, up some stairs, along another corridor and up one final set of stairs until she was outside a beech door with 'Dr Pearson' written on a small plaque.

The student smiled sweetly and then disappeared off round a corner as Jessica tapped gently on the door.

A booming voice welcomed her in and then Jessica settled in for a lesson in how much she didn't know about the world.

'So, bats do it...?' Jessica said, still not entirely sure she was getting it.

Dr Pearson was a big man in all ways. Tall, broad, Santa Claus beard, massive hands that could burst eardrums whenever he banged his desk – which was a lot. The eye specialist at the hospital was on holiday, leaving Jessica with the next best thing – a professor in optometry.

The chair creaked under his weight as he rocked backwards, nodding enthusiastically. 'Exactly like bats. Dolphins can work with echolocation as well. It's an ability that definitely exists in the animal kingdom.'

'What about humans?' Jessica asked.

Pearson tilted his head to the side, giving it the unmistakable 'dunno-about-that' look. 'It's unproven,' he said.

'But unproven doesn't mean it can't exist...?'

'Correct. I've seen videos on the Internet and attended a couple of conferences where people have spoken about echolocation in humans. To say it's an unknown phenomenon is an understatement of massive proportions. You're talking about perhaps a dozen people worldwide who claim to be able to do this.'

Jessica was distracted by the sheer amount of clutter around the doctor's office. There were faded posters on the walls showing various parts of the human anatomy, most focusing on the head. There were two separate skulls that she hoped were plastic on his desk – and some sort of spherical sculpture or model that was probably the human eye. There were all sorts of wiry bits coming from the back of it that made it look more alien than human.

She was far from a clean freak – let alone someone with OCD who arranged movies and music in alphabetical order – but the way the book spines on his shelf were mixed was an absolute disgrace.

There should be a law about it.

Tall, thick books were matched next to smaller ones; some had been stuffed in between other publications, pages facing outwards; hardbacks were with paperbacks; textbooks with smaller novels. It was pure Sodom and Gomorrah territory.

'Sorry...?' Jessica said, realising she'd missed the tail end of what the doctor had been saying.

He didn't seem to mind. 'I asked if you're able to tell me why you'd like to know. I understand if it's confidential, or police business.'

Jessica considered him carefully and then spoke: 'I have a witness to a crime,' she said, 'but he's blind.'

'Ah. I see the problem.' He cleared his throat noisily. 'Sorry, poor choice of words. Y'know... it might be a coincidence, but a young mother was due to visit me a few years ago because her son was clicking. His GP didn't know what it was and it went through a couple of professionals until it was referred to me.'

'What happened?'

'She pulled out of the visit the day before.' He straightened himself in his seat. 'I won't pretend I wasn't disappointed. I never knew any names ahead of time, but there was a professional curiosity.'

Jessica wondered if it had been Evie and Samuel who were referred. If it was true that only a dozen people worldwide had taught themselves to echolocate, then it seemed likely.

'Was there a reason for cancelling?'

'Sick of doctors, apparently. Can't really argue with that. If he was blind, then he would've no doubt been through all sorts of procedures and operations. At some point, it's natural to throw one's hands up and say, "enough". I didn't push back because it's not my place.'

Jessica was staring at the eye sculpture, trying not to be creeped out by it. 'One final time,' she said. 'I think I've followed things – well, most of it – but feel free to assume I'm an idiot. From what you've said, although it's unusual, it's possible for a blind person to see...?'

Pearson smiled, fatherly. 'Sort of. You and I see because the cornea at the front of our eyes bends light through our irises. Are you with me?'

Jessica most definitely was not. She nodded anyway.

'The retina then turns that into a series of light impulses through many, many nerve endings. Those are carried via the optic nerve to the brain.'

'My witness had his corneas replaced but it didn't work.'

'I'm not completely surprised. Technology and procedures are catching up fast, but for some people, the hard truth is that their blindness is irreversible. Doesn't mean others shouldn't try – but that's the way things are. Anyway, echolocation means seeing in a different way. It pushes the boundary of what we mean by the very verb "to see".'

'How?'

'Think of the films you might have watched of a submarine using sonar.' Pearson drew a circle in the air with his hand. 'It's impossible to see when underwater, so a submarine sends out a soundwave and waits for it to bounce off something. When the sound returns to the ship, it shows how close another object is. On film you'll see the spinning dial going round and then there'll be a blip of a dot or something to show that.'

'I get it.'

'A person who claims to be able to echolocate does much the same thing. They may tap a stick or click with their mouth to create a soundwave. That noise then reflects from various surfaces around them. That much is fact. What's unclear and unproven is how the individual then processes that reflecting sound to create such precise images of what's around them.'

Jessica didn't reply straight away. She wasn't sure how to phrase things. 'It sounds, well... impossible. How can anyone be able to interpret between the distance and depth of one surface and another?'

Pearson shrugged. 'I don't necessarily disagree with you. When I say this is unproven, that doesn't mean there haven't been studies. A blind person who can echolocate has activity in their visual cortex when they do this. It's the interpretation of that activity which is unproven. Studies are rare because the condition is so unknown. What is undeniable is that certain individuals *can* do this.'

It was a lot to take in. Blind people being able to see? What was next?

'Is it like the old thing where people say if you lose one sense, the others make up for it?' Jessica asked.

'If you like – but magnified many times over. Assuming echolocation works, you have to understand that the way a person can see is completely different to how you or I do. If you're in front of a traffic light, all those little nerve endings and impulses tell you the colour of the light. Echolocation would allow the individual to see the shape of the traffic light – the post, the box and so on – they'd know something was there and be able to avoid walking into it – but they'd not be able to see the colour.'

Jessica sat deeper in the chair and let out a long, long breath. She wondered what Samuel might make of Pearson's higgledy-piggledy bookshelves.

'I know,' Pearson said. 'It's difficult, isn't it? Are you going to end up asking me to explain this to a jury one day?'

Another long breath. 'In the nicest way possible, I really hope not.'

He laughed.

'What I'll tell you is that your witness, whomever he might be, however old he is, must be one utterly extraordinary individual.'

Jessica nodded in agreement. 'From what I've seen, he most definitely is.'

TEN

Jessica had concluded that the employment agency for which Evie and Deborah both worked was almost impossible to find – and that was with two working eyes. She walked up and down Deansgate, passing shops, restaurants and pubs, somehow unable to find the address that she'd printed out the day before. She double-checked it on her phone, but it was correct.

She passed a bike shop, a diner, a church and an Italian place, then headed back the way she'd come, wondering if there was some sort of Platform-Nine-And-Three-Quarters spookery going on. Jessica eventually found the unmarked door next to a hole-in-the-wall takeaway. There was no number, merely a faded plaque at the side on which 'Fit To Work' was engraved.

Jessica headed up the stairs and then spent even more time waiting before the manager was free to speak to her.

Tina was all perfect nails, coiffured hair, spotless make-up and creaseless, pressed clothes. She was the type of woman who left Jessica wondering whether some people had twenty-six hours in their day. She was sitting behind a spotlessly clean desk with a cardboard folder in front of her.

'Terrible news,' she said. 'Absolutely terrible. I was devastated when I heard – we all were.'

'Did you know Evie well?' Jessica asked.

'She's been working here for years – longer than most of the staff.' Tina clicked her fingers. 'I could've placed her somewhere in a permanent role like that. Employers are crying out for hard-working, reliable staff, but she didn't want the hours, what with her son and all.' She paused. 'Terrible news. Just terrible.'

'I assume you've got a list of the companies where Evie worked over the years...?'

Tina opened the folder and took out two sheets of paper. She passed them over and said Jessica could take photocopies if she wanted. Jessica scanned the list, but it was mainly cleaning or production-line work.

'All those companies are regular clients,' Tina said. 'Evie was mainly placed around the hours she requested. We all understood the situation with her son so didn't offer anything that didn't fit around the days she gave us.'

Jessica finished scanning the pages and put them down. 'Were there ever any problems?'

'Not really – only the odd time when the trams are playing up, that sort of thing. Nothing that was down to her. Employers understand when public transport is at fault.' She tapped the wooden desk. 'We've all been there. I wish I had a hundred people like Evie on the books.'

Jessica pointed to an item on the list – the name of a school. 'Is that cleaning work?' she asked.

'Clerical. Once or twice a year they ask us to provide someone to work on their database.'

'Is she qualified for that?'

Tina snorted. 'She's *over*qualified! It's only the hours that stopped her doing more of it. I could have probably got her an office manager's position if things had been different for her at home.'

'How do you mean "overqualified"?'

Tina reached into the folder once more, perfect nail scraping gently on the desk. She pushed another pair of pages across the desk. 'That's her CV,' she said. 'It's from a few years ago so it doesn't include much of the work she's been doing here – but you can see her qualifications.'

Jessica scanned the relevant section and then looked up. 'Evie had an accountancy degree?'

'Like I said, *over*qualified. I told her for years she didn't have to take the cleaning jobs if she didn't want, but it was all about the hours. She put her son ahead of everything.'

'Do you have kids?'

Jessica didn't know why she'd blurted that out as a question. The answer was irrelevant, but the question left her thinking of Caroline and Russell, of how there should have been a child in her house years before and now, finally, there was. It just wasn't hers.

Tina shook her head, turned to her monitor even though she didn't type anything. 'No,' she said. 'You?'

'No.'

A moment or two of silence hung and then Jessica added: 'Did Evie do any accountancy work?'

Tina spun back in her seat so that she was facing Jessica. She sat up straighter, focused on the conversation once more. 'That sort of thing is rarely offered to agency workers because it's so confidential. I don't know of many – if any – companies who'd open up their books to a freelancer. It'd only be something small, with a handful of employees. Perhaps even one or two employees.'

Jessica glanced down towards Evie's CV, reading it

through once more. 'Do you have a recent payslip of Evie's?' she asked.

Tina bit her lip, nodding slowly. She clicked the mouse a couple of times and then tapped some keys before the printer behind her burred to life. She passed Jessica one more sheet of paper, with Evie's name and address at the top – and a paltry sum of money at the bottom.

'Is this a standard number of hours for her?' Jessica asked.

'She normally did between twelve and twenty-four depending on what she had going on with her son. She told us when she was available a week or so in advance and we worked around that.'

Jessica stared at the amount Evie had earned for that week. There'd probably be some sort of government tax credit as well – but it wasn't a lot to live on.

Tina's point that most companies wouldn't want a free-lance accountant to be going through their books line by line was fair enough – but the men who'd broken into Evie's house had asked specifically about money.

'*Where's the money?*' – that's what Samuel had heard.

Jessica doubted the intruders were talking about the pitiful wage Evie made from the agency – so if it wasn't that money they were after, what did they *actually* want?

ELEVEN

Jessica was sitting on the bench outside the clinic waiting for Caroline to emerge. She checked the time on her phone for what was probably the twentieth time – but that didn't make her friend come out any quicker.

A pair of blokes were sharing a cigarette as they hovered on the pavement at the end of the path, those crucial few centimetres away from NHS land. Jessica was only watching them in the sense that she was staring off into nothingness, but they noticed her anyway, giving the 'you stuck here too?' flick of the head. They probably thought she was a lesbian who was there for her partner. Before either of them could instigate a conversation, Jessica took evasive action by going for a wander and phoning Izzy.

'The guv's gunning for you,' Izzy said as a greeting.

'What have I done?'

'Those balloons with "old fart" on the front. He knows they're from you.'

'Why does everyone assume that when anything slightly dodgy happens, it has to involve me?'

'You did buy the balloons, though.'

'That's not the point. Just because someone left half a dozen balloons in his office calling him an old fart, that doesn't mean it was me.'

Izzy laughed. 'You're prime suspect – the only suspect, I think. He's talking about the culprit – uniform or not – having to do the night shift on Black Friday next month.'

'There is no way on earth I'm heading off to Asda at midnight to stop a bunch of nutters rioting over cut-price TVs. Some bloke got stabbed last year in an argument over a foot massager! One of the specials got punched in the back of the head by a bloke who was trampling over a woman to get a half-price beer fridge. I'd rather sign up for New Year's Eve than work Black Friday.'

'Tell it to the judge.'

Jessica was wondering if she could get away with sneaking some unused balloons into the drawer of Detective Inspector Franks – her nemesis – when Izzy asked if she was on shift for the day.

'I'm still at the employment agency,' Jessica replied. 'They were giving it the whole data protection thing, so I've been going round in circles. I told them it doesn't apply for a dead person – you know the drill. I'm just finishing up – then I'm off to talk to Evie Briers' old neighbours.' She paused and then added: 'Are you busy?'

'Massively. We've dragged some bloke in for groping that woman on the bus last week, so that'll be a delightful inter-view, then we've got reports back for the community centre break-in, plus some bastard's nicked the rest of my Maltesers. I only answered the phone for a break.'

'I thought it was for my charming wit.'

Izzy laughed. 'That too, darling. Now, what do you need?'

'Even though she was working as a cleaner, Evie Briers has an accountancy degree. Can you ring round some of the local accountants and mention her name? See if anyone knows her, if she's worked for them, that sort of thing. Get Arch to do it if you're busy.'

Jessica could just about make out the sound of a pen scratching before Izzy replied, saying she'd sort it and then adding: 'Arch found your bloke with the stolen driving licence, by the way. He was right happy with himself. Got him on CCTV in some bar at Deansgate Locks the other Friday. The manager reckons he called in the next day to ask if his wallet had been handed in.'

Jessica hrmmed a reply. She wasn't sure if she believed Chatresh's account of why his driving licence might've shown up on a bloke who'd had his head kicked in but it sounded like it all checked out.

'Any sign of who might've robbed him?' she asked.

'You'll have to ask Arch. Anyway, I do have some other news, if you're interested. One of the constables found Samuel Briers' father.'

'Where?'

'He's living in Canada. We woke him up this morning to tell him what had happened to Evie.'

'What did he say?'

'Not much. He and Evie broke up years ago, she had custody of Samuel, all that. He can't come home, apparently. He's going through some citizenship thing and can't leave the country. Sounds like a right piece of you-know-what.'

Jessica could picture Samuel describing her necklace back to her. '*One utterly extraordinary individual*' – that's what Dr Pearson had said – except he was a kid unwanted by his own father.

Izzy said she had to go and so Jessica checked the time and then repocketed her phone. Caroline should be out any minute... which was what she'd told herself twenty minutes previously.

The pair of smokers had disappeared, but when Jessica

turned back towards the clinic, she noticed another man sitting on the bench where she'd been. *Her* bench. He was in the centre, taking up most of the space, staring at an unlit cigarette in his palm.

'Hi,' Jessica said, drawing his attention. She hoped it was the sort of 'hi' that brimmed with a hidden message, one that screamed, 'How about you move over to the side?' Unfortunately, the one-word greeting was met with only a smile.

'Hi,' he replied.

'You're not supposed to smoke that here,' Jessica said, trying not to sound like too much like one of *those* people who looked to take offence at everything. She nodded at the 'no smoking' sign.

He followed her gaze and then smiled back. 'I've not had a smoke in almost four years.'

The man shuffled to the side – finally – and Jessica squished herself into the opposite corner.

'I like to keep one on me just in case,' he added, pushing the cigarette into his wallet.

Jessica turned to the side, viewing him properly this time, rather than pegging him as a bench-stealer. He was bald, but it suited him. Not the sort of desperate dusting of hair that some blokes held onto no matter what. He was trim in a suit and shirt, earring in his right ear, blue eyes. None of that bullshit about blue like the ocean or an endless expanse of sky, they were normal. *He* was normal.

'In case of what?' she asked.

The man nodded at the clinic. 'I'm supposed to be having a wart cut off my foot. Nothing to worry about, but I don't really do hospitals.'

Jessica didn't reply with words but she rocked in agreement. She didn't *want* to do hospitals – she'd had more than enough grief involving them – but she frequently had no choice.

The man offered his hand. 'Mark,' he said.

'Jessica.'

They shook and then he squeezed his wallet into his back pocket, cigarette and all. There was a delicious silence for a few moments. Awkward in any other circumstance except that Jessica knew he was hunting to find the right words. She actually enjoyed the anticipation.

'I don't suppose you're here for a wart, are you?' Mark said.

Jessica spat out a laugh and then couldn't stop herself. It took a few seconds to regain her dignity. 'Is that a chat-up line?' she asked.

Mark shrank back into his corner, unsure whether to grin or recoil fully. 'Sorry,' he said.

'Truth is, I'm a stalker,' Jessica replied with a smile. 'I only stalk the chronically sick, though. I'm hoping to strike it rich by marrying some billionaire with lung cancer.' She crossed her fingers and held them out for him to see. 'I go round all the hospitals, thinking today will be the day.'

It was Mark's turn to laugh. He snorted through his nose and then tilted his head at an angle, lopsided smile on display. '*Billionaire?* You're a bit hopeful aren't you? Not even going for a millionaire?'

'You've got to aim high.'

He paused, glanced away towards the clinic doors and then back again. 'Do you ever go out with people whose bank balances don't stretch to ten figures?'

'Exclusively.'

'So, um...' he gulped, coughed slightly, clearly hoping she'd take it from there.

At one time she might have done – but there was no chance Jessica was letting him off the hook. It had been a long time since someone had actually asked her out. She was revelling in the moment.

'...Do you, er, fancy a coffee sometime?' he added. 'Or a meal...?' Mark looked past her, not quite meeting her eye.

Jessica made him wait, just for a second or two, and then she pulled out her phone, unlocked the screen and handed it to him. 'Type your number into there,' she said, 'and then go and get that wart sorted out.'

TWELVE

Making house calls wasn't nearly as much fun when Jessica was by herself. For one, she had to do her own navigating, which, given the labyrinthine nature of Manchester's road network, was rarely much of a laugh. Second, with no one to play off, she was left listening to the inane 'banter' on the radio.

After twenty-five minutes of trying to figure out where she was in relation to where she was supposed to be, Jessica eventually found herself in front of a smart semi-detached on the edge of a leafy estate. It was the sort of place dominated by families, young professionals and 'have you seen our missing cat?' posters. Not even a hint of morning-after-the-night-before vomit in the gutter, or used condoms flung under the nearest bush. Very cosy. Bit of a step-up for the people who'd been living in the same block as Evie Briers.

Jessica knocked on the front door and waited. When there was no answer, she tried again, before crouching to peer through the letter box and getting only a face-full of dark bristles. The downstairs curtains were pulled, the driveway empty, the garage clamped closed.

After double-checking she was at the right place, Jessica went next door and tried there instead. This time, a man with a criss-cross tank top over a shirt answered. He had neighbourhood watch organiser written all over him.

'Can I help?' he asked, with the distinct air of someone who didn't want to help.

'I'm looking for Peter and Veronica Haversmith,' Jessica replied. 'I think they live next door.'

The man turned past her towards the house next-door as if to confirm that, yes, it most definitely was a house. 'What do you want them for?' he asked.

'Nothing serious. Do you know if they work during the day? Or how I might be able to get hold of them?'

'You're not a bailiff, are you?'

Jessica showed him her warrant card, which certainly got his attention. He blinked at it, then her, then the card once more.

'Police...?' he said, as if the massive word 'police' and the logo on her ID wasn't enough of a clue.

'Do you know how I might be able to speak to either of them?'

'There's nothing wrong, is there?'

Jessica stood waiting, wondering if he might come out with something that wasn't a question. It took a few moments, but it eventually dawned on him.

'They're on holiday,' he said. 'Went last week.'

'Do you know when they might be back?'

'I think they're on a cruise. Veronica mentioned something about it being three weeks – "trip of a lifetime", if I recall correctly. Is there anything I can help with...?'

'How long ago did they move in?' she asked.

The man peered upwards, counting silently. 'Three months, maybe four. Not long.'

'Any particular problems?'

'Like what?'

'I'm not sure. I'm not saying there should be anything wrong.'

He nodded. 'They seem friendly enough,' he said. 'They say hello in the mornings, we wave back and forth – that sort of thing. I helped them with a bit of weeding and Peter cut my lawn.'

Jessica smiled sweetly, assured him there was nothing wrong and then thanked him for his time.

House two was a mile or so down the road, not quite as smart as where the Haversmiths lived but still better than the block in which Evie had died. There was a park at the end of the street and the area was nice enough that the various pieces of equipment hadn't been covered in graffiti and then smashed to pieces. The swings weren't wrapped around the top of the frame and the bin for dog waste hadn't been set on fire.

Jessica tried ringing the bell, but there was nobody home. There was no answer at either of the adjacent houses, nor anyone in across the road. The estate was full of working people, which was a surprise in itself. There was usually someone home on any given street: some bloke off on the sick, a housewife or husband watching daytime TV, or somebody who worked nights and was begging to be woken up by a police officer asking inane questions.

Jessica returned to the house for one final bell-ring, which was when she noticed the 'to rent' sign on the path at the side of the property. The bottom of the post was rotted with moss and soil and it looked like it had been snapped, rather than carefully pulled from the ground. Jessica dialled the number of the estate agent and waited for the falsest of false 'Hello, how can I help you?'

She gave the address and said she'd seen a rental advert

and was wondering if it was still available. The agent said he'd check and then Jessica listened to thirty seconds of a computer keyboard being bashed around.

'That's gone, I'm afraid,' the man said. 'We do have some other properties that might suit your needs. Could I take your name, please?'

'How long ago did it come off the market?'

'Three months ago. Where did you see the ad?'

Jessica told him not to worry about it – and then hung up.

Sally Nugent had a brand-new car on the drive. The registration plate was the giveaway – but there wasn't much more to make it look new. The side windows were clogged with jingly-jangly crap, a fluffy pink heart was dangling from the mirror and there were eyelashes on the headlights. It was like she'd gone into the showroom, said, 'Can you fill the car with as much shite as possible', and then driven off.

On the plus side, she did at least answer her front door.

She was in a baby pink towelling tracksuit, the type of crime against humanity that was hard to forgive. Her jaw was in perpetual motion, masticating away on gum like a hungry bovine.

'Y'a'ight?' she asked – although it took Jessica a second or two to realise that there were words among the gooey, saliva-filled chomp.

'Are you Sally?' Jessica asked.

'Who's asking?'

Jessica's warrant card came out once more and Sally scowled at it, still chewing rhythmically.

'What y'after?' Sally added.

'Do you know Evie Briers?'

'What's she done?'

'I'm sorry to break it to you like this, but she was killed two nights ago.'

The chewing stopped, Sally's mouth hanging open. 'She what?'

'Someone broke into her flat the night before last. We don't know all the details, but I'm afraid she's dead. I was hoping to ask you a few questions.'

Sally continued to stare at Jessica and suddenly things weren't quite so funny. 'You better come in,' she said.

Sally's gum had been replaced with a carton of coconut water. 'Detox,' she said by way of explanation. 'I drink one of these for breakfast, another for lunch, and then fish or chicken for tea. I love it.'

The frown didn't make it seem like she loved it.

'Did you know Evie well?' Jessica asked when they were settled in the kitchen. There were high stools and a breakfast bar.

'Not really – I was in the flat below, so we said hello every now and then. I can't believe she's dead. What happened?'

'We're still figuring that out at the moment. Can you tell me what she was like?'

'Normal, I suppose. She'd smile and say hello.' Sally put a hand to her mouth. 'Oh, God. What's going to happen to her son?'

'I don't know.'

'Poor kid.' Sally guzzled some of the coconut water through a straw, staring into nothingness. Despite her spoken concern, Jessica wasn't seeing it from the way she was acting. She was picking at her nails, frowning at something amiss, glancing towards the clock above the television, reading the label on the back of the carton.

'What?' Jessica asked.

They locked eyes and then Sally knew the façade was up. 'Call me a bad person if you want,' she said with quiet defiance, 'but I couldn't put up with that clicking noise. You could hear it through the floor. Morning, noon and night – *click, click, click*. Sometimes I'd just want a lie-in – you know what it's like. Long week at work, two hours in the gym the night before, you want to stay in bed at the weekend. Not possible when there's a constant noise coming from above. Have you heard it?'

Jessica let it all sink in for a moment and then said: 'I don't think you're a bad person.'

Sally eyed her suspiciously, opened her mouth to say something and then closed it again. She'd been ready to unleash her righteous indignation and now there was no need.

'Oh,' she said eventually.

'Is that why you moved out?' Jessica asked.

A slight shrug. 'Sort of. Not just that – I'd been there a while. Time to move on, sometimes, innit?'

'Aside from the clicking, was there anything else that concerned you about living there?'

'Like what?'

'Late-night noise, kids hanging around, general antisocial behaviour...?'

She tugged at her tracksuit bottoms, having a good ol' scratch at her thighs. 'A few boy racers now and then. One of the mums down the road contacted the council. She came knocking on all the doors asking us to sign a petition because she thought her kids might get run over.'

'How long ago was that?'

'Years – two or three.'

'Anything more recent?'

Sally shook her head slowly. 'Should there be?'

'Not really – just examining all possibilities. Did you get on with the other neighbours?'

'I suppose. It's not like we were having big nights out together or inviting each other round for coffee. We said hello, the odd nod here and there. You'd hold the door open – the usual sort of thing.'

'And the landlords...?'

'Shaun and Julie?'

'Right.'

Sally blinked, nodded quickly and then broke into a smile. 'Yeah, sorry. They're lovely. I was struggling one month because I'd lost my bank card, but they didn't mind me taking a few extra days to pay. Then there was a problem with the shower head making the pressure really low, but they had that fixed. They got a man round to sort out a dodgy plug socket too. Never had a problem with them.'

The smile widened, a kid trying too hard to convince her parents she hadn't nicked the sweets found in her bedroom.

'Did you see them much?' Jessica asked.

'Who?'

'Shaun and Julie.'

'Oh... sorry, I'm not with it today...'

Sally eyed the back of her drinks carton with suspicion. If that's all she was surviving on then Jessica wasn't entirely surprised she seemed a bit spaced out. She could barely think straight without a mid-morning trip to the canteen vending machine – and a good three quarters of the officers around her were smacked off their tits on McVitie's – or the cheapest supermarket version. It was a time of austerity, after all.

'We used to text each other,' Sally added. 'They came round once or twice a year to make sure everything was all right, but that was it. No need for anything more.'

That sounded about right – and had been the same in every place Jessica had ever rented. Everyone wanted a simple life. Landlords wanted their money; tenants wanted a roof, some peace and privacy.

'When did you leave?' Jessica asked.

Sally counted on her fingers. 'Three months ago. Maybe four? It was definitely summer.'

'Late June or July, then?' A pause and then: 'Is that a problem?'

'Not necessarily – but there were four flats in the block. Three of you all moved out at roughly the same time. Certainly within a few weeks of each other...'

Sally couldn't look at Jessica any longer. She put the drinks carton down and then brushed her hands on her lap, shooting a quick glance towards the window. 'What are you saying?'

'Nothing – I was just wondering if something happened that made you all decide to go at the same time.'

There was another glance to the window and then Sally shook her head furiously. 'Just one of those things, I guess.' She stood quickly and took a step towards the door. 'I am a bit busy, actually...'

As hints went, it was up there with kicking a puppy to show a person didn't like dogs, or booting a bloke in the balls to tell him a date was off the cards. Jessica knew when she wasn't welcome, so stood as well. She passed Sally a business card, telling her to call or email if she thought of anything that might be useful.

Sally said she would and then repeated she was 'gutted' about Evie. She tagged on the old classic: 'If there's anything I can do...' even though the second part of the sentence might as well have been '...don't bother contacting me'. They shook hands and then Jessica was gone, wondering what on earth had happened three months previously.

THIRTEEN

Jessica was driving back to the station when the Bluetooth speaker on her dashboard kicked in with a frazzled series of buzzing belches and flashing blue LEDs. She shouted 'answer', there was a beep and then Izzy's tinny voice crackled.

'You busy?' she asked.

'Twenty minutes away, depending on traffic. Are you angling for more chocolate?'

'Some of us are working today, not just skiving off to pretend we're doing interviews.'

'Oi! I have been doing interviews.'

And ferrying Caroline to and from the clinic, of course... Still, with all the unpaid overtime Jessica had done over the years, it was about time she got some of it back.

'Three of the constables have been phoning round various accountants,' Izzy continued. 'We started with the city centre and then tried east towards Evie lived, then others dotted around Greater Manc. We also searched for her name in relation to accounting, finance, money, economics – all that sort of thing.'

'And?'

'Nothing. No one's heard of her. She's as well-known as an *X Factor* winner three months after their first single.'

'Bloody hell. More people know me than one of them.'

'Precisely. If she did work as accountant, then either it wasn't for a proper company, or they're keeping quiet about it.'

The Bluetooth box fizzed and, for a moment, Jessica thought the call had dropped. Izzy's voice jumped in and out of being heard and then it was clear once more.

'...prison.'

'What about prison?' Jessica asked. 'My signal's conking out.'

'I said someone's found Mr One-Leg-Shorter-Than-The-Other Carl Brompton. He's been living at Hotel Smack since leaving prison.'

Jessica glanced up to the road sign she was passing under. There was a bewildering range of arrows that only vaguely pointed her in the direction she was heading. It was an indication she'd lived in the city for far too long that she knew precisely where she was.

'That's only five minutes from where I am,' she said. 'Has anyone called them?'

'I figured you might want to.'

Jessica glanced to the dashboard clock. It was a little after two and she had an inbox full of things to deal with back at the station, plus she had to find out what Archie had discovered from the CCTV at the bars.

But the truth was – and everyone knew it, *especially* Izzy – she liked being out and about. Needed to be. If it wasn't for being able to lean on her sergeant, Jessica would spend most of her day at a desk. It had been her main concern when applying for the inspector's role in the first place. Some people suited the desk life; others, like her, had to see the whites of people's eyes, to hear the quiver in their voices. Jessica was a rank above

Izzy – but wouldn't be able to do the job her way without that help.

Jessica flipped her indicator lever up and drifted into the left lane. 'You know me too well,' she said.

Hotel Smack was an old house nestled on the edge of a cricket pitch not far from Heaton Park. What had once been a Victorian mansion had now been converted into a hostel for a dozen or so men who were either on probation with nowhere to live or who had recently been released from prison. When it had first opened, there had been a massive outcry among locals. 'We don't want our kids finding used needles', 'Why can't former prisoners be housed on the edge of someone else's estate?', 'What about our house prices?' – and so on. It was all very *Daily Mail*. Inevitably, the place had opened anyway and things had gone quiet. No needles were found and everyone's house prices had continued to spiral out of the reach of anyone under the age of thirty.

The grounds offered a wide expanse of carpeted lawn interspersed by trees that were beginning to wither with the season. There was a cricket pavilion over the back of a twiggy hedgerow and a crumbling driveway arching its way from the road to the house.

Jessica parked under the shadow of a steepling old tree and then stepped across the mulch of leaves, mud and twigs, heading for the door. The house would have once been glorious: four storeys, with thick, Gothic beams. The sort of place built for ghost stories.

There was a buzzer box next to the front door and Jessica jabbed the button marked 'reception'. As she waited, she turned to take in the rest of the grounds once more. She wondered how such a beautiful place had become known as Hotel Smack. It was a nickname used widely at the station, probably unofficially by the probation service as well. She'd never known it as anything else, even though the sign read: 'Middleton House'. It wasn't as if there'd ever been any major trouble with drugs at the house... it was just one of those things: ex-prisoners equalled drugs. Even in PC times, the name had stuck.

'Can I help you?'

Jessica jumped at the sound of a male voice. She spun back around to see a man in the doorway wearing a shocking cream jumper with green and red triangly bits. They might have been trees but Jessica didn't want to go cross-eyed by staring at it too closely. It was the sort of thing a grandmother might foist upon some poor child one Christmas.

'Sorry,' the man added, not sounding too sorry. 'Didn't mean to startle you.' He had thinning grey hair and glasses that shielded a set of weary eyes.

'Tim,' Jessica replied, reaching for her warrant card. 'We've met before.'

His gaze arrowed in on her and then he started to nod slowly. 'I have absolutely no idea who you are,' he replied.

Jessica blinked. That was bloody charming, that was. Christ, you spend a lifetime wanting to make an impression, to be remembered, and then some bloke you've met at least four times doesn't know who you are. Four times! She'd visited twice before to talk to a resident, they'd met once in court – and then he'd been at some civic function she'd been roped into against her will. Four times!

Tim glanced at her warrant card and then angled back towards the house. 'You after someone in particular?'

'Carl Brompton.'

'Not seen him in a couple of days.'

'I thought his release conditions meant he had to sleep here?'

'I did report the breach to probation but' – a shrug – 'out of my hands then, innit?'

Tim had the weary, rolly-eyed gaze of a man who'd seen and heard it all before. The poor sod probably hadn't thought he'd end up working as a de-facto caretaker for a bunch of blokes either fresh out of prison or lucky not to be there in the first place. What would the job advert even say? *Wanted: Poor sod for thankless task. Pitiful pay, dodgy jumpers a must.*

'Any idea where he might have gone?' Jessica asked.

Tim adjusted his glasses and hugged himself with his arms. It was a bit chilly, but he'd not invited her in, so he could hardly complain.

'I don't ask, they don't tell. I lock the door at the same time each night. If they're in, they're in. If they're supposed to be here but they're not, I report the breach. Nothing's changed.'

He was giving off a distinct, 'Go on, piss off' vibe. Something that Jessica well knew. Not only had she seen it in action many times before, she was still trying to master it herself.

'Can you call me if he shows up?' she asked.

Tim shook his head. 'Not my job, that. Residents are guaranteed privacy. They're not going to trust me if I go running to you every time you want to talk to one of them, are they?'

Jessica stared at him, trying to get some sort of evil-eye action going on, wanting him to wilt under her gaze.

No chance.

'I'll leave you a card anyway,' she said. He didn't even bother to look at it as it went into his pocket.

'Well... I'll leave you to it,' Jessica added.

'Right you are.'

Tim didn't say goodbye. He simply turned his back and headed inside, then pulled the door closed. Jessica didn't exactly blame him – he was the middleman caught between his residents and the police and probation service. He wasn't supposed to take sides.

Still, they'd now met five times and he probably still wouldn't remember her.

Jessica was back at her car when she noticed a shuffling shadow close to one of the spindly, autumn-ravaged trees. In the middle of summer, when thick green leaves covered the branches, it might have been a decent spot for some privacy.

Not so much now.

Games of hide-and-seek wouldn't last long in the grounds of Hotel Smack during autumn and winter.

Instead of getting into the car, Jessica ambled across the damp grass. The figure behind the tree twitched as if to move off but then froze like a bunny in the headlights. He had a crooked back and was wearing a thick olive green coat a few sizes too big for him. A charity-shop special. The hood was up, but Jessica realised she knew the man as she approached. She'd arrested him at least twice. The first was years and years back when she was in uniform. He was hanging around cash machines at the university, not exactly robbing people but causing a public nuisance by asking for money in a not-so-polite way. She also remembered nicking him for shoplifting cheese from one of the express supermarkets on Deansgate. The sad truth was, he was homeless and had been for a long time. He'd be periodically picked up for various crimes, get a few weeks in prison, and then the cycle would begin once more.

'Hello, Donal,' Jessica said.

The man winced away at the sound of his name, looking at her sideways through the gap between his hood and the rest of the coat. Even though his back was bent, he was taller than her.

'I was hoping you could do me a favour,' Jessica added.

She took out her purse and produced a ten-pound note, which suddenly had his attention.

'What?' Donal's voice was gruff with the merest hint of Irish.

'Do you have a phone? Or access to one?'

He nodded towards the house and muttered a cloggy, 'There.'

'Do you know Carl Brompton?' she added.

'Aye.'

'Next time you see him, give me a call, okay? Ten pounds now, another ten if you call me.'

His grey eyes met hers before shooting to the money. He held his hand out greedily.

'Do we have a deal?' Jessica asked.

'Aye.'

She passed him the money and a card. Both disappeared into the pocket of his coat and then he shuffled backwards.

'You can call me anytime,' Jessica added. 'Even if it's three in the morning.'

'Can I have the other tenner now?'

There was the slightest twitch of his lips into what was almost a smile. He held a hand out hopefully.

'Nice try,' Jessica told him. 'Call me if you see Carl.'

Jessica was in the station's car park thinking about her avalanche of emails. She fought back a yawn, wondering whether Russell might have a quiet night. It was fine having Caroline living in the spare room, but her son had one hell of a pair of lungs on him.

She was almost out of the car, honest she was, when she fell back into the driver's seat, phone in hand. She scrolled through the list of names and there he was – 'Mark: hospital weirdo'. She'd typed the name in herself before handing him the phone, wondering if it would put him off. Either it hadn't, or he'd not noticed. There was no getting out of it, really...

Unless he'd typed in the wrong number by mistake!

That would be a bonus – not even her fault then. How could it be her fault if he'd entered a wrong digit here or there?

Her thumb hovered over the name. It had been a long time since she'd done anything like this. She actually craved a cigarette – and she'd not smoked at all in years, not regularly since she was a teenager. Now she really wanted one. A reward and a punishment in its own right.

She pressed Mark's name and watched the screen change colour. He definitely wouldn't answer. Even if he'd typed the number in correctly, he'd be somewhere without service. Happened all the time, didn't it? All the network operators were cowboy charlatans, what with their dodgy coverage maps and all.

It rang. Once, twice and then...

A man's voice: 'Hello?'

'Oh, um... hi. It's Jessica from the clinic earlier.'

'Oh, hello! I was hoping you'd call.'

'Right... so I was wondering if you might like to do something in a couple of nights' time...?'

FOURTEEN

Jessica was on the main floor where the constables worked, bobbing back and forth on one of the spinny office chairs. The bin in the corner was filled with chocolate wrappers and a deflated set of 'old fart' balloons that DCI Topper had apparently dumped while trying to find out who'd left them in his office. He'd not seen Jessica since, which was probably a good thing.

Following the afternoon before and a good hour that morning, Jessica was finally through her emails, plus the assorted memos, forms to sign off, Post-it notes that had been left on her desk – and everything else designed to make her life just that little bit more difficult.

She and three constables were crowded around Izzy's desk, though the rest of the floor was largely empty. Either officers were busy or there was some special offer at the café down the road.

'We're still waiting on reports from Evie's apartment,' Jessica said. 'I spoke to someone at the lab, but they say tomorrow at the earliest. They snagged a bunch of hairs – but they could be Evie's, Samuel's, or anyone else's. No obvious shoeprints or fingerprints were found and, though it would have been nice, neither of the robbers dropped a passport. As such, we're still unsure who either of our men were. We only have Samuel's word and, well...' She tailed off, not needing to add that he was blind. 'We do have the post-mortem. Evie cracked her head on the corner of her kitchen counter, causing severe bleeding on the brain. That would indicate that, at least to some extent, the men who broke into her apartment didn't actually mean to kill her. It's impossible to know whether she slipped or was shoved. As for getting in, they would have had to get through both the main door and Evie's own door. There's no sign they forced their way into the apartment, but they might well have simply knocked and then pushed their way in. Evie's best friend, Deborah, said the main door was rarely locked, but that's not been confirmed. Either way, they'd have had to get through Evie's own apartment door. Deborah said Evie didn't know too many people. The teachers at Samuel's school have more or less confirmed that, as far as they know. She didn't use social media – lucky her – and her only family is Samuel's father, who's in Canada. That said, if she *did* open the door, then the attackers could be someone she knew.'

One of the constables took his turn to pipe up: 'The CCTV from the nearest shop wasn't working – and the one closest to that didn't show anything. We got a blurry traffic cam match of two males crossing the road near the stadium, but it's hard to identify anyone specifically, let alone clean it up enough to get a face. The time could be about right, but then it might just be two men walking home from the pub. Aside from that, ANPR has given us a list of cars in the area, but there are no obvious flags. Someone's been on to the taxi companies asking about nearby drop-offs or pickups – but that's not thrown up too much.' He looked up to Jessica. 'In short, we've got nothing.' He paused. 'Not yet.'

That was more or less as Jessica suspected. She told them about Evie's neighbours all moving out at roughly the same time three months previously – not that it meant much by itself. For the time being, the crime had been kept relatively quiet – predominantly as there wasn't much to go public with. It was probably an attempted burglary gone wrong – but what were the thieves trying to steal? They only had the say-so of a blind teenager that it had been two men in the first place – and that wasn't something the higher-ups were willing to tell the media. There was little point in asking people whether they'd seen two men in the general area if it actually turned out Samuel was mistaken all along. A public appeal might well come – but not yet.

'What's come in overnight?' Jessica asked.

Izzy tapped something on her keyboard and then turned towards the rest of the group. 'There was a burglary at Robinson's Garage just down the road. SOC are there right now. A domestic got out of hand in the flat above a pizza shop on that rank out by the BP on Hyde Road, Mrs Heath called twice more about those kids hanging around the garages opposite her house—'

There was a collective groan – Mrs Heath was a serial caller. Kids outside the front of her house, kids walking along the alley at the back of her house, kids playing football near the trees, kids listening to music, kids on the bus. She really didn't like young people.

'—Someone's tortoise has gone missing, some woman saw lights in the sky and thought it was aliens.' She looked up. 'Actually, four different people all saw lights in the sky, so perhaps it was aliens.' Back to her screen: 'Cows got onto Ashton Old Road overnight, possible burglary in Levenshulme turned out to be a squirrel.' She paused for breath. 'Quiet night, really.'

Jessica looked around the circle.

'I'm not doing it,' Archie said quickly.

'Me neither,' chirped in the first constable.

'Don't look at me,' Izzy replied.

They'd all spoken so swiftly that the final member of the group hadn't managed to get his mouth open. PC Pen Thief wasn't a newbie – but he still had a lot to learn.

'Bollocks,' he muttered under his breath.

'You visit Mrs Heath,' Jessica told him. 'Give her a bit of sweet-talking, drink whatever herbal tea she offers you, agree that things were better in the old days and show off your arm muscles, whatever it takes.'

The constable cursed once more.

'What have the night crew done?' Jessica asked.

'Well, they haven't been abducted by aliens, if that's what you were asking,' Izzy replied. 'Other than that, pretty much everything's in hand except the burglary.'

'Good. What about an ID for that body in the ditch?'

Izzy shook her head. 'Not that I've heard.'

Archie's turn: 'I went round the bars Chatresh said he was in, but there was only watchable CCTV in one. He's definitely there – but no particular sign of someone who robbed him. The owner says he called in the next day to ask about a missing wallet – but there weren't any other reports of stolen things that night. I spoke to city centre about pickpockets in the area, but they couldn't really help. He said it was stolen, but he might've left it in the toilets.'

Jessica said she was waiting for a fingerprint report to come back from Chatresh's licence – and that she'd put in a follow-up call. She slapped her knees. 'Okay, Iz, you're in charge. If we can't find out who broke into Evie's flat, then let's at least figure out what she had going on behind closed doors. Deborah reckoned Evie might have another job and Samuel heard a man asking for money. Arch – you're with me.'

FIFTEEN

In the days since Evie's death, her apartment block had transformed into one of those places that would end up being called a 'blight on the neighbourhood' in some planning report from the not-too distant future.

The glass of the main door was covered with thick chipboard daubed with a 'do not enter' sign, though that was somewhat offset by the enormous penis that had been graffitied underneath. What was it with people drawing dicks on everything? It was a purely male trait – no one went round scrawling the female anatomy on unassuming walls.

A bouquet of flowers had been left on the patio at the front, covering the patch of scorched concrete; with another resting underneath one of the front windows. As Archie fiddled with the padlock, Jessica stooped to check the flowers. The first was a set of lilies that had started to wilt from being left outside. The card was from Deborah, simply saying 'miss you. RIP'. The second left Jessica feeling as if she'd been punched in the gut. There were a dozen white roses, plus a small cream card inscribed with only three letters.

'What?' Archie said.

Jessica didn't know how long she'd been staring at the card, but she gulped and blinked away the sting at the back of her throat.

She held it up for him to see – the letters slightly crooked, written in felt-tip: 'MUM'.

Archie stared at it, lips tight, not knowing how to reply. What was there to say?

'Did it open?' Jessica asked, relieved that her voice hadn't cracked. She returned the card to the bouquet.

Archie pulled the door open and headed inside. He flipped the switch on the wall and light beamed from above. It took Jessica's eyes a moment to adjust, but there was a door on the left and the right, with a set of stairs directly in front. Four individual mailboxes were underneath the light switch and there was a small rug in the corner, covered with mud and filth.

'Door doesn't shut properly,' Archie said.

He was trying to wrestle it into place with his shoulder, but it was sticking in the frame, swollen from the Manchester climate. He tried turning the key, but it wasn't working.

'It must lock somehow,' Jessica said, realising she was being unhelpful only after she'd spoken.

Archie flashed a 'don't-you-think-I-know-that' look and then continued battling with the wood. In the end, he managed to lock it only by heaving it upwards and then twisting the key at the same time.

'It'd look locked without actually being locked,' he said. 'No one's going to fight that bloody thing every time they get home.'

Jessica didn't disagree. She'd have been the same – she'd have pulled the door closed and left it at that, rather than fighting it into submission to actually turn the key.

'Do you think this was one house originally?' she asked.

Archie turned in a circle, gave it the whole one-hand-on-hip builder's nod. The one that oozed a confidence to say he knew what he was talking about, even though he probably didn't.

'I reckon so,' he said. 'Knock it into four, stick a few locks on the doors and that's quadruple the rent.'

They headed up the stairs and Archie used a second key to unlock Evie's front door. This one was far more normal – Yale lock, twist, push and in.

The curtains were pulled and the inside was shrouded in darkness until Archie flipped the light switch to reveal the mess. Someone had tried to clean up – but they'd made about as much effort as Jessica did to appear interested during team briefings. The dust that was used to look for fingerprints had been swept into the corners and there were still smears across the countertops.

The vague stain of blood was still there, too.

The apartment was largely open-plan and Jessica found herself drifting along the short hallway, past a door on either side, into the kitchen.

It was like a flare had been dropped in the centre of the apartment, a beacon demanding attention. The once cream tiles of the kitchen floor were now blemished indelibly by a dim crimson. Evie's blood had streamed into the gap between the tiles, pooling outwards towards the fridge and crusting into an inky scab.

Jessica crouched to examine it more closely, twisting back to look towards the front door. She could picture Samuel standing at the counter, clicking to see what was going on, anguish in his voice.

What a horrible, horrible mess. In more ways than one.

As she stood, Jessica's head started to spin. She clasped the counter, squeezing her eyes closed and trying to force the sensation away. With the card outside and now this, it was all a little too much. Jessica wasn't even sure why it was this in particular that had hit her. She'd seen much worse in the past... and yet she'd not met Samuel at any of those.

'You're going to get the men, aren't you?'

He'd really done a number on her.

Jessica reached for the sink and twisted the cold tap. There was a sputter and then the merest trickle of water. She tried the hot and a thick spurt of liquid gushed into the sink, splashing up and over the top.

Jessica swore under her breath as she turned the taps back off, before trying again. The second attempt was no different to the first – the cold tap didn't work properly. She tried the bathroom next – where this time the taps did work, for both the sink and the bath.

It was a morbid sight: bottles of shampoo, conditioner and liquid soap that were half used and now wouldn't be finished. Some hair ties, a comb. The unspoken, dreary part of a person's life. What happened to all this stuff when they were gone? There'd be clothes, too. Shoes. All the normal things that were left for somebody else to clear away.

'Jess.'

She followed the sound of Archie's voice back towards the kitchen and the open-plan living room. A sofa separated the room, but that was it – there were no other walls in the main area. There was almost no clutter, either. Minimal furniture, with a television unit at the front and everything else tucked away into a cabinet against the wall. The apartment was nowhere near as messy as she'd first thought, it was only the fingerprint dust in the hallway that had made it look so.

Archie was crouching at the side of the cabinet, pointing at the wall. 'See this?' he said.

'It's a wall.'

He waved her down until she was crouching next to him. There was a plug socket next to the unit but it was loose and a pair of wires were visible at the side.

'What do you reckon?' he said.

'It's still better than the electrics at the station.'

'But we don't have blind kids, do we?'

Jessica realised what he was getting at, but Archie spelt it out anyway.

He wafted a hand towards the rest of the room. 'It's only the floors that are messy – and that's due to our lot – but look at the rest of the place,' he said. 'Everything's tidied away, there are no random ornaments or bits of furniture lying around. She'd have kept the house clear so Samuel didn't walk into anything by accident.'

'Deborah said the same thing.'

Archie pointed back towards the socket. 'So this is a bit odd, isn't it? She keeps everything in place and yet there are live wires there.'

'The tap in the kitchen's on the blink, too.'

Archie stood and moved into the corner. There was a tall uplighter about the same height as he was. He twisted the switch on the front but it didn't come on. He turned it back and nothing happened. 'There's a bulb in there,' he said. 'It's plugged in. It just doesn't work.'

'The landlady said the other flats needed a bit of work, but she didn't mention this one.'

'We could call her and ask...?'

Jessica left Archie looking around the flat as she headed out into the main communal area. She didn't have either Shaun or Julie's numbers on her – but their letting agency was easy enough to find online.

It was Julie who answered, a mix of polite, professional and chirpy. She was surprised to hear Jessica's voice but pleased to hear the house itself would be released back to them within a day or so. She insisted Evie hadn't contacted them about any repairs to the house, let alone frayed wires or taps that didn't work. She even called through to her husband to double-check.

Jessica thanked her and then hung up. Not entirely surprised. Even if Evie had reported those things, Jessica doubted the owners would be shouting up to say they'd not had the work done.

Back in the apartment, Archie was in Evie's bedroom. He was sitting on the floor hunting through one of the divan drawers. 'See this?' he said.

Jessica took the frame from him and twisted it around. It was a certificate to show Evie's accountancy degree – a BSc signed and stamped from the University of Salford.

'It was at the bottom of the drawer,' he said.

'Have you found anything that looks like a payslip or a contract?'

'Only for her agency work.'

'There was nothing on her phone records, either. If she was working for someone on the side, she wasn't calling them from her own number.'

'We should get a proper search team in here,' he said. 'Y'know, rip up the floorboards, check in the walls – that sort of thing.'

Jessica peered around the room. It might be an idea – probably was – except what would that leave for poor Samuel and Deborah to clear up? Would Samuel return? Or would Shaun and Julie have to do it? It was grim enough as it was.

'Bit much, isn't it?' she said.

Archie shrugged. 'I've always fancied myself with a sledgehammer.'

He turned back to the drawer and continued flicking through the various items. Jessica rounded the bed and pulled out the drawer on the other side before starting to do the same. Her side was mainly packed with shoes.

'How'd you think you'd get on with a blind kid?'

Archie's question came utterly out of the blue. Jessica

peered up over the bed and she realised he was watching her. There was a curl at the front of his hair, still wet from whatever gel he used.

'Sorry,' he added. 'I didn't mean—'

'Probably badly,' Jessica replied. She looked back down to the drawer, hunting through the shoes in case there was anything underneath – and being sure not to look Archie in the eye. 'No patience,' she added. 'I mean, if you had a kid who was blind, you'd find a way. You'd just get on with it and that'd be the norm. But with you asking me now, I don't know what I'd say.'

Archie didn't reply instantly. When he did, it was three short words: 'We broke up.'

Jessica didn't look up from the shoes, even though she'd finished sorting. She figured Archie wouldn't want her to look at him. She definitely wouldn't want it if the roles were reversed.

'When?'

'Maybe a month ago. I kept it quiet because, well, y'know what things are like at the station.'

'You're going to take as much stick as you give out – and by "you", I actually mean *you*.'

He sighed and then laughed. 'Aye, well... I guess I've got my fair share coming in that case. Should've kept my mouth shut a bit more.'

There was a rustling from the other side of the bed and Jessica knew he wanted her to ask. She wasn't usually one to give in but he had that kicked-puppy-dog look about him. She also wasn't quite sure how many people he knew with whom he could be himself – or at least the version of him that she knew. She didn't much care for his cheeky-chappie front.

'What happened?' she asked.

'Just one of those things. She reckoned I was putting other things first – the job, mates, United – all that. She was like, "If it's like this now, what's it going to be like when we have kids?", then I was like, "Kids? Who said anything about kids?" Then we were just back and forth. She said a few things, I said a few things. Turns out we probably should've had a chat about what we actually wanted a long time ago.'

Jessica didn't reply. She continued rummaging, letting him stew. If he was after relationship advice, she didn't exactly have the best track record herself. She slipped the drawer closed and then shuffled around the floor until she was facing the nightstand.

'I ran into her at the United game last weekend,' Archie added.

Jessica opened the bottom drawer and started to flit through the mounds of socks and tights.

'Thought I'd say hello, but she wasn't having it. Told me I had to grow up, which is a bit bloody rich, seeing as she sleeps with a soft toy dinosaur.'

The middle drawer was underwear. Nothing particularly exciting.

'Anyway, it's probably for the best, innit? No point in wasting loads of years if you want different things at the end of it.'

There was make-up and body sprays in the top drawer, plus more hair ties, some pins and clips, a brush. The usual sort of stuff. Jessica slid the small wooden unit to the side. She wasn't sure what she hoped to reveal – but it certainly wasn't the mounds of dust stuck to the carpet.

'It's bloody hard work, though. You go from having a shag pretty much every night to being stuck in a desert. Sometimes I can't even think straight.'

Jessica ducked lower to peer under the bed, but, after seeing nothing, went to move the nightstand back into place. That was when she noticed what was wrong.

'Well, I didn't expect that,' Jessica said.

'Didn't expect what? A man has needs. It's not like—'

'Not you and your bloody "needs" – but let's not mention them again – I meant *that*.'

Archie clambered over the bed to see what Jessica was pointing at. The skirting board that ran around the room had been painted royal blue to offset the cream of the walls. At first glance, the section behind the nightstand was the same as everything else in the room – except there were two vertical slits around thirty centimetres apart.

Jessica reached forward and pulled the wood away from the wall. It resisted a little but then easily came away from the wall. It had been attached with double-sided tape, enough to keep it in place, but not the usual sort of material that would have been used to attach it to the wall.

There probably should have been a wall behind the board – but there wasn't. A ragged hole had been chiselled into the bricks, leaving coarse sandy edges curved around darkness.

Jessica lay flat on the carpet, switching on the flashlight of her phone and shining it into the gap.

'There could be a rat in there.'

Jessica turned and glared up at Archie. 'You're not helping.'

'I'm just saying.'

'Say nice things.'

'Okay – perhaps there's a baby unicorn and a rainbow in there.'

Jessica rolled back and angled her phone towards the gap. The light instantly caught something smooth and translucent. Jessica reached for it and then pulled her fingers away, suddenly wary that it *could* be a rat.

Bloody Archie and his big mouth.

'What is it?' Archie said.

She stretched forward, fingering the smooth plastic of a sandwich bag. Confident it wasn't a flesh-eating rodent ready to bite, Jessica yanked the bag out of the gap and then reached in to remove a second. She pushed herself into a sitting position and then unsealed the ziplock at the top.

Money.

A small stack of tens and twenties. Some were crumpled, others relatively crisp and new. The sort of mix that would end up in a coffee-shop till at the end of the day.

'How much?' Archie asked.

Jessica looked to the second bag, which was much the same as the first. 'Five hundred,' she said. 'Perhaps six.'

'Not that much.'

Jessica agreed. She squidged herself towards the gap and shone her light fully inside. The crevice stretched behind the layer of plaster towards the outer wall. There was a thin layer of insulation but plenty of space at the bottom.

'There's nothing else in here,' Jessica said.

'Do you reckon she's got more hidden around the flat?' Archie asked.

'Maybe... I doubt it. If she was hiding money, there's lots of room here. Why would she spread it around?'

'True.'

Jessica pushed herself up onto the bed. She checked the second bag of money and then resealed it. She spoke through a sigh at the senselessness of it all: 'It doesn't seem like a lot to get killed over.'

The bed sank as Archie sat next to her. He picked up one of the packets of money, twisting it in his hand but not opening it. 'It doesn't sound like they meant to kill her,' he said. 'Besides, five hundred quid's like a lottery win to some people. To others, it's five hundred more to go up their arms. Muggers have killed people for a tenner in this city.'

Jessica huffed out another long breath. She knew he was right – of course he was – but bloody hell. Is that what a life was worth?

'Where'd you think she got the money?' Archie added.

'I reckon if we can find that out, we'll have a good idea of who killed her.'

SIXTEEN

Jessica wasn't entirely sure what would happen to the money. For the time being, it would be submitted as evidence, even though it wasn't actually proof of anything specific. In theory, it belonged to Samuel, passed down with his mother's death – and yet it could never be that straightforward. Was it the money for which Evie had died? Plus, was it earned legally or by other means?

After requesting a search team to go through the house properly, Jessica found Archie in the living room of the apartment. He was sitting on the sofa, seemingly staring at the wall. When she entered, he turned to look at her, but there was something different. He was biting his lip, hesitant and suddenly unsure of himself.

'You up to much?' she asked.

He glanced away from her, eyeing the front door. 'What are you doing with the money?' he asked.

'What do you *think* I'm doing?'

'I don't know, I—'

'Are you seriously asking if I'm going to nick it?'

'No.'

'So why ask?'

'No reason.'

She stared at him but he couldn't meet her gaze. She was glad she hadn't let him finish his sentence.

'What's going on?' she asked harshly.

'What do you mean?'

'You. One minute, you're all laughing and joking, then you're telling me about your break-up with Arwen – that's all fine – but then you're acting weird. Trying to listen into my phone call to Iz the other day and now asking about money.' She waited for a response but, when one didn't come, she added: 'You've been like two different people since you came back from suspension.'

He really wasn't able to look at her now, staring at his own feet instead. 'Just... things...' he mumbled.

Jessica continued staring at him and then put a hand on his shoulder. 'Is it about the crash?'

It was only a few months since Archie had driven into a man that had been pushed in front of his car. Things like that didn't simply go away.

'No.'

'Arwen?'

A shake of the head. 'Not really.'

'There are people you can talk to, y'know—'

'It's not that, either.' He looked up, staring through her, imploring her to know what was wrong because there was no way he was actually going to speak the words.

'I don't know what to say,' Jessica admitted.

Archie gulped, licked his lips. 'Just... be careful.'

He turned away again, this time all the way so that he was looking out the window.

'What does that mean?'

No reply.

'Arch?' Jessica added.

'Nothing. Forget I said it.'

'Be careful about what?'

'Nothing.'

'You must've said it for a reason?'

Archie rose abruptly, crossing to the window and staring beyond. Jessica stood, waiting for an answer, but then he picked up a set of keys from the hook on the wall next to the fridge. He pressed something on the fob and then half turned back to Jessica.

'I didn't realise Evie had a car,' he said.

Jessica moved to the window and watched as Archie plipped the fob, making the rear indicator lights blink on a small car a little down the street.

'Looks new,' he added.

Jessica stood for a moment, wondering if he'd finish his earlier thought. When he didn't, she headed for the front door.

'Bring the key,' she said.

Jessica ran a hand across the top of the vehicle. It was smooth and shiny, metallic blue. New, but without the bells, whistles and dangly pink crap that dominated Sally Nugent's car.

'What is it?' she asked.

'A car,' Archie replied.

She fixed him with a full-on death stare. 'Not in the mood, Arch. Not after the bullshit upstairs.'

'A Suzuki,' he replied. 'Two years old.'

'How much?'

'About twelve grand new. Perhaps seven-ish now, maybe eight, depending on the mileage.' He unlocked the car and walked round to the driver's side before opening the door and checking the dashboard. 'It's not done many miles.'

'How does a part-time cleaner afford a car like this?'

Archie relocked the car and then walked around the back.

He flicked away at a piece of dirt or grit and then leant in to examine the rear window.

'Do you remember the garage from this morning?' he asked.

'What garage?'

'From the overnights. There was some burglary last night.'

It took Jessica a moment to even remember there'd been a garage, let alone the name. 'Robinson's,' she said. 'Something like that.'

Archie nodded her across and pointed to the sticker in the back window. It was almost too much of a coincidence, too obvious, yet there it was in pure sticky-back plastic: SUPPLIED BY YOUR FRIENDS AT ROBINSON'S.

SEVENTEEN

Jessica didn't say a word to Archie on the journey across to the city. '*Be careful*' – what did he mean? Be careful around him? In general? At work? There was no point in trying to get him to explain any further because the moment was gone. She knew him too well, or at least she thought she did. When he clammed up about something, that was the end of it. He'd only say more when he was ready.

She turned the radio on and figured he could sod right off in the passenger seat. What an arse.

It only took them twenty minutes to reach Robinson's Garage. Multicoloured triangular flags were flickering from a long string across the top of the lot and there was a weird wind-puppet, sock-man flailing his arms from on top of the main office at the far end. 'Robinson's' was stencilled in huge red letters on the back wall, but the rest of the space was, predictably, filled with rows and rows of cars. From what Jessica could tell, it was the usual sort of second-hand crapmobiles. It took one to know one – and Jessica had bought enough deathtrap cars in her time to spot another. There wasn't much like the newer car that Evie had.

She parked and then headed for the main building with the flapping puppet on top. One of the windows had a wooden board across it and the pole stuck to the upper corner that would have once had a CCTV camera on the top was now lying flat on the ground. The camera itself had been smashed to bits. Jessica took a moment to take it in as Archie caught her up. He had followed like a chastened puppy, which was pretty much all he deserved. She had enough of the cryptic ask-me-if-I'm-okay, give-me-attention-please status updates from lurking on Facebook, let alone having to put up with it at work. From one of her supposed *actual* friends.

After entering the office, Jessica and Archie were met by a smartly dressed woman sitting behind a desk. Her perfectly plucked eyebrows arched in confusion at their appearance.

'Oh,' she said. 'I thought you were finished looking over the place.'

'How long ago did the Scene of Crime team leave?' Jessica asked.

'Maybe half-hour. Not too long. There was a couple in uniform, too. I didn't realise you'd be back.'

'We want to be thorough,' Jessica replied, leaving it vague enough so that she wasn't giving a precise reason for them being there.

The woman introduced herself as Janet, saying she was the secretary and that the owner – Mr Robinson – wasn't there.

'What actually happened overnight?' Jessica asked.

The office was a small brick building latched onto the back of the lot. There was a front door, a fire door, a small kitchen, the office in which they were sitting – and then one final room where the door was closed. The word 'MANAGER' was engraved in copperplate type on a shiny plaque. Pound-shop chic.

'We've had a bit of a clean-up now,' Janet replied. She stood and walked around the desk, pointing towards the window next to the main door with the board on the other side. 'Someone smashed their way in through there. They pulled down the security camera outside as well. I got an alert from the security company at about three a.m. By the time I got here, whoever had broken in had already made off.'

'What did they take?'

'Nothing, as far as I can tell.' She unlocked the manager's office and led them inside, pointing to a safe in the corner. 'The laptops are kept in there, with the float, and all car keys are secured in a separate safe that's built into the floor underneath here. They didn't get into either of those. I told your other lot that whoever broke in probably didn't know what they were looking for. Figured they'd find a few sets of keys easy-peasy and then go for a joyride.'

The manager's office was nothing special. There was a framed certificate on the back wall that looked suspiciously as if it had been printed off the Internet. 'Owain Robinson' was in huge letters across the centre and it had apparently been awarded for 'corporate excellence' – whatever that meant.

'Did anything show up on the security cameras?' Jessica asked.

'Just a shadow – nothing I could make out. Your other lot took away the hard drive and said they'd have a look.'

Jessica nodded her approval and then indicated the poster. 'I take it Owain Robinson is the boss?'

'Owner, manager and company director.'

Janet spoke proudly, standing tall on her heels as if she'd just been paid a compliment.

'Where is he?' Jessica asked.

'He's not on site today, I'm afraid.'

She spoke with authority, even though she wasn't answering the question. She'd do well in Parliament.

'Do you know where he is?'

'Not exactly.'

Jessica waited, focusing on the woman until something approaching an answer came.

'I left him a message,' Janet added.

'So he doesn't know the garage has been broken into?'

'No...'

'Isn't that something he'd like to know?'

'As I said – I left him a message. Sometimes he's hard to reach. He might be in Grimsby and it's difficult to get hold of him when he's there. Something to do with phone reception. It's perfectly normal. He always calls in eventually.'

It didn't sound perfectly normal...

'What's in Grimsby?' Jessica asked.

'Robinson's has a second branch. I've left messages on their answer machine, but it's been all go this morning with the police arriving and then you and everything. We've had customers, too.'

Janet moved out of the office, beckoning them as well. As Jessica turned to head out, she noticed a framed photograph on the wall. It showed a man leaning against the type of prestige car that wasn't for sale on the lot outside, a shiny black Jaguar or something like that. It was fair to say the man filled out his shiny grey suit and the sun was glimmering from his bulbous, bald head. He looked a bit like a giant condom.

'Is that Owain?' Jessica asked.

'That's Mr Robinson, yes,' Janet replied.

Jessica took another moment to take in the photo and then turned back to Janet. 'We're just going to have a look around the lot outside, if that's all right. Make sure nothing was missed, that sort of thing.' She poked a thumb towards Archie. 'My colleague here drives one of those cars with a ridiculously big exhaust and could do with something that doesn't break noise-pollution laws.'

'We have a fine selection here – plus all sorts of financing options. If you have any questions, our salesmen will be delighted to help you.'

Jessica thanked her and then led Archie out of the office.

There didn't seem to be any particular order to the cars. It was a higgledy-piggledy mix of shapes, sizes, brands, prices and colours.

'You talking to me now?' Archie mumbled.

Jessica stopped and turned to look at him. They were about the same height, but she pushed upwards so she could peer down upon him. 'What were you going on about back in Evie's flat?'

'Nothing, just talking nonsense. I didn't mean anything by it.'

'So why say it?'

'I don't know.'

'Did you think I was going to take that money?'

'No...'

'You don't sound very sure.'

Archie bit his lip, turned towards the cars and then back to her. 'Can we just forget it? I'd been talking about Arwen and... y'know...'

He was the type who only showed any degree of emotion when United were either losing or had lost, so it wasn't a surprise that the sentence went unfinished.

Jessica spent another moment or two hovering over him and then dropped back to her regular height. 'Fine – but the next time you mention your "needs", you're getting a knee in the bollocks. Deal?'

'Deal.'

They weaved their way between the cars, heading for the nearest man in an ill-fitting suit. The salesman was young, probably not long out of college, and wearing clothes his mum thought he'd grow into one day. He was polite and eager – at least until Jessica told him who they were and he realised a sale wasn't forthcoming. She showed him a photo of Evie Briers, asking if he knew her. The salesman squinted at the photo, puffed his lips together and then shook his head.

The second salesman was older, with just a little whiff of desperation about him. Either that, or it was his ropy after-shave. He had the look of a man for whom a yawn was always near, yet never quite there. When Jessica showed him the photo of Evie, his eyes narrowed and then widened before he shook his head.

'Sorry,' he said. 'Never seen her.'

'Are you sure?' Jessica replied. 'Can you look again?'

He did – but for barely a second. 'I mean, she might have been round looking for a car,' he said, 'but we get lots of people through here. She doesn't seem immediately familiar.'

'She's called Evie Briers.'

Another shake of the head. 'Sorry – doesn't ring a bell. Should I know her?'

'We think she might have bought a car from here.'

He looked at the photograph once more, but it was more for show.

'There are four different salespeople working here depending on the day of the week. Mr Robinson is in some-times, too. I don't know her, I'm afraid.'

Jessica exchanged a quick glance with Archie, knowing that he'd seen it too. For a used-car salesman, the bloke wasn't the best of liars. She wondered if he'd be able to sit opposite a customer banging on about 'seasonal tyre proofing' with a straight face.

He was given an out as a couple walked onto the lot hand in hand. He apologised to Jessica and then started strolling towards the couple, a predator stalking its prey.

'Well, he's talking out of his arse,' Archie said, echoing her thoughts. The salesman had definitely recognised Evie.

Jessica headed back towards the office, knocking politely

and then entering. Janet was back behind the desk, fingers clacking on the keyboard. She stopped and looked up at them, eyebrows expectant.

'Is that everything?' she asked.

Jessica flattened the photo of Evie Briers on the desk between them. 'Do you know her?' she asked.

Janet frowned down to the photo and started to shake her head slowly. 'Should I?'

'She bought a car from here.'

'Did she?'

'You must have records.'

Janet peered up defiantly, features harder. 'We do.'

'Could you search for her name?'

'I could...'

They stared at each other, with Jessica realising that Janet wasn't simply a secretary. She knew where the bodies – hopefully metaphorical – were buried. The whole '*Mr* Robinson' thing told its own story, too. At the absolute least, she had a slight infatuation with him, more likely they were playing horizontal hide the sausage.

'*Will* you search for her name?' Jessica added, a little more firmly.

'If you have a warrant, I will.'

Jessica took a step back, reluctant to concede defeat but knowing she could get a warrant if she wanted one. Of course, by then the records could have been conveniently lost.

'Tell *Mr* Robinson I need to speak to him,' she said.

EIGHTEEN

Jessica was busy hitting the delete key as she scrolled through her emails. It was quite the daily ritual, cathartic in many ways. Community coffee morning. Delete. Some bullshit MP visit. Delete. Time to change passwords – again. Delete. A force-wide initiative about smiling more often. Delete.

'You should probably read those, you know...'

Izzy was sitting at the still unfilled desk in Jessica's office. When she'd been a sergeant, a second officer had shared the space with her. Since Jessica's promotion, DI Franks had preferred to keep his own space, which was fine with her. Other officers had been allowed to leave without being replaced and, somehow, she'd ended up with a large space to herself. Some said it was because nobody dared to spend any significant time in her company. *Some* brave types.

'I need a PA,' Jessica replied. 'Someone to sum all these emails up into one or two sentences and then tell me anything important. Otherwise, it's three hundred words about a new cleaning rota.'

'Did you get the one about the Christmas party?'

'That's months away.'

'Yeah, but they need numbers. The guv normally gets a round in, so...'

Jessica clicked a couple of screens until she was looking at the force's Facebook page. It was managed by some bod in the media team who was paid more than most starting constables. Not that the fact pissed off actual officers, of course...

There was a photo of the man found at the side of the road. It was graphic, with a warning above the top, but his face was so bloodied that the major identifying feature was his tattoo. She scrolled through the meagre comments underneath.

'Nobody's got a clue who he is,' Jessica said, spinning on her chair to face Izzy. 'No fingerprints showed up on the driving licence in his pocket – so we can't ID him from that.'

'Nothing on the list of calls either,' Izzy confirmed. 'I checked in this morning with the hospital.'

'And?'

'He's on a ventilator. Alive, but not by much.'

'Wouldn't someone miss him? It's been three days now. Surely someone's wondering why their husband, boyfriend or dad hasn't come home?'

Izzy sipped from a plastic coffee cup, fresh from the machine. 'He might be single and living on his own.'

'His employer, then, wondering why he's not turned up for work for three days.'

Izzy raised her mug. 'Everyone's been too busy to do much digging. When he comes round, we can see what he has to say, but there's too much going on at the moment. I've got one constable off on the sick, another on holiday; Franks has borrowed one for who knows what reason – and then Archie's going through the menopause. I don't know what's up with him half the time.'

'Me either.'

'I wondered if United was on a poor run of form or some-thing, but I don't even think it's that.'

Jessica thought about mentioning the break-up, but it wasn't her place. She didn't think that was the reason for his apparent personality switches anyway.

'Be careful.'

She also didn't believe him when he said he didn't mean anything by it. She'd seen his eyes and it had been a clear warning. She'd get it out of him sooner or later – but, in the immediate term, Izzy was right. They were short of officers and she needed him in a fit state of mind to work.

'What's going on with the garage break-in?' Izzy asked.

'One of the PCs took statements this morning. The SOCOs looked for prints and so on, but there's no way we've got the budget to look for blood, sweat or hair, especially as nothing was taken. I think the salesman recognised Evie, probably the secretary, too.'

'Loads of people would have bought cars from there, so what does it matter if she's one of them? Why would they get so arsey about it?'

Jessica closed the Facebook window and pressed back in her seat. 'That's the default position for some people. Start off arsey and then get arsier. There's a whole scale of arsiness.'

Izzy finished her drink and started to look around the floor. 'Don't you have a bag for recycling?' she asked.

'There's a bin in the corner.'

'Didn't you get the email about GMP wanting to raise internal recycling rates by a quarter this year?'

'Probably. They're not going to raise our salaries by a quarter, are they?'

Izzy placed the empty paper cup on the corner of the desk but didn't say anything. Jessica plucked it up with a wink and dropped it into a bag underneath her feet that contained other recyclable items.

'See,' she said, 'I'm not a planet-hating, swan-strangling nutter. I recycle – I just resent all the corporate reasons for it.

Like a hotel saying they don't want to wash your towel because they want to save the dolphins. Just tell me you can't be bothered and leave it at that.'

Izzy yawned wide, covering her mouth and finishing with a grin. 'I've applied for another job,' she said.

Jessica stared at her. 'What?'

'Primary school teacher.'

Jessica continued to gawp. '*Teaching?*'

'What's wrong with that? Amber starts school in a year. I was thinking of either doing one of those PGCE things so I could be full-time in a year, or starting off as a teaching assistant. Malcolm makes decent money, so we could get by in the short-term.' She paused, bit her lip. 'We're also talking about having another baby.'

Jessica stared at her colleague. Her friend. It felt like a punch in the face. A sort of good punch in the face.

'Um...' Jessica didn't know what to say. She eventually managed 'congratulations', but she was a worse liar than that desperate bloke at the car lot.

'I've not told anyone else,' Izzy added, not minding Jessica's reaction. 'I've kind of spread myself around – applied for a teaching assistant's position that would start in January, gone in for the PGCE course and then Malcolm and I are trying as well. I've not actually figured out what to do yet.'

'You're definitely leaving, though? I had no idea.'

'Not definitely. Staying is the other option.'

'I might arrest you, dereliction of duty or something like that. Chain you to your desk.'

Izzy smiled sadly, lips tight. 'Some weeks it feels like that anyway.'

Jessica rocked slightly on her seat, making it bob from side to side. 'It's my fault for giving you too much.'

'It's really not. Look at this week alone. People off sick, others on holidays, more sequestered to work elsewhere. No one ever gets replaced. The pay never goes up. There's never any real appreciation. It's not worth it.'

'How about I top up your salary with biscuits. A packet of choccy digestives a week?'

A hint of a smile: 'I still might stay – I've not decided yet.'

'Tunnock's teacakes – none of the cheap knock-offs? One box a week...?'

Izzy laughed. 'Make it two and you're talking.' She batted away a yawn and apologised, back on message as if she hadn't just dropped the pipe bomb. 'Are you going to ask for a warrant for Robinson's?'

'Not yet,' Jessica replied. 'I want to talk to Owain Robinson first. There's not a lot of point. At best, there'll be a record to say Evie bought a car from there – but we could get that from the DVLA anyway. There might be a finance record, something like that, but she might not have even bought it from them. Those garage stickers never come off, so she could have got it second- or third-hand.'

'I'll get onto the DVLA.' Izzy pressed herself up and then broke into a smile. 'What's going on with you anyway?'

'What do you mean?'

'You've been smiling too much.'

'What? When?'

'All day. One of the constables was worried you'd taken a blow to the head.'

'Cheeky sod.'

Izzy stood with one hand on her hip, waiting.

'I'm going out with someone tomorrow,' Jessica eventually said.

She'd be a good poker player because Izzy reacted with only a blink: 'What's he like?'

'I'm not sure. I met him as he was about to get a wart removed.'

Izzy laughed. 'I know that's what turns me on when it comes to men. I like verrucas as well. Or is it verrucae?'

'He seems nice,' Jessica added. 'Not a psycho.'

'You really need higher standards than no warts and not a psycho.'

'True – but have you *seen* the standard of blokes we have around here? Take out the warts and psychos and there's not much left.'

'You could always ask out Not-So-Fat Pat...'

Jessica reached into her recycling bag, removed Izzy's empty cup and threw it at her. The aim was good but the cup wasn't, dropping well short and plopping on the ground. 'Why don't you sod off to be a teacher,' she said, definitely not meaning it.

NINETEEN

By the next day, the flapping sock man on top of Robinson's Garage was looking a sorry sight. Due to a lack of wind, there was very little flapping going on, more a sort of droopy floor-licking.

The same pair of salesmen from the previous day were again traipsing around the forecourt waiting for anyone walking by to show even the smallest amount of interest in a vehicle. They'd been joined by a new bloke, spiky-haired and sharp-suited. There were still no customers, though.

Jessica and Archie headed for the office, offering weak smiles to the salesmen from the day before and dodging the new bloke before he could accost either of them with the usual, 'Can I help you with anything?' spiel.

Janet was looking as immaculate as the day before, typing furiously on her keyboard as Jessica knocked and entered. Her brow furrowed as she started, 'I didn't expect—' before Jessica cut her off.

'Is Mr Robinson in today?' she asked.

'I'm afraid not. You really should have called. I could have saved you coming down.'

'Have you heard from him at all?'

For a moment, Jessica thought she was going to be met with a brick wall of defiance but Janet quickly caved. 'No.'

'He still doesn't know there was a break-in at his garage?'

'Like I said yesterday, it's not unusual for him to be off the grid for a day or two.' She cleared her throat. 'I don't suppose you're any closer to finding the culprit from the other night?'

Jessica turned back to the window that was now full of glass instead of chipboard. 'We're still working on it,' she said. 'It would really help if we could talk to Mr Robinson...'

'I wish I could help.'

'Does he have any family?'

Janet peered past Jessica towards a calendar on the wall. 'He's got a wife in Spain. They're separated.'

She didn't physically squirm but she might as well have done. Either that or added, 'the cow', at the end of her sentence. There was clearly very little love lost between the women.

'Could he be in Spain?' Jessica asked.

'No.'

'Are you sure?'

'He'd have said.'

'Any kids?'

'No.'

'I could really do with talking to him.'

Janet let out a loud huff: *me too* – she didn't say.

'Did you ever socialise outside of work?' Jessica asked.

Janet's eyes narrowed. 'What are you trying to say?'

'Nothing – but colleagues can be friends away from the office. Trip to the pub, afternoon coffee on a day off, that sort of thing.'

The other woman shuffled backwards in her seat, a little embarrassed at her defensiveness. 'I suppose we've been out for the odd drink. A meal here and there. Sometimes we're here from first thing to last. Open at half eight, close at half eight. It's not like you want to go home and cook after all that.'

'You can say that again.'

Jessica smiled and, for the first time, there was a chink in Janet's demeanour. Her lips curled into a slight smile of sisterhood.

'I don't want you to take this the wrong way,' Jessica said, 'but is there any reason to be worried about him?'

Janet slumped even lower, head bowed slightly. From nowhere, she seemed like she might cry, her breaths becoming shallower and more frequent, top lip trembling ever so slightly. 'I went to his house last night, but no one answered. His car's either in the garage or not there. He could be in Grimsby but, well... I'm sure he'd have called in once he got my message.'

There was a chart on the wall, part nursery-school project, part something to do when there were no customers. A list of names was listed on the right-hand side of the chart and there were cardboard cut-outs of cars stretching across the rows next to each name. The word 'Manchester' was across the top and then halfway down the columns was a thick black line and the word 'Grimsby'.

'Each car is a sale,' Janet said.

Jessica walked over and looked at the chart more closely. 'Mick' was the best seller in Manchester with eleven cars by his name. Someone named Aziz in Grimsby had twelve.

'Grimsby are leading this month,' Janet added. 'The lads outside are on edge about it – especially with Christmas coming up. The winning site gets a bonus each month.'

Jessica counted the number of cars quickly in her head. Grimsby was ahead by three.

'It's a couple of days behind,' Janet said. 'Mr Robinson does the updates every two or three days, but with him not being here, it's a bit behind.'

'Do you ever contact Grimsby for their numbers?'

'No – I think Mr Robinson enjoys it. This whole rewards chart was his idea. It's certainly raised productivity.'

'Did you try calling them again this morning to ask if they'd seen him?'

Janet nodded. 'Of course.'

'And?'

'Answer machine.'

'Is that normal?'

The secretary shifted uncomfortably, standing and smoothing her skirt. 'I don't have a lot of contact with them. It's Mr Robinson's side project. Aside from sharing the name and competing for sales, there's not much need for us to work together. He handles that side of the business anyway. I'm just the secretary.'

Jessica doubted that – but she did sense concern. Janet was worried about Owain. It was getting quite creepy how she constantly referred to him as 'Mr Robinson', though.

'Where does he live?' Jessica asked.

Janet crossed her arms. 'That's confidential.'

The three of them stood in silence for a few moments before Archie chipped in. 'I'll get on to Companies House,' he said. 'Easy-peasy. Probably have it in fifteen minutes. I'll spend that long on hold.'

'Either that or council tax,' Jessica replied. 'Simple search for his name. Can't be too many blokes named Owain in Manchester.'

They'd barely taken a step to the door when Janet lunged forward, hand on Jessica's shoulder. She immediately realised she'd gone too far, pulling her hand away and apologising.

'It's in Chorlton,' she said, before reeling off an address. Archie made a note of it and then they headed back towards the car.

'Good work,' Jessica said when it was just her and Archie.

'But get onto Companies House anyway. Find out if Owain Robinson uses an accountant to file his returns.'

TWENTY

Owain Robinson's house was detached with a large double garage and an elaborate pattern created from bricks as a driveway. From the outside, it looked like a good four or five bedrooms, well beyond the salary of a detective inspector, let alone an undersized detective constable.

'He must've sold a bunch of cars to buy this place,' Archie said as Jessica parked in front of the house.

'This is the suburban dream, isn't it?' Jessica replied as she clambered out.

They stood at the side of the car, peering towards the house. 'Not my scene,' Archie said, shaking his head.

'What *is* your scene? Friday nights on Canal Street?'

'Oh, ha-ha, very funny.'

Archie indicated the houses around them – all large with lush front gardens and manicured topiary. It'd be a sea of blue signs come election time, probably with the odd purple chucked in for good measure.

'I need a bit of character,' he added. 'Bit of rough and tumble, where you can come out your front door and find an abandoned shoe that someone's left behind the night before. I like that randomness.'

'You like finding odd shoes?'   •

'Not just shoes – that sort of thing. Y'know what I mean. *Real* Manchester. This is all a bit vanilla. A bit, y'know...'

'What?'

Archie tilted his head, lowered his voice. 'A bit... *London*.'

Jessica almost laughed at him. 'It's not a swear word, Arch. You can say it out loud.'

'Gentrification, that's what it is.'

'You really have graduated from Mr Men books, haven't you? You don't have to have an entire population living in workhouses to prove it's northern or working class.'

Archie continued shaking his head. 'Nah, not having it.'

Jessica wondered if he'd ever grow out of it. Loving the area in which a person grew up was one thing, but he seemed to think it was terrible if anything changed.

She passed him and headed along the driveway to the front door. She knocked firmly twice and then rang the bell.

Archie was hovering next to her, bobbing on his heels, likely bored from being in the car all morning. 'Want me to check round the back?' he asked.

'Give it a minute.'

Jessica tried the bell once more and then pressed herself against the glass, shielding the glare and trying to squint through the dimples.

'Curtains are pulled,' Archie said. He had leapt over the flower bed like an arthritic ballerina and was standing at the main front window, fingers cupping his forehead against the glass.

Jessica tried the letter box, fingering around in case a key was left dangling on a string. It didn't seem like the area for that – and she couldn't find one anyway. Archie was checking the flowerpots, so she did the same, looking for signs the soil had been disturbed and then picking up the smaller ones and checking underneath.

'Find anything?' she called.

'Nothing.'

What they *had* managed to do was attract attention from the local branch of Nosy Bastards Anonymous.

A man with glasses and an olive green trainspotter's mac was hovering at the end of the driveway, smiling awkwardly. 'Can I help?' he asked, nodding towards the house next door. 'I'm from number twenty-two.'

'We're looking for Owain Robinson,' Jessica replied.

'And you are...?'

Jessica offered her warrant card and the man looked at it closely before relaxing with a loud exhalation. He must have thought he might have to perform some sort of citizen's arrest if they were potential burglars. With his crisp chinos and smart shoes, Jessica wasn't convinced he had hidden ninja skills... although that probably *was* how ninjas hid in plain sight. Nobody would expect martial arts and monkey flips from the bloke with a thermos.

'I'm Brian,' the man said, pointing towards number twenty-two once more. 'I run the neighbourhood watch scheme. Gotta keep an eye out for each other, haven't you?'

Archie stepped back over the flowers until he was at Jessica's side.

'Have you seen him?' Archie asked, indicating Owain's house.

'Not for a day or two. I usually give a wave if I see him in the morning.'

'Do you see him most mornings?'

'I guess so. He does seem to go away for a couple of days at a time though.' There was a quick pause and then: 'Not that I'm checking up on him or anything. Don't want you to think I'm some kind of snooper.' He laughed at himself.

'Oh, we don't,' Jessica said with a smile, thinking that she definitely *did* think of him as some kind snooper.

'I did notice someone knocking on his door last night,' Brian added. 'A woman with blonde hair. She drove off when no one answered. I think she's been here before...'

He left it at that, proving how much of a snooping nosy sod he really was. Jessica thanked him for his time and then stood waiting for him to disappear back into number twenty-two.

'Still think this is suburban paradise?' Archie asked.

'Big Brother paradise, maybe. It's like GCHQ around here.'

They turned back to the house and Archie asked once more if he should skirt around the back. He seemed determined to hop over a fence, whatever happened – either that or get in before her.

Jessica approached the door and tried the bell once more, not expecting anything to happen but figuring it couldn't do any harm.

'We could probably be back here with a warrant in a couple of hours,' he offered.

'You wanna do overtime tonight?'

'Not really.'

Jessica pressed against the glass. It was double-glazed, the type of door that needed to have the handle yanked upwards from the inside in order for it to lock. She leant on the handle and... it crunched downwards.

She was so surprised that she almost fell into the house, only managing to avoid landing on her face by grabbing onto what turned out to be a radiator inside the hallway.

'Was it unlocked?' Archie asked, following her inside.

'Either that or I've being doing weightlifting in my sleep.'

They stopped in the hallway and Archie closed the door, not wanting to draw any further attention from the neighbours. Jessica then edged forward, turning to find herself in the living room.

They both stopped, staring into the gloom.

'Bloody hell,' Archie muttered.

Jessica turned on the lights but it only illuminated what she could already see.

The place was a mess.

Cushions had been torn from the sofa and thrown across the room and the sofa itself was upside down, the bottom slashed open to expose soft foam. There was a large display unit against one of the walls – but the drawers had been pulled out and tipped over. The carpet in the corner had been dragged back, a bureau had been hurled to the floor and there were books and movie cases thrown all around.

Jessica didn't want to move any further into the room because it was unquestionably a crime scene. She backed away into what turned out to be the kitchen, where it was a similar story. The drawers had been pulled out and emptied onto the floor, which was a sea of glimmering cutlery. It was like someone had force-fed Haribo to their hyperactive children and then let them loose in the kitchen section of IKEA. The oven door was hanging ajar, the microwave, too. The cupboards were a mix of open and closed, with various tins and packets strewn across the countertops.

Jessica was already putting on a pair of nitrile gloves when she heard Archie calling her from the hallway. She followed his voice back through the living room to the stairs.

'You really need to come up here,' Archie called.

His voice was steady but it didn't take a speech expert to detect the quiver.

The stairs creaked with squalid dread as Jessica headed up one slow step at a time. She knew that she didn't want to see whatever it was that awaited her and yet it was only going to be one thing.

Archie was standing on the landing, facing anywhere other than the open bedroom door.

'Is it...?' Jessica started.

Archie nodded, gulped a 'yeah', but she had to push forward anyway.

The carpet was a plush, fluffy cream. Nice between the toes, Jessica thought. Anything other than having to look at what was actually on the bed. The bedspread was chocolate brown – but that didn't mask the stain that had spread from the main part of the bed down to the floor.

The man was flat on his back, wearing a pair of tartan pyjama bottoms but naked from the waist up. The hairs on his chest were matted with thick, dark blood, but, above all that, Jessica couldn't stop looking at the hole underneath Owain's chin.

It wasn't a regular type of burglary gone wrong, some random act of violence; Owain hadn't been knifed or strangled.

He'd been shot.

TWENTY-ONE

Janet was in tears. She was piling through the tissues as Jessica sat on the other side of the desk and Archie hustled around making tea.

It was only lunchtime, but Robinson's car salesmen had been sent home for the day. There wasn't much appetite for selling once they'd found out their boss had been killed in his own home. It really took the thrill out of flogging a banged-together motor with a dodgy exhaust.

'I can't believe it,' Janet said. Her eyes were puffy and red, with smeared dark lines of mascara leaking from the corners. She blew her nose long and loud.

'Are you sure it's him?' she added through the tissue.

Jessica remembered the photo in the other office, Owain Robinson's big bulbous head and what she'd seen on the bed. 'It's him,' she replied.

'But who'd do that? I don't understand.'

'That's what we're hoping to figure out.'

'He was just a normal bloke.'

Archie took that moment to arrive with a mug of tea. He placed it on the table in front of Janet and then hovered next to the door.

'How well did you know Owain?' Jessica asked.

'I've been here for five years now. He's never shouted at me, not once. He was a good man. Always got a kind word, always encouraging to the staff. I've seen him go out of his way to look after customers, ferrying them around, and so on.'

She blew her nose once more and then took a sip of tea. She'd untied her hair, letting it hang loose around her shoulders, wavy and limp at the bottom.

'But how well did you actually *know* him?' Jessica added, making the emphasis as obvious as she could without asking outright.

It took Janet a while to answer. She sniffed and tried to compose herself, gazing off towards the water cooler in the corner before replying: 'We were... close.'

'As in...?'

'After his wife left, we were together a bit. Not a regular thing...'

It sounded clear that not being a regular thing was Robinson's choice and not hers.

'It's going to take a while for our team of investigators to go over the house and look for clues, so I was wondering if you know of anyone who might hold a grudge?'

'Like who?'

'That's what I'm asking.'

Janet shook her head rapidly. 'He wasn't like that. There was never any trouble around here.'

'What about his wife? You said she was in Spain and that they're separated – do you know if it was amicable?'

'So he said.'

That was something to check, but Jessica doubted there was anything overly suspicious going on there. This felt far more immediate than something to do with a marriage break-up. Someone had broken into the garage and Robinson's house, possibly on the same night. Given the state of the house, it seemed clear that a person – or persons – had been searching for something.

As Janet blew her nose once more, Jessica signalled to Archie and he produced the photograph of Evie they'd shown the previous day. He laid it on the table and then stepped away. Neither of them said anything as they waited for Janet to straighten herself out. Eventually, she had nowhere to look other than at the picture.

'Do you reckon she killed him?' Janet croaked.

'That's incredibly unlikely,' Jessica replied, understating it, considering given that Evie herself was dead.

'So why are you showing me it?'

'Because I need you to look at it properly and tell me if you know her.'

Janet didn't really look at the photo – but then Jessica had a good inkling she didn't need to. Janet knew full well she'd seen the woman in the picture. It had been written on her face when the question had been asked the day before. The salesman outside as well.

'I think she might have bought a car from here,' Janet said slowly, choosing her words. 'Is this a different photo?'

'It's the same as yesterday.'

'Perhaps the light is different?' She glanced up to meet Jessica's gaze but realised she wasn't fooling anyone.

'You *think* she might have bought a car?' Jessica pressed. 'We already know that. The DVLA tells us the car Evie owns comes from here. She bought it five months ago. One previous owner, eleven thousand miles on the clock.'

Jessica paused, let it sink in that they weren't a pair of chumps who believed everything they were told.

'So how come you remember her if she bought a car five months ago?' Jessica added.

Janet snivelled into a fresh tissue and patted her eyes with another. She sipped her tea, took her time, but then seemingly realised she had no one to protect any longer.

'She was here a couple of evenings a while back,' Janet said. 'I didn't know her name. I assumed she was some woman Mr Robinson had picked up.'

'I don't mean to be crass, but did he "pick up" many women?'

Janet shook her head. 'He wasn't like that.'

'How do you mean she was here?'

'We close at half eight, but she'd show up at maybe twenty past and wait until everyone was leaving. Mr Robinson brought her inside after everyone had gone and I thought, well... you would, wouldn't you?'

Yes, Jessica thought, *she most definitely would.*

'What about the car?' Jessica asked.

'I came in one morning and Mr Robinson asked me to put through the paperwork on it. We'd only had the car in for a day or two and he said he'd sold her the car the night before and that I could send off the forms.'

'Do you sell many cars at night, after closing hours?'

Janet's only reply was to dab away at her eyes. She ended up smearing her mascara even further, dragging a dark line out around her cheeks. It looked like some naughty child had drawn on her with a biro. The implication was clear, though: of course they didn't sell many cars after hours.

'Do you know how Evie paid for the car?' Jessica asked.

Janet shook her head. 'No idea. If it was cash, then it wasn't left in the safe overnight.'

That was interesting – largely because Jessica had seen Evie's bank records and knew there were no large purchases made through either a credit card, a loan, or her regular accounts. The only way she could have paid legitimately for something like a car was with cash.

'How good was Mr Robinson with numbers?' Jessica asked.

'Not great. I did a lot of the paperwork because he couldn't do mental arithmetic and he couldn't figure out calculators. He never did percentages, he'd offer a fixed amount instead. A customer once wanted ten per cent off an eight thousand pound car and Mr Robinson got confused and said a thousand was too much. He was a good salesman, though. We can't all be good with maths.'

'But it's fair to say you did a lot of the little things around here – including the paperwork.'

'We all have our skills.'

Janet smiled through watery eyes and Jessica had the sense this was more like the real her. She actually was a nice person and her loyalty to Owain Robinson was the only thing that made her quite so obstinate.

'Did you do the company accounts?' Jessica asked.

Janet shook her head. 'I put through the amounts for payroll, but the accounts themselves aren't my thing,' she replied.

'Did Mr Robinson ever ask you about it?'

'Why would he?'

'Because, as best we can tell, he didn't have an accountant. If he did, he still filed his own tax records – both personal and for the company. He had an accountant up until a little over a year ago, but then he sent an email saying he didn't need their services any longer. He was filing accounts for himself and two garages, all while you say he couldn't do percentages. Does that seem right?'

Janet stared at Jessica, looking for answers she wouldn't get. 'I don't understand.'

'I'm not sure we do, either.' Jessica pressed herself up. 'You're going to have to go home,' she said, trying to be kindly.

Janet blew her nose one final time and then creaked her chair away from the desk. 'Can I come back tomorrow?'

'I don't know.'

With a meek nod, Janet took the answer and then started clearing her things into her handbag. She didn't argue when Jessica asked her to leave the notepad she picked up, nor the pen drive she said was her own personal one. She swept the desk clean of tissues by dumping them all into the bin and then left without another word.

'Well, that was fun,' Archie said grimly when they were alone.

'I know you make bad tea, but I've never seen it have that effect on anyone before.'

Neither of them laughed. Jessica didn't know why she'd said it. Better than thinking about Owain Robinson's body, she supposed.

'What do you think they were looking for?' Archie asked.

'Who?'

'Whoever broke in here and his house. They were obviously after something.'

'I don't know – but if Evie Briers was doing the books here, then we could have a serious problem because someone was after her as well.'

They stood in silence for a short while.

'What now?' Archie eventually said.

It took Jessica a few seconds to reply, not because she didn't know the answer, more because she couldn't believe the words were coming from her mouth. 'Well,' she started, 'I *really* have to be back in Manchester by eight o'clock – but let's all go to Grimsby.'

TWENTY-TWO

'I can't believe we're going to Grimsby.'

Archie was moaning again from the passenger seat.

Jessica was sitting comfortably in the left-hand lane, watching the M62 zip by. For once, there were no snarl-ups, not even a hint of some prick in a jack-knifed lorry out to ruin everyone's day. She'd not even been overtaken by some maniac in a BMW weaving between lanes at 100mph while talking on a mobile phone.

It truly was an odd journey – and the rolling greenery of Yorkshire was, for once, beautifully drenched with sunshine.

Not that Archie was having any of it.

'*Grimsby?*' he added.

'What's wrong with Grimsby?'

'It's even got Grim in the name. It's like calling a place Shitsville.'

'What's in a name? Archie Davey rhymes with starchy gravy – but I'm not complaining.'

She got a snigger for that.

'I don't even know what county it's in,' he continued. 'It's past Yorkshire, so what is that? Holland or something? Belgium? Nothing good's ever come from Belgium.'

'What about chocolate?'

'Nah, I'm not having it. You can get chocolate from anywhere.'

'Grimsby isn't in Belgium anyway.'

'It may as well be.'

'Just like Manchester and Liverpool are pretty much the same place.'

Jessica kept her eyes on the road but she felt Archie's *Exorcist*-style head-spin to face her. He went quiet for a bit after that.

Only a bit, though. Ten minutes later, he was off again, a fidgety child in a car seat, asking, 'Are we there yet?'

'What's actually *in* Grimsby?' he said.

'One of Owain Robinson's garages.'

'What else? You hear about buildings, statues and art from other places. Britain's full of culture – but what's in Grimsby?'

Jessica had to admit he had her there. She had very little idea. 'There's definitely a fishing port,' she said.

'No one's going for a day out to look at a bunch of boats. No one I'd like to meet, anyway.'

'It's probably all cobbles and hanging baskets. I don't know, I've never been.'

After almost two and a half hours in a car, Jessica was able to confirm that it definitely wasn't all cobbles, let alone hanging baskets.

Grimsby was, well, grim – especially on the side streets close to the docks. The sunshine over the Pennine moors had given way to murky grey skies and a fizzing breeze. Large vacant expanses of concrete and tarmac were mingled with huge, seemingly empty, red-brick and plastic-fronted warehouses, all backing onto rippling brown water.

If that wasn't bad enough, the car's satnav was having

something of a meltdown, advising them to turn left – which would have been fine if it wasn't for the two-metre high fence and, ultimately, the ocean.

In an effort to offset the electronic device's rogue advice, Archie was on his phone trying to figure out where they should be going. The problem was, he couldn't get anything like reception. He was holding his phone above his head and leaning forward towards the windscreen, saying things like, 'I've got one bar', 'Have they heard of 4G round here?' and 'Are we in Hull? This says we're in Hull', none of which was helping.

Jessica eventually found a parking space on the side of the road and they clambered out of the car, both holding their phones high, hoping for the mythical God of Mobile Phone Reception to smile brightly upon them.

'Did you say Montague Street?' Archie asked. His arm was strained to the heavens and he was looking directly up.

Jessica checked the card she'd taken from Robinson's Garage in Manchester. The addresses of both garages were listed at the bottom.

'That's what it says,' she replied.

Archie had his tongue out, which presumably helped him think. He turned in a circle; looking down to the pavement, then up, then down again. He licked his index finger.

'It's that way,' he said, pointing away from the water.

Jessica's phone was even less compliant than Archie's, so she had little choice other than to follow, even though she didn't have much faith in either his mobile reception or his navigational skills. Those instincts proved correct when he got to the corner, stood still, and then pirouetted.

'I *think* it might be over there,' he said, sounding as certain as a call centre worker assuring a customer that their delivery would definitely be there within the hour.

Jessica continued following as Archie headed into a dead

end with his head down. He only looked up when he was swallowed by the shadow of the wall in front and then turned in a circle and continued back the way he'd come as if it hadn't happened.

A pair of haulage lorries barrelled past them as they clung to the edge of the road where there was no pavement. Archie didn't stop at the next corner, taking another left and leading them onto a pavement. They were now finally on something resembling an actual street, with a long line of terraced houses on either side of the tight road. Cars were parked along both sides, with an invasion of green wheelie bins pervading everyone's minuscule front yards.

'Montague Street!' Archie proclaimed proudly. The crusted brown sign high on the wall even proved him correct. He put his phone away smugly, as if he'd achieved something far more complicated than being able to walk in a straight line.

Jessica checked the address on the Robinson's Garage business card once more and then set off along the line of houses. The area was typical of many in Manchester: pebble-dashed outer walls speckled with satellite dishes and weathered burglar alarms that almost certainly didn't work. She got to the end of the street to find more of the same.

No sign of the garage.

Jessica turned in a circle, wondering how they could have missed an entire garage. She followed the intersecting street, passing a narrow back ginnel at the rear of the houses and stopping at a boarded-up hovel. The white paint was chipped, exposing the faded red bricks underneath. All of the windows were covered with graffiti-ridden wood and there was a phone box outside, the cord hanging loose with no receiver on the end.

'Is that it?' Archie asked.

Jessica checked the address on the card but only then realised how vague it was. 'Robinson's Garage, Off Montague

St, Grimsby'. There was a postcode listed but that wasn't much help for now.

As they stared at the run-down wasteland, a woman was passing, her two-berth pushchair shunted forcefully in front of her. She was wrapped up for the cold in a long coat that had furry bits sticking out of the hood and arms. Shopping bags hung from the back of the stroller as she motored along as if in a race.

Jessica just about managed to flag her down before getting run over. She smiled weakly as the two children in the pram stared up at her goggle-eyed.

'Hi,' she said.

'What?' the mum replied, angling the pushchair away.

Jessica pointed to the building. 'How long has that been empty?'

The woman shrugged. 'I dunno.'

'A few months? Years?'

'Like, forever.'

She grunted something Jessica didn't catch and then hurtled off along the pavement, not looking back.

'She was friendly,' Archie said.

Jessica was ready to query whether they were in the right place – except it was obvious they were. The street sign on the wall was clear.

They continued a short distance to the end of the next street, where there was a mini-market on the corner. It was the usual bizarre mix for that type of shop: international calling cards and pay-and-go SIMs alongside multipacks of Wotsits, discounted Coco Pops, out-of-date Jaffa Cakes, dustpans and cat food.

The woman behind the counter was flicking through a copy of some lifestyle magazine. She was young, perhaps even a teenager, and seemed surprised that someone was actually there.

'Is there a garage round here?' Jessica asked.

'For cars?'

'Exactly – somewhere that sells cars.'

'There's a place out by the train station.'

Jessica had driven past that on the way in. It was more of a dealership than a second-hand seller. 'Is there anything on these couple of streets?' she asked.

'Not here.'

'But this is Montague Street?'

The server pointed behind them, through the door. 'That's Montague Street over there. There's no car place, though.'

Jessica thanked her and then they headed back the way they'd come.

'I don't understand,' Archie said.

Jessica checked the business card once more but there was no doubting the address. There was only one phone number listed – but it had an 0161 prefix and was back in Manchester. Whichever number Janet had called for Grimsby wasn't listed on the business cards.

Unsure of what was going on, Jessica called Izzy – except the sergeant wasn't picking up. She tried the desk number and her mobile, but there was no answer. Archie dialled one of his constable mates, but people were either busy, or their colleagues were deliberately ignoring them. Jessica would believe either version.

'You're going to have to do it,' Archie said grimly.

He wasn't wrong. Jessica called the dreaded number linked to the main reception area of the station. It rang once and then Not-So-Fat-Pat's voice chuntered. He was using his official phone voice, welcoming them to Longsight Police Station and asking how he could be of service.

As soon as he realised who it was, the gruffness bored through. 'What d'you want?' he asked.

'Can you do me a favour?' Jessica asked.

'What did your last slave die of?'

'Doing an Internet search for me. Thanks for asking.'

Pat didn't laugh. He'd not been the same since going on a health kick and dropping a good third of his body weight. He'd lost his humour with the fat – though the attitude had remained: 'Get on with it then,' he said.

'Can you look up Robinson's Garage in Grimsby and let me know the address?'

'Christ, anyone would think mobile phones hadn't been invented. What are you calling me from?'

'I'm not – I'm a voice in your head,' Jessica replied, before adding: 'Can you just do it?'

Pat mumbled and grumbled, but Jessica didn't exactly blame him. He'd apparently been 'off the carbs' for months, which was enough to make anyone fantasise about the odd axe rampage.

'You got a pen?' he said.

'I don't need one – just tell me,' Jessica replied.

'Fine – it's off Montague Street.'

'Is there more than one Montague Street in Grimsby?'

'Are you having a laugh? I've got things to do.'

'Can you please just look for me...?'

There was more grumbling and then, eventually: 'There's just the one, your highness. Anything else? You want me to guide you through a list of Henry VIII's wives? How about a rundown of all fifty American states?'

'You've been *really* helpful,' Jessica replied, remaining polite against all her instincts. She hung up before Pat could carp on about something else; it had been the nutritional value of avocados the last time she'd been caught in a conversation with him.

'What did he say?' Archie asked.

'This is it. We've not made a mistake. There's no garage here.'

Archie's eyes narrowed. 'I don't understand. If there's no garage, then what's going on with that sales chart in Manchester?'

Jessica started to walk back towards the car. 'Something fishy, that's for sure.'

Archie sniffed the air. 'Aye. That'll be the boats over there.'

She didn't break stride. 'You're an idiot.'

TWENTY-THREE

The curry mile was glowing with fake pumpkins and ghostly shadows. Hallowe'en was still a couple of weeks away but that didn't mean the area wasn't all set for visitors armed with camera phones and hashtags.

Takeaways and restaurants dominated both sides of Wilmslow Road, with an apparent competition between establishments as to who could have the brightest lights. There was a giant blinking vampire over one place, with a flashing pumpkin above the takeaway next door. Groups of teenagers were massing on a corner close to a milkshake bar, with couples strolling up and down, peering at the menus in windows.

Jessica had parked close to the massive Asian supermarket, straightened her work suit as best she could, and then made a dash for it across the road.

Mark was already at the restaurant and Jessica saw the momentary look of relief on his face as she ducked around the greeter at the entrance and pointed towards him.

'I'm so sorry I'm late,' Jessica started as she fought with her coat. 'I had to go to Grimsby, then I had no reception, then my phone died, then I got it charged in the car, but I still had no reception. I've not been home.'

She slumped into the chair opposite him.

'*Grimsby?*' he replied. 'What's in Grimsby?'

'Fish.'

'Do you work with fish?'

It was only then that Jessica realised she'd not told him what she did for a living. She had no idea what he did either. Mark had put down the menu he'd been holding and she had a moment to take him in. There were actually two earrings in his right ear, both small hoops, which suited him. He had long, dark eyelashes – the type that some women would murder for – which only drew more attention to his blue eyes. There were crinkles at the corners of his eyes, but it was more experience than age. She'd never really gone for bald men in the past but, with him, it worked. It helped that his head wasn't reflecting the light like a bloody Belisha beacon.

Jessica was saved from having to answer straight away because a waiter breezed into their conversation, asking if they wanted drinks and poppadoms. The question was still hanging by the time he'd disappeared. Mark hadn't added anything else, leaving Jessica little option other than to outright ignore it, or simply answer.

'I'm police,' she replied breezily. Easy as that. 'CID,' she added. 'A detective inspector.'

His head tilted slightly and then his bottom lip pouted out as he nodded. 'Blimey. Old Bill, eh? What sort of things do you detect?'

'Mainly how to get stuck in traffic.'

Mark laughed, which was better than she'd hoped for. 'Does this mean you're going to check up on me? Run me through your system, or whatever? Make sure I'm not a secret axe murderer?'

Jessica smiled, not quite a laugh. A bit too close to the truth.

'I've always assumed that's what police officers do when they meet someone for the first time,' he added. 'I probably would.'

'It doesn't work like that. Everything's logged.'

Mark nodded along. His words could have sounded hostile but they hadn't. More that he'd watched a bit too much television.

The waiter was back with drinks, fussing over whether they'd decided upon something and apparently blinded to Jessica's unease at being late and unprepared. She went for a light classic – biryani – as there was little attractive about ordering the hottest thing on a menu for a first date. A person knew they were completely comfortable with another when they could go into an Indian and get the vindaloo without fear of judgement. Mark ordered some sort of fancy spinach thing and then they were alone once more.

'What do you do?' Jessica asked.

'I'm part of a team that designs apps. It's an independent start-up.'

He took out a card and showed her the logo – some sort of slanty fancy font in bright colours. They were based at MediaCity across the river in Salford. His full name was Mark King.

''*Appy Days*?' Jessica said with a smile, reading the card.

'Don't you like it? I didn't choose the company name, by the way.'

'What sort of apps do you make? Those ones that are free but then cost a fortune to actually do anything?'

Mark laughed through his nose. He left the card on the table, implying it was hers to take. 'Mainly for businesses,' he said. 'Anyway, we don't want to talk about work all night, do we?'

Which was music to Jessica's ears. She'd had a long enough day as it was.

'How are the warts?' she asked instead.

'Wart,' he corrected. 'Singular – and it's gone. You never did tell me why you were hanging around the clinic.'

'My friend was getting some regular baby check-up thing. I was the free taxi.'

'The best kind of taxis.'

'Exactly. Uber without the sex pests.'

It might have been her grumbling stomach anticipating food, perhaps even that she'd stopped for the first time that day, but Jessica suddenly felt a little looser. She sat lower in her seat, bit off the corner of her first poppadum.

'I don't really do hospitals, either,' she said, parroting what he'd told her when they first met.

'Does anyone?'

'My ex-fiancée spent a year in a coma.'

Mark blinked, mouth open. 'Oh.'

He had a swig of his drink. Neither of them looked away from each other even as the silence hung.

'I didn't expect that,' he added.

Jessica hadn't either. It had simply blurted out.

'My friend was in hospital after giving birth when there was that bomb scare in Manchester six months ago. She had to be evacuated to one of the nearby houses.'

'I saw that on the news,' he said before taking another swig and then a puff of breath. 'Your hospital tales definitely beat mine. I feel a bit silly now.'

Jessica managed a weak smile. 'You're still here.'

'Why wouldn't I be?'

'I don't know – this sort of thing would usually send someone running for the hills.'

'I try not to run on the flats, let alone the hills.'

Jessica munched the poppadum, using it mainly as a

distraction because she couldn't think of something either amusing or interesting to say. All she ended up with was: 'Why don't you like hospitals?'

It was Mark's turn for a bit of obstruction. He finished his drink and flagged down the waiter to order another. Their main food then arrived and Jessica was busy tearing into the giant naan when he answered.

'My dad was a doctor,' he said. 'A GP. He was seemingly always on call and I didn't see him that much. Then my parents broke up and my dad had a heart attack about a week later.' He shrugged, though his narrow smile said more than his words. 'Just one of those things, I guess.'

'Basically, we can both agree hospitals are churches for the devil.'

He raised his glass and they clinked. 'Amen. Hallelujah.'

They drank and that was that. Some sort of solidarity in any case. They had a few minutes of eating, with Jessica taking extra care to make sure she was chewing with her mouth closed, that she didn't talk with her mouth full, and that there was nothing wedged into her teeth. It was only then she realised how much hard work it was to eat in front of a stranger. All those things about manners she'd been taught when she was a kid went out the window as soon as she was comfortable with someone.

'There's something you should probably know,' Mark said when they had both finished.

'Go on,'

'My life begins again in eight months.'

It took her a moment to clock what he was on about. His smile made it clear he wasn't some whack-job religious nutter.

'You're thirty-nine?' she asked.

'Exactly. I'm looking forward to it in some ways.'

'Me too,' Jessica said.

'You're thirty-nine?'

'I've got the creaky knees to prove it.'

'My knees used to be right and left, now it's good and bad.'

Jessica laughed – that was the type of thinking she could get on board with.

'Did you ever think it'd come down to this?' Mark asked, gulping down the rest of his drink once more. He was on the cider, which glowed bright orange like the pumpkins outside.

'What?'

'When you were, say, twenty, forty was the end of it all. Someone's officially old at that point. Then, from nowhere, *you're* turning forty and you don't know where twenty years went. You always assume adults know everything and then, before you know it, *you're* an adult but nobody's ever given you that lesson to make sure you have all the answers.'

Jessica wanted to reply but didn't know what to say because he'd already put it into words better than she could.

'What are you going to do to celebrate?' she asked.

'No idea. Something I've never done before.' He paused, bit his lip.

'You can ask,' Jessica said, knowing what had been on his mind since she first mentioned it.

'You said "*ex*-fiancée"...'

There was the merest of lumps in Jessica's throat as she remembered the basement room and those long nights. 'He didn't wake up from the coma,' she said. 'That's it, really.'

Both their drinks were empty now, but the waiter was busy doing magic tricks for a trio of young women near the window

'What about you?' Jessica asked.

'What about me?'

'You know why I'm single. The whole coma thing...'

He winked and smiled. 'I'm too hideous. I was voted most likely to be single at forty when I was at school.'

She held his gaze, waiting for the actual answer. Mark's

features hardened and she noticed the rugged definition of his jawline.

'Divorced,' he said. 'My wife met someone else and left me two years ago. She moved to London and took our daughter with her. I only get to see her once every six weeks.' He paused. 'My daughter, not the ex-wife.'

They stared at each other for a few moments more and then both started to laugh.

Mark spoke first: 'We're quite the pair, aren't we?'

It was hard to disagree.

TWENTY-FOUR

Jessica was beginning to feel sorry for Mr Desperation. The seller from Robinson's Garage in Manchester was actually named Billy and he had such a droopy expression that Jessica couldn't help but want to pat him on the head. He was sitting low in his chair, in genuine danger of disappearing underneath the table.

They were in a coffee shop close to the garage as he explained that he didn't know what to do with himself. He was unsure whether he was out of a job and, if so, what he should do instead. He'd even dressed himself in his regular work suit as if he couldn't remember what else he could be doing.

He stirred his cappuccino absent-mindedly and ran a hand through his sandy, gingery hair.

'I don't suppose you know of anything going, do you?' he asked, apparently being serious.

'With the police?'

He sat up a little straighter, as if she'd offered him an inter-view: 'Anything. I'm a good salesman. I was in a call centre before this. I've got references.' He dug his phone out of his pocket, apparently ready to give her a name and number there and then.

'I'm not sure I can help,' Jessica replied. 'I was more hoping to talk to you about Robinson's.'

'Oh.'

He slunk back into his seat. Jessica didn't think it was worth pushing him on whether he recognised Evie, seeing as Janet had already confirmed it.

'Maybe I could get a job in Grimsby...' Billy added, largely talking to himself and proving he really had hit rock-bottom.

'That's partly what I wanted to ask you about,' Jessica replied. 'Have you ever visited the Grimsby garage?'

Billy shook his head. 'I've never really thought about it.'

He spoke with something close to outright hostility, as if they were the enemy.

'Did any of the other salespeople?'

'Go to Grimsby? Not that I know of. Why would we?'

He had a point. Archie had perhaps put it best – *No one's going for a day out to look at a bunch of boats.* Jessica doubted the tourism industry was massive on the East Lincolnshire coast and so why would someone visit an alternative branch of the place at which they worked? If it was in somewhere like Liverpool, they might stumble across it while on a weekend visit. Grimsby was far enough away that there would never need to be a crossover.

'Did you have much contact with the salespeople at Grimsby?'

'I don't understand. Why would we?'

'Perhaps at a trade conference? I don't really know how car-selling works – but something like that, where you get together? Or with Christmas parties, where you all have a meal once a year?'

'We never really did that. We did our thing, they did theirs.'

'How about calling their office to see if they have a car in stock?'

'No need. It's all on the computer system. Mr Robinson told us to go to him if there was ever anything we needed from the other branch.'

'When I was in the office, there was some sort of sales chart on the wall...?'

Billy slapped the table gently, making the froth leap from the top of his cup over the saucer onto the table. He didn't notice. 'We had a real chance of winning this month. That's another five hundred quid we won't be getting.'

'How did it work?'

'Simple, really. Everyone in Manchester got one point for a sale, regardless of how much it cost. Same deal in Grimsby. Whichever site sold the most cars in a month shared a bonus.'

'Sounds like quite the competition.'

Billy laughed humourlessly, raised his eyebrows as if to say, 'You don't know the half of it.' What he did say probably summed it up better: 'Bastards. Absolute bastards.'

Jessica couldn't stop the small giggle from escaping and then apologised. 'I didn't mean it like that,' she said.

It did at least get a genuine smile from Billy. 'Don't worry. I've never met any of them, but it's like they're taking money from us every month. Some of the others have kids and every time Grimsby win, they say it's like that's money being taken out of their children's mouths.' He shrugged, conceding the unmade point. 'Yeah, I know. Mad, isn't it?' A pause and then a smile. 'They're still bastards, though. There's this guy named Aziz who works there – and he's always their top seller. I keep hoping he'll get a job somewhere else. I've not even met the guy and I hate him.'

'How often do you win?'

'Maybe once every four months. Not often. A couple of times we've been leading with a day to go and then Grimsby have sold four or five in a day. Mr Robinson used to sit in his office and give us updates through the day. Last month we were level on the thirtieth. We sold three cars that day and thought we had it in the bag. Would've been five hundred between five of us. Then Mr Robinson said they'd sold five in Grimsby – including two in the final hour.' Billy sank lower into his chair. 'One of the lads was almost in tears.'

Given what Jessica knew about the Grimsby site – or the apparent lack of it – things were taking a truly disturbing turn.

'We won twice in a row at the start of the year,' Billy added. 'Absolutely smashed them in January. We thought it was going to be a big year, but then they won every month from March onwards. We wondered if they're allowed to sell for lower prices, or with bigger discounts, but Mr Robinson says it's a level playing field. It's his competition and he pays out either way, so I guess that's fair enough.'

Billy had barely touched the drink, but he spooned a blob of froth into his mouth and sucked it down. The bit he'd spilled had started to morph into a light brown smudge across the table surface. If he left it for another month, he could enter for the Turner Prize.

'Did you visit the Grimsby lot?' he asked.

Jessica hadn't expected his question and found herself fishing for a lie that was probably better than the truth – at least for now. 'There are other local officers out there,' she said. 'We're focusing on Manchester for now.'

'Right.'

'Did you have a close relationship with your boss?'

'Mr Robinson?'

'Right... it's just the very fact you call him that. It suggests a certain degree of formality.'

'I never really thought about it. I suppose we got on all right. He was happy when we were selling, like most bosses, I reckon. What's yours like?'

The directness took her her by surprise. 'He's fair,' Jessica replied.

'Exactly. So was Mr Robinson. Gave us a kick up the arse when we needed one, paid out our bonuses when we beat Grimsby. I've worked for worse people.' He spun his cup around so that the handle was facing him. 'I've just realised something,' he added.

'What?'

'It sounds a bit silly...'

'I've heard a lot of silly in the past.'

He nodded to acknowledge but didn't reply instantly. He continued spinning the cup and then ran his finger around the rim to scoop up the rest of the foam, before licking it clean.

'Did you ever have a strict dad or a teacher?' he asked.

'My mum was harder on me than my dad.'

Jessica didn't know why she'd answered. It was all a bit personal – not usually the type of thing she'd open up to anyone about, let alone a stranger.

'Mr Robinson was like that,' Billy said. 'He'd haul you over the coals about missing targets and that, but every now and then, he'd say something really nice – "you did really well on that sale", or that you'd handled a situation well. That sort of thing. I know it's weird, that he was just a boss, but those moments kinda made it worth it. It's not like it was a bad place to work, but you had to work so hard for those little bits of praise that it really meant something. One of the lads had been there for ten years, so Mr Robinson got him tickets to see United. It was out of the blue and it's that sort of thing that made you want to work harder.'

Jessica let Billy finish his story without interrupting. She knew what he meant – praise from her mother was worth so much more because it came along so rarely. She'd not had much in a while, largely because her mum was too busy dropping sledgehammer-like hints about grandchildren. She had the subtlety of an erupting volcano.

'I know it sounds a bit wild west,' Jessica said, 'but did Mr Robinson have enemies?'

'Not that I know of. You'd be better off asking Janet. I just sold cars.'

He exchanged a wide-eyed look with Jessica to say that Janet knew their boss a *lot* better than any of the salespeople.

'I understand,' Jessica replied, not doubting it. Somebody else was off interviewing her at that very moment.

'Do you think it was linked to the garage?' Billy asked.

'We don't know.'

'I mean... you hear things, don't you? Not about Mr Robinson, but in general. Gangs and turf wars, rivals trying to put each other out of business, that sort of thing. You don't know if it was that, or just some random burglary.'

Jessica let him talk, wondering if something specific would emerge, but it sounded like he was generalising, trying to make sense of something he didn't understand. She asked if he had anything else he wanted to say but got a sad, slow headshake in return. With that, Jessica left a ten-pound note on the table along with her desk's phone number, asking him to contact the desk if he thought of anything.

She was on the way back to her car when she managed to get Archie to answer his desk phone. It had taken four attempts to get through.

'You skiving?' she said into her own phone.

'Christ alive, I was having a piss!' he replied. 'I just rushed back to my desk thinking it was someone important.'

'I *am* important.'

Archie laughed but he didn't sound amused. 'I am allowed to have a wee, y'know.'

'On your own time, you are. You're supposed to be finding my murderer.'

'This is workplace bullying. I'm filing a complaint. First you drag me out to Grimsby, then you ban me from having a slash.'

'What have you been doing all morning?'

There was the sound of fingers bashing a keyboard and then Archie's voice was suddenly serious. 'You won't believe this – but Brian and his neighbourhood watch lot didn't see a thing on the night Owain Robinson was killed. We picked up some CCTV from outside someone's house at the other end of the street, but it only shows that Janet woman's car arriving and leaving at the time she said she was there. It's really dark, though – so anyone could have walked past and not been seen.'

'I believe that all too well. What about the Grimsby employees?'

'The local plod have been round the other dealerships in Grimsby asking about Robinson's – but no one's ever heard of it. Janet said she didn't know anyone, so we only had first names from the sales competition board. We've not found a single one.'

'Not surprising. Billy said Grimsby usually win the monthly contest, so they get a bonus.'

Archie huffed so loudly that Jessica could almost feel the breeze through the phone. 'The cheeky bastard. That Robinson bloke had a right scam on the go – making his salesmen compete with a garage that doesn't exist. Have we been checking alibis for the salesmen? If someone found out, they'd be well pissed. I would be.'

'Annoyed enough to kill someone?'

There was a humming sound from the other end of the line. 'Probably not – but still. If he'd do that to his own employees, what would he do to other people he didn't know?'

TWENTY-FIVE

Jessica shook the other woman's hand and then plopped herself in the seat on the opposite side of DCI Topper's desk.

'Tess,' the mystery woman said.

'Jess.'

The newcomer smiled. 'Tess and Jess. Nice. Sounds like a TV show.'

'If I can get my holiday days sorted, we could be rescue rangers.'

Topper smiled between them. 'Thanks for coming,' he said as the three of them sat.

'You're welcome,' Tess replied. 'Anything to get away from HQ is a bonus in my book.'

Tess was close to Jessica in age, but, at least in the latter's eyes, that was largely all they had in common. Tess seemed the sort who worked for some international fashion house as opposed to the police. She was in a slim-fitting grey suit with matching shoes and hair that didn't look like it untied itself with no reason or warning.

'Tess is a financial specialist,' Topper explained. 'I requested some help yesterday evening and, well, here she is.'

She offered a lopsided grin in Jessica's direction, slightly embarrassed. 'I wouldn't say "specialist",' Tess replied. 'I just offer advice now and then.'

Jessica returned the smile. 'If you know your twelve times table, it puts you on a pedestal above pretty much everyone here.'

'Ha! Well, I don't know about that.'

Tess shuffled a thick wad of papers onto the corner of Topper's desk. 'I've not had long to look through the books of Robinson's Garage, but I can make a few conclusions if you're ready.'

Jessica held up a finger to stop the other woman from continuing. 'Feel free to explain the financial stuff as if I'm a person who hypothetically doesn't understand a tax return form.'

Tess's lips creased into a small smile and then she was off: 'Last year around fifty-five per cent of Robinson's revenue came from the Grimsby garage. You're looking at close to half a million pounds from that one site. That's not profit – that's money that goes in and out. Profit is a lot lower because the mark-up on used cars isn't as high as, say, the mark-up on a new vehicle. The profit on a second- or third-hand cars can be as low as five per cent. When you add the Manchester branch to the list, there's almost a million pounds of turnover, with a listed profit of around one hundred and fifty thousand pounds.'

'Is that profit all for Owain Robinson?' Topper asked.

'It could be. There are no shareholders and he's the sole director. He does draw a high five-figure salary from the company so, actually, that profit is sitting in his business bank account for now. He could take it as a bonus dividend if he wanted – but then he'd be taxed for it.'

Jessica wasn't sure she was following. 'I'm not sure what that means for the Grimsby garage, seeing as it doesn't exist.'

Tess nodded to accept the point. 'This is where it gets a little clever, depending on your viewpoint. HMRC will have an idea of roughly what percentage profit each type of business might make. Say you own a sandwich shop and you declare it only makes one per cent profit a year. All the other money you make is spent on supplies – bread, butter, lettuce, Marmite, ham, and so on—'

'If that's your idea of lunch,' Jessica said, 'let's never go for a sandwich together.'

'Ha! Anyway, if you were to claim you make such a small amount of money, they'd compare your profits to the profits of all the other sandwich shops. All those other shops make on average a thirty per cent profit. Some might be twenty-five per cent, some thirty-five – but there's a spread there.' She paused. 'Pardon the pun – but you get what I mean. The place that claims it only makes one per cent will stand out. It's likely they're hiding money away, perhaps keeping back cash and only declaring the card purchases. I've simplified it a bit, but that's how a scam might work. The best way to not get caught is to ensure your business runs at a similar margin to all the other similar businesses.'

Jessica was nodding along, Topper too.

'With the garage, a similar thing would apply. Let's say a normal profit margin for a second-hand dealership is fifteen per cent. You're really unlikely to be investigated by the tax inspector as long as your books say you make something in that region. Perhaps twelve per cent, perhaps even ten – but there's a spread you'd stay within. That doesn't mean there couldn't be an anomaly. You might be wildly down for a couple of years because you're building a new office, or you're investing in stock. But they'd look for a pattern. Say you declared a loss four years in a row, HMRC might then get interested as they'd wonder where all the money had gone.'

'How does this relate to Owain Robinson?' Topper asked.

'Because that Grimsby branch was listed as operating for two years and his declared profit margin was fourteen per cent. It's not going to attract any attention from tax officials or anyone really. Half a million isn't a huge amount of turnover in real terms. Money goes into the business account, money goes out – and at the end there's his fourteen per cent profit. Nobody bats much of an eyelid.'

'But there is no garage in Grimsby,' Jessica said.

'No – anyone can register a company with Companies House with any address, even if that's a PO box. Tax authorities aren't going around making sure everything is legitimate – they don't have the time or the staff. Even if you're unlucky, they're only looking at the numbers on a spreadsheet to see if something feels right. Owain Robinson had the Manchester garage registered as the place for financial correspondence. All his letters, bills and tax documents went there – even for the Grimsby branch.'

'Is that normal?' Jessica asked.

'Perfectly. Think of, say, Marks and Spencer. They have a head office that'll deal with those sorts of things. For Mr Robinson, Manchester was his head office. He filed his own tax forms, so there's less chance of anyone noticing the small matter that half his business is fictional.'

'I guess that's where Evie Briers comes in,' Jessica said. 'She was an accountant who needed money, so she did a bit of work on the side to make everything seem legitimate. Owain Robinson wasn't good enough with numbers to make it happen himself. In return, Evie got a car and some cash.'

Tess held her hands up to say she didn't know.

'Whoever filed his accounts would have done it online,' Tess said. 'He signed to say he'd done his own, but who knows?'

'Where did the money come from?' Topper asked. 'The second garage doesn't exist – but you said half a million went through his bank account anyway. A bit is still in there but most of it went in and then came back out again. So where did that half a million come from?'

Tess smiled thinly. 'I'm afraid that's not a question for me. I can tell you how much was attributed to the Grimsby garage – but if you're saying that place doesn't physically exist, that's either half a million he's magicked out of thin air, or he had another source of income.'

Topper thanked her and they all shook hands. Tess said she'd have a closer look at the books if she could – but that she was busy doing a job for the Serious Crime Division, with time at a premium.

After leading her back to reception, Topper returned to his office and sat opposite Jessica. 'Don't think I've forgotten about those balloons,' he said.

'Not me, guv.'

He didn't seem convinced, but there were more pressing things. 'What's going on with the Briers case?' he asked.

'Forensics came in about an hour ago,' Jessica said. 'They found plenty of hairs in the flat – most were either Evie's or Samuel's – but there were a couple of others next to the door.'

'And...?'

A small smile. 'A match. DS Diamond is talking to the media team right now about how best to find our man.'

Topper nodded, not asking for a name. He pointed towards the now empty chair. 'What about this?'

'I'm thinking I should definitely get Tess to do my tax return.'

'Other than that.'

'If Robinson wasn't selling cars to make half a million, he's into something else. Probably the usual – drugs, weapons...' Jessica paused, remembering her night in a pub car park that wasn't in the too distant past, 'girls...'

Topper rubbed his forehead hard and then set about his eyes. 'I bloody hope not,' he said. 'Not again.'

'Is someone on-site at Robinson's Manchester garage?' Jessica asked.

Topper reached for his phone: 'We'll be tearing that place apart within the hour.' He glanced up to the clock – it was lunchtime. 'Okay – two hours.'

•

TWENTY-SIX

'Kale and spinach,' Not-So-Fat Pat said, holding up his lunch for Jessica to see. 'This isn't a regular wrap, either. The flatbread is made from quinoa and chickpeas. You use a coffee grinder to turn the quinoa into a flour and then—'

Jessica stared at the green stuff poking out of the wrap. 'Are you sure that's food?' she asked.

'You should get on it,' he said. 'Never been healthier.'

He took a step away from the reception and smoothed his nearly flat belly. Give it another couple of months and he'd be skinnier than her. Now the quadruple chin had melted away, there was definition to his cheekbones. She didn't know how old he was, but he was looking closer to thirty than fifty.

'I was about to go on a doughnut run,' Jessica replied, even though she wasn't.

His eyes narrowed. 'The devil's work.'

'You can't tell me you don't crave a Krispy Kreme at lunchtime – or one of those steak bakes from Greggs. Think of all that oozing gravy and the perfect flaky pastry...'

Pat leaned closer, glaring daggers. 'I always knew you were pure evil.' He pressed back and took a bite of his wrap. 'Kale and spinach for me. I've entered a half-marathon for Easter – was wondering if we could get a station team together. Bit of friendly competitiveness, raise a bit of money, that sort of thing. Shall I put your name down…?'

'And you called *me* pure evil! Are you mad?'

Pat had another bite of his overly green lunch. 'Some of the girls are taking me out at the weekend. We're starting on Canal Street and then seeing where it leads.'

'*Seeing where it leads?* You know Canal Street's the gay area, don't you?'

He shrugged. 'You only live once. I'm going to jiggle ma booty!'

Pat gave a demonstration that left Jessica wishing she could gouge out her own eyes. Some things couldn't be unseen.

'You should come,' he added, once his buttocks had stopped vibrating.

'I think I'm washing my hair or, y'know, slitting my wrists.'

'Go on. You know that constable who transferred in last month – Steve something – I've got a cracking bit of goss about him. You and me make a good team.'

'We've never made a good team, Pat. Yesterday you were moaning because I asked you to do a quick search for me. You've spent the last three years threatening to bill me every time you take a phone message.'

'That was the old Pat.'

'*Yesterday* was the old Pat?'

He finished his wrap and then licked his fingers clean. 'That doesn't count. I was on a starve day. You can't judge a man on his starve days, else where will we be as a society?' He nodded towards her, one eyebrow cocked. 'We should go out sometime.'

Jessica took a half-step away, eyeing him carefully. 'Are you asking me out?'

He batted away her concerns, laughing to himself. 'As if! But I am back on the market and everyone needs a good wing-woman.'

Jessica had never been more grateful to hear her phone start to ring. The number was unknown but it could have been someone banging on about mis-sold insurance for all she cared.

'Sorry,' she said, holding her phone up. 'This is important.'

Jessica shuffled through reception out the front door of the station onto the car park.

Wing-woman?

Is that what things had come to – playing second fiddle to Not-So-Fat Pat with his bloody kale wraps?

It was a male voice on the other end of the phone. Stumbling and uncertain, so low that she could barely make it out.

'That Inspector Daniels?' he mumbled.

Jessica's instinct was to correct him, but she'd be there all day if she started getting into details when it came to her name.

'Yes,' she replied.

'It's Donal.'

Jessica almost replied 'Donal who?' – but then it hit her. The shambling homeless bloke she'd found hiding behind a tree outside Hotel Smack.

'Are you all right?' Jessica asked.

'Aye... it's yer man.'

'Carl Brompton?'

'Right – he's here.'

Jessica was already scrambling for the car keys in her pocket as she told him she was on her way.

Donal was still hanging around the spindly tree when Jessica pulled into the grounds of Hotel Smack. He reeled away, attempting to hide behind the thin branches as Jessica approached with Archie at her side. Jessica held out an arm and told Archie to wait by the car as she headed across the grass by herself, Donal's dark eyes watching her every step of the way.

She stopped a short distance from the tree and dug a ten-pound note from her pocket holding it out until Donal mooched carefully towards her, like a puppy in training eyeing a tennis ball with suspicion.

'Fair's fair,' Jessica said. She nodded towards the house: 'Is Carl inside now?'

Donal snatched the note away sharply, as if worried it might be withdrawn. It disappeared into one of his pockets. 'Yeah.'

'When did he get here?'

'Hour or two ago – saw him coming up the driveway.'

'Was he alone?'

'Yeah.'

'Thank you.'

Jessica waited for a moment, wondering if her source might want to add anything. When he didn't, she drifted back to the car and Archie and then they headed along the driveway to the front of Middleton House.

Tim didn't take long to answer this time. He was wearing another shockingly offensive woolly jumper with a bewildering pattern of horizontal blue and black lines.

'Whoa,' Archie said, which summed the situation up.

Tim examined Archie without a word and then turned to Jessica. She was hoping for recognition this time around but his gaze was as blank as before.

'Can I help you?' he said.

She showed him her warrant card again. 'I was here the other day – DI Daniel – I'm looking for Carl Brompton.'

Tim studied her even more carefully, although gave no

indication he remembered her. 'Who says Mr Brompton is here?'

'I do – and, at the absolute least, he's breached his bail, so I want a word.'

There was a sigh and then Tim told them to wait as he disappeared back into the house and along the hallway. A couple of minutes later he reappeared, this time with another man at his side.

Carl Brompton's limp was even more pronounced than Izzy had made out. He plonked all his weight down on his left leg and then pivoted upwards, almost falling onto his right before quickly shifting back to the left. As Jessica watched, she noticed how different it sounded when he was walking on his right foot compared to his left. One was a heavy thump, the other more of a slide. If she could hear the difference, then a blind boy with heightened senses definitely would.

As they moved along the hallway of Middleton House, Brompton started to lag behind Tim. He was a good few steps behind when Tim stopped to make sure he was still being followed.

Brompton's birth certificate said thirty-five – but his weathered features read fifties. There were deep lines cut around his eyes and forehead, a scar across his chin and another by his left ear. He was wearing camouflage gear but there was a hole in the knee of his trousers and another under the armpit of his top.

Tim was peering between Jessica in front and Brompton behind. The tension was hard to miss, with Brompton backing away slowly and Archie edging forward in case he made a run for it.

'Is there a problem?' Tim asked.

'I just want to talk,' Jessica replied. She risked a quick glance to Tim before returning her focus to Brompton. 'Do you have an office or a spare room we can borrow for ten minutes?'

Tim waited for a few moments, the tension obvious. 'Just through there,' he said, indicating a door on the opposite side of the hall.

'After you,' Jessica replied, motioning towards Brompton who had stopped backing away. He was eyeing Archie, knowing the constable would beat him in a race to the back door if it came to it.

For a moment, none of them moved. Brompton's gaze was flicking quickly from Jessica to Archie and back again as he tried to figure out what he should do next.

'Who are you?' Brompton asked. His accent was local, his voice hoarse.

Jessica moved forward slowly, taking out her warrant card and offering it towards him, even though he was too far away to read it. 'Detective Inspector Daniel. This is Detective Constable Davey.'

'What d'you want?'

'A word.'

'About what?'

It might have been the crack in his voice, perhaps even the way he was struggling to stand, but Jessica knew Carl was their man. He'd been in Evie's house on the night she'd died in a pool of her own blood on the kitchen floor. He was the person Samuel had heard sliding across the smooth floor.

Archie saw it, too.

Brompton exhaled a long, loud breath and he slumped even further. His head dipped to the floor as if his spinal cord had been severed.

'We know, mate,' Archie said. He spoke kindly but there was a brimming undertone of Manc menace there, too.

'Know what?'

'It's over, Carl.'

There was an agonising moment, slow motion perhaps, where Brompton dropped to his knees. He had one hand tugging at his hair, the other tearing at the sleeve of his top. 'It wasn't me,' he moaned. 'She slipped. It wasn't even me.'

Jessica took a step forward, but Brompton wasn't moving anyway. He fell forward, bashing his forehead on the mat without trying to protect himself. Archie moved quickly, lunging ahead and hooking a hand under the other man's armpit to support his weight. Brompton slumped sideways, resting on Archie's knees and whining to himself.

'It wasn't even me,' he said. 'She slipped.'

Archie's handcuffs were off his belt loop in the time it took for Jessica to start speaking. 'Carl Brompton, I'm arresting you in connection with the murder of Evie Briers...'

TWENTY-SEVEN

Jessica was sitting on one side of the interview room table as Archie strode back and forth like an overly short sergeant major.

'Will you sit down,' Jessica said. 'You're making me nervous.'

Archie did sit, apologising as he did so. Then he started fiddling with the file on the table in front of them.

'How did you do that voodoo thing?' Jessica asked.

'What thing?'

'The whole, "We know what you did" malarkey. It's never worked for me.'

'Dunno – that's the first time it's ever worked for me. Normally they tell you to sod off, aim a kick at your knackers and make a run for it. Police work's a piece of piss when they fall on the floor and confess.'

'There's no way that's counting as a confession,' Jessica said. 'If he gets a half-decent solicitor, they'll say he was talking about some girl he knows tripping over the stairs or something. All he said was that it wasn't him and that "she slipped". We need him to say something useful on tape.'

Archie turned to her and held out a hand, waggling his fingers.

'Ooooooooh,' he said spookily, 'you *want* to *buy* Archie a Yorkie bar... ooooooooooh...'

'I really don't,' Jessica replied.

Archie stopped doing the annoying thing with his hand. 'I guess the voodoo's worn off.'

He pressed back in his chair and then sat forward, resting his elbows on the desk and pressing his chin into his palms. He glanced up at the video camera above Jessica's head, then lowered his voice, scratching his nose at the same time so that his palm was covering his mouth.

He'd spoken so quietly that it took Jessica a moment to figure out what he'd said.

'If you get a minute later, I could do with a word.'

She opened her mouth to reply but then closed it again, nodding in silent acknowledgement instead.

Before anything else could happen, there was a sharp knock on the door. Jessica called that she was ready and then a uniformed officer led Carl Brompton into the room. Brompton had regained the use of his legs and wasn't struggling as he limped towards the chair on the other side of the interview room. His face was a smeared mess of tears and snot – and it didn't look like he'd made much effort to clean himself up.

The duty solicitor trudged solemnly behind, briefcase in hand, before taking a seat next to Brompton. He was trying to keep a straight face but he looked like he could really do with a good night's kip.

'You look upset,' Jessica said after the formalities were out of the way. Brompton was staring at the table, not cuffed to the huge bolt in the centre. He was rocking gently back and forth. 'Carl,' Jessica added, hoping to get his attention. 'Would you like to tell me what you're upset about?'

'I didn't do it,' he said.

'Didn't do what?'

Even with three sets of eyes on him, Brompton offered no reply.

Jessica left it a few moments and then asked Carl where he was on the night Evie died. He snivelled to himself, wiping his nose on his sleeve.

The solicitor adjusted his tie slightly as he replied: 'My client's memory isn't the best.'

'It's only five nights ago.'

Archie opened the file in front of him, removing the photo of Evie Briers and sliding it across the table. She was in a park with Samuel, smiling with a flower pushed into her hair over her ear. Samuel was grinning, too: a mother and son who had overcome the obstacles put in front of them.

'Do you recognise her?' Jessica asked.

Brompton shifted in his seat, so that he was facing the wall.

'You're going to look at the picture,' Jessica said. 'You're going to look at it and tell me whether you know her.'

She waited. Archie started to fidget and so did the solicitor. Brompton continued sniffing and sobbing, occasionally using his sleeve on his nose.

All the while, Jessica waited.

'Perhaps we could move on,' the solicitor suggested.

Jessica didn't acknowledge him. It might not have been a full confession but she had something close to a partial one – and that'd be enough to get extra time from the magistrates.

Not to mention the hairs that had been found close to the door of Evie's apartment...

They had ninety-six hours if it came to it. She'd send him back to the cells and then bring him back up a couple of times a day until he looked at the damned picture.

Jessica waited some more. There was a clock on the wall, a small tilt of the head away, but she didn't move.

Five minutes, ten, perhaps even fifteen – and then Carl slid back until he was facing the table. His eyes were puffy and raw and dried snot had crusted to his top lip. His gaze darted to the photo and then lingered.

'"She slipped",' Jessica said. 'That's what you told us at Middleton House. I heard it, so did Constable Davey – and so did Tim. What did you mean by that?'

The solicitor tried to interrupt, but Brompton took a deep breath, stretched a hand towards the photo and then withdrew it.

There was a moment of silence and then: 'I didn't know her name,' he said croakily. 'She was just some woman. I didn't know there'd be a kid there.'

From nowhere, the room felt a degree or three colder.

'Samuel,' Jessica said. 'That was the kid's name.'

Brompton nodded.

'What happened?' she asked.

'I dunno. We were supposed to give her a fright – but then the kid was there and he was making this noise, this weird sound with his throat. I was trying to hold onto him, but I guess she panicked.'

'You mean *Evie* panicked?'

Brompton nodded softly again. It was a few seconds before he spoke. 'I don't know. One minute she was standing and then she was on the floor. I think she slipped.'

'Who were you there with?'

Nothing – and then, eventually, a slight shake of the head.

Jessica remained calm, let the silences hang. 'Did the other person push her?'

It was barely perceptible but Brompton shrugged.

'I need you to say it, Carl.'

The words came out as a croaky mumble but they were there: 'I don't think so.'

'So, to be clear, you're saying you were in Evie's apartment when she died?'

The solicitor pressed forward, just about getting out the word 'now' before Brompton spoke over him. 'Yeah.'

'You were there with one other person?'

No reply.

'But you say Evie slipped and hit her head on the counter?'

The reply came instantly this time: 'I don't know. It was too quick. I was holding onto the boy. He was making this noise. No one meant...'

'You didn't mean for her to die?'

Brompton shook his head slowly. He'd gone from not looking at Evie's photo to staring at it.

'Who were you with?' Jessica tried again.

She didn't get any response this time, not even the headshake. She left the question hanging for a few seconds before moving on.

'You asked Evie where the money was?' she said.

Brompton blinked up from the table. His eyes were watery and there was a small pool of tears on the table. 'Huh?'

'When you got into her apartment, you asked her where the money was. What money were you talking about?'

'Oh.'

Brompton's mouth remained open. Jessica felt a tingle – this was it, a link from Evie to Robinson to the big trail of money. It was all about to come crashing down.

Except it didn't.

'I heard it on TV,' he said.

'Heard what?'

'These blokes were trying to scare these other blokes. Busted in through the front door shouting, "Where's the money?"'

Archie shuffled in the adjacent chair. His nerves were hers.

'I don't understand,' Jessica said.

'We were trying to scare her. Figured if she had some money, then great. If not, she'd be well frightened. Didn't know she was some mum with a kid. I didn't know any of that.'

Jessica believed him. The search team had discovered nothing squirrelled away in Evie's flat. No other bundles of money hidden in the wall – just the little over five hundred quid Jessica had found. It was probably just-in-case money – Owain Robinson had paid her with a car, after all. There was likely a bit of cash on the side but not loads. Why would anyone try to rob a single mother for cash?

'Did someone pay you to scare her?' Jessica asked.

A nod.

'How much?'

Brompton licked his lips, rubbed at the scab above his lip.

'How much was her life worth, Carl?'

'Hundred each.'

Jessica let it hang because the words spoke for themselves. A young woman's life was worth two hundred quid. Two hundred sodding, bastarding, arseholing, pissing quid.

'Why were you supposed to scare her?'

'Don't know.'

'Okay – *who* paid you?'

Brompton sat in silence, breathing through his blocked nose. It was so loud that it sounded like he was snoring, even though he was wide awake.

In-out.

Hee-haw.

'Who was it, Carl?'

'No.'

'Was it a man?'

He shook his head.

'A woman?'

Another shake.

'It must be one or the other.'

Brompton continued shaking his head. He muttered 'no' once more, but that was it.

Jessica nudged Archie and he found the photo of Owain Robinson, slipping it across the table. Jessica didn't have any evidence, but perhaps Evie had been threatening to blackmail the garage owner, so he wanted to scare her? That didn't explain what had later happened to him though.

'Was it him?' she asked.

Brompton glanced to the photo but his brow rippled before he caught himself. He didn't say no – but he might as well have done. He'd never seen Owain Robinson before.

'Who was your accomplice?' Jessica tried once more.

She waited.

'We've got your hairs,' she said, matter-of-factly. 'We know you were there. You're in enough trouble with this, so telling us who you were with will help when it comes to sentencing. Judges look kindly on this sort of thing.'

She looked to the solicitor, wondering if he might chirp up. There was no particular reason for him to help her – and he didn't. Perhaps Carl's tongue would loosen after a bit longer in the cells with the solicitor explaining what would happen.

Either way, for now, Brompton still wouldn't answer. He rocked back into his chair and snorted loudly, trying to clear his blocked nose.

Jessica was thinking about ending the interview anyway – but the gentle knock on the door did that for her. She gave the time and suspended it, leaving Archie to watch over things as she edged into the corridor. A uniformed officer was waiting for her.

'I was told to come find you,' he said.

'Why?'

'The search team at Robinson's garage has found something.'

TWENTY-EIGHT

Jessica was standing in front of a whiteboard waving a pen around as if it was a lightsaber. Someone had doodled the obligatory cock in the corner of the board, with an impressive amount of detail given the state of the board marker. There was definitely perverted talent there.

It would usually take a few minutes to shut everyone up ahead of a team briefing – but it was late in the day, people were keen to get home and the night crew were getting ready for handover. There were a little over a dozen officers present, some CID, some uniform, nobody seemingly paying much attention.

'Some great work today,' Jessica said, giving the whole, upbeat *aren't-we-sodding-wonderful*-tone those trainers banged on about at management coaching.

There was a mass muttering from the officers wanting to go home.

'Trading Standards are on-site at Robinson's Garage and they've recovered tens of thousands of pounds in counterfeit clothes and shoes from underneath the main office. I spoke to Shah earlier and he reckons it'll turn out to be one of the city's biggest ever hauls. If that's not a result, I don't know what is.'

Jessica didn't quite expect a standing ovation but a mumbled chorus of approval would've been nice.

'HQ have been called in to follow the money trail – which at least means they can do the boring stuff. It looks like Owain Robinson used a fake garage in Grimsby to funnel this money through, with the likelihood being that Evie Briers was doing his books to hide the anomalies.'

Nothing.

Someone at the back let rip with a yawn that would have dislocated the jaw of a regular man. It was like one of those snakes in a nature programme just before it started to eat something three times its own size. The constable's mouth snapped shut and he stretched his arms high, before offering a watery-eyed apology.

'If that wasn't enough,' Jessica continued, 'Carl Brompton has been arrested for the murder of Evie Briers. We've got his hairs at the scene, though he says someone else was present and that it was all a big accident. He says he was paid to give her a scare – but he won't say who coughed up the couple of hundred quid – and he won't say who was with him in her apartment. Of course, Samuel Briers is unable to give us any sort of physical description other than that the second man was tall.'

There was a cough from the side and Jessica scowled towards the culprit, wondering if it was a genuine cough, or some sort of scoff.

'Samuel might be blind – but he was right about one of the men dragging his leg – which is what led us to Carl Brompton in the first place. If he says the second man is tall, I'm inclined to take his word for it.'

If it *was* a scoff, then the officer was now silent.

'Owain Robinson and Evie Briers are both dead – but, for

the moment, there's nothing specifically to link what happened to them. Our best chance of figuring that out is persuading Carl Brompton to tell us who hired him to scare Evie. I'm not holding my breath on that, so a priority has to be to look for further links between them. This whole thing is quite the mess. HQ are running a money trail on Robinson, while we are following up on Evie. Everyone's supposed to be liaising together but, well, we know how that goes.'

This *did* get a reaction – everyone knew precisely how it went. Whenever anyone from HQ was involved, especially if it was the Serious Crime Division, that meant a chance they could claim all the credit while dumping anything negative at the feet of the mere mortals working at Longsight. Serial murders, gang violence, anything to do with fraud or finance would often end up being dealt with at HQ.

Jessica started to write on the board, linking the names and then drawing a question mark. 'Who hired Carl Brompton to scare Evie?' she asked the crowd. 'Why target her? Someone – or a group of people – was giving Evie grief for weeks leading up to what happened, so what was going on there? Also, who's Carl's friend? We're after a tall man – which I realise isn't much, but it puts Constable Davey in the clear.'

That got a laugh.

Archie folded his arms in the front row and slouched a little lower, muttering under his breath. 'All right, piss off,' he eventually told his colleagues. At least it came with a grin.

Jessica calmed the crowd and then continued: 'Who does Carl Brompton hang around with? He's a well-known shoplifter and has spent God knows how long inside – so there's quite a big list of potential bastards he could know. This is going to mean a trip to Hotel Smack for some poor sod as well.'

Boooooooo...

It was fast turning into a panto.

'We've also got to talk to the garage staff again. How much did they know about the Grimsby operation and the counter-feit goods under the office? I can't believe someone was able to drop a load of knock-off Nikes into a building and have no one notice. Anyone who knew about it is a potential suspect.'

Jessica stopped to assign a few roles for the next day. Between Middleton House and the Robinson's employees, it was going to be another busy day.

'At the risk of treading on anyone's toes at HQ, let alone Trading Standards, it'd be really good for us to find out where Robinson's counterfeit goods came from. Chances are Robinson pissed off someone he was either buying from or selling to. He's the middleman – so who's he buying from and who's selling knock-off tracksuits and trainers around the city? That's clothes shops, eBay traders and so on. We can start with the usual suspects. Sergeant Diamond has the details of people we've done before for selling dodgy goods, so that's more doors to knock on.'

Jessica ran a hand through her hair, trying to remember everything. They really needed more officers. She'd already handed out more work than they were going to get through in a day. Other officers from HQ and Bootle Street in the centre would be helping as well – but there were never, ever enough officers.

She turned to Izzy: 'Any news on that community centre break-in?'

There was a quick update – but not much. A warrant was out for the person whose fingerprints had been found on the windowpane that had been kicked through, but no one had answered his front door and there had been no sightings.

'There was a jogger mugged at knifepoint last night,' Jessica said. 'There's also some protest going on at the uni tomorrow about, I don't know, animal rights or something. Tuition fees? Whatever it is this week. We're sending a couple of officers there, so we'll be at least two faces down. Oh – and we've also got an unidentified man still in a coma at the hospital. Another picture and appeal is going in the papers tomorrow – plus ITV are on board for something on their evening news. It might be a night team job, but someone's going to have to monitor anything that comes from that.'

Jessica glanced to Izzy, who gave a small nod.

'I think that's it,' Jessica said.

Chairs scraped, feet scrambled, like the bell going to signal the end of a lesson at school.

'Oh – and I'm off for two days and I have absolute faith I'll get back to discover that everything outstanding has been solved.'

That got a laugh, too. An unintended one.

Officers filed out, either finishing their shift or ready to start, leaving Jessica and Izzy alone in the smallest of the incident rooms. Jessica yawned and then Izzy joined in before they both started laughing at the other.

'Quiet day,' Jessica said.

'Aren't they all?'

'I talked to the guv and we're going to leave Carl in the cells overnight. The duty solicitor's gone home, so he's on his own down there. Give him a whole night on a stone slab to see if he wants to say something useful.'

'I thought you were off for two days?'

Jessica pushed on the back to the chair and hauled herself up. 'I might pop my head in.'

She turned around the room, before realising what she'd forgotten.

'What?' Izzy asked.

'Archie – he wanted a word.'

'It'll only be about getting time off for a United game. It always is.'

Jessica nodded. Izzy was probably right. It was always football, wasn't it? She'd get a text or a call that night with a fixture list alongside a 'just this once' add-on that, of course, meant he'd be asking for something similar in a month.

'See you tomorrow,' Izzy said.

Jessica only realised what she'd replied when she was back in her car: 'Yeah – see you tomorrow.'

TWENTY-NINE

Jessica was in the corridor outside interview room number one, sipping vending machine coffee. In terms of taste, it was a bit like licking rainwater off a dirty window. For texture, it was more like the gunk at the back of a microwave. Still liquid and yet somehow gritty at the same time. Scientists should probably look into it – a new state of mass that was neither liquid nor solid.

That and the 'day off' wasn't including so much of the 'off'.

'You're brave,' Izzy said as she approached.

'I think I'm immune to it now,' Jessica replied. 'I've built up a tolerance over the years. It used to take a sip or two and I'd be on the toilet for a morning. Now it's a good few cups.'

'Charming.' Izzy poked a thumb along the corridor in the direction from which she'd come. 'Carl's not doing well. He's got withdrawal symptoms. Practically scratching the walls.'

'What's he on?'

'Prescription something or other, plus methadone and some other things. They had a doctor come in this morning to check him over. He's addicted to all sorts. I think Cadbury's Creme Eggs were on the list.'

'That Creme Egg addiction is a right nasty one. Probably the worst. You can get heroin all year round – but they only do Creme Eggs for about four months. I've seen a bag of mini eggs go for ten grand on the black market when autumn comes round.'

Izzy ignored her. 'Anyway, the doctor reckons he's fine to be interviewed. The duty's been down for about a half-hour, so we're all set.'

'You know I should be at home watching TV, don't you? There are important DNA tests being announced right now. There's this girl who's pregnant and the father could either be her boyfriend or the boyfriend's dad. I'm missing this.'

'My money's on the dad.'

Jessica headed into the interview room and checked the recording set-up. No point in getting Carl Brompton to say something interesting if the only observer was four blank walls.

It wasn't long before Brompton was brought in, the duty solicitor at his side. Brompton looked like the definition of a rough night – dark bags under heavy eyelids, swollen cheeks, a red raw nose from being blown and hair jutting off at odd angles as if he'd been plugged into the National Grid. It was like Jessica and most of her colleagues the night after the Christmas party.

'Bad night?' Jessica said, not particularly trying to be a smart-arse, more stating a fact.

Brompton grunted something that might have been 'yes'.

'It doesn't have to be like this,' she told him. 'You know you're going to be charged for Evie's death, you know you're going to be remanded – but you can help yourself. There are cushier cells at Strangeways than we have here. Better blankets, comfier beds. Their canteen food is practically Michelin-starred compared to ours.'

He didn't reply.

'I just want two names,' Jessica added. 'Who were you with at Evie's house – and who paid you to scare her?'

She glanced to the duty solicitor, who was also looking to Brompton. He was peeping over his glasses, apparently unsure what was going to happen. Jessica wondered what his advice would have been. Legally speaking, it probably *was* in Brompton's best interests to give up the names; personally... it depended on who those names belonged to. Prison could be a dangerous place if the wrong person felt aggrieved. Brompton had seen enough of jails to know that for himself.

He didn't reply, staring at the table instead.

'How about you don't give me a name,' Jessica said.

It finally got a response as Brompton peered up with wide eyes lined with popping red veins.

'We can start with a gender. Were you paid by a man to scare Evie Briers?'

Brompton looked back to the table, conceding nothing.

'How about no gender. Was the person older than, say, forty?'

Nothing.

And then, just as Jessica was about to move on, he looked up. Brompton glanced firstly to his solicitor and then to Jessica. 'I don't know who it was,' he said.

Jessica waited a moment to see if he'd add anything.

'Do you mean you saw the person but didn't recognise him or her?'

'Right.'

'But you could identify this person if I were to show you a photo?'

For a moment, Jessica thought she had him. He'd volunteered the information, after all. But then Brompton returned his attention to the desk. He was picking at a fingernail, perhaps even the skin around the cuticle. Either way, he was back out of the conversation.

'That's something,' Jessica said. 'You saw the person handing over the money. We're getting there. Next up is male or female...?'

Brompton took a deep breath and asked for some water. A minute or so later and he had it, gulping down the entire cupful in one go and asking for another. He sipped the second more slowly and then started scratching his arms.

'Is there a reason you don't want to talk to me?' Jessica asked. 'You've been in court enough to know how these things happen. Time off for pleading guilty, bit of leniency for cooperation. Judges love this sort of thing. If there's someone or somebody you're worried about, we can help.'

Brompton said nothing, leaving his solicitor to chime in and remind her that his client was free to say nothing at all.

'Who were you with at Evie's apartment?' Jessica asked. 'Can we at least get an answer to one of these two things?'

Brompton looked up once more and finished his water.

'What do you want?' Jessica asked, trying not to let her frustration show.

'Huh?'

'It doesn't suit any of us for this to continue. What do you want in exchange for the two names? I'm not saying I can make it happen – but if you tell me what you're after, I can at least see if it's possible. It's better than keeping you in our cells for four days.'

Brompton turned to his solicitor and Jessica realised this wasn't something they'd discussed. Plea deals didn't really exist in UK law and the solicitor probably wanted Brompton to talk as much as she did. He wouldn't fancy ninety-six hours of this, either.

'Chips,' he said.

Jessica blinked. '*Chips?*'

'From Leo's.'

He scratched the back of his neck and then his forearms.

'If you want to give me a name or two, I'll see what I can do,' Jessica said. She looked to the solicitor, wondering if he'd object. If he did, then he didn't say anything.

The next thing Brompton said make Jessica's blood run cold. It was only a word, just five letters, but that was all it needed.

How could she have been so stupid?

'Donal,' Brompton said. 'It was me and him at the flat.'

THIRTY

'Shit.'

Jessica muttered the word under her breath so that only Archie could hear.

'I mean, it's just...' She shook her head. 'Actually I was right the first time. *Shit.*'

Archie was unexpectedly distant, checking over his shoulder to make sure there was nobody anywhere near them in the canteen.

'How bad is it?' he whispered.

'Well, Donal Doherty has skipped out of Hotel Smack and nobody's seen him since yesterday – so pretty bad.'

'Aah... how much did you pay him?'

Jessica glared at him. 'It's only you who was there, Arch.'

'What are you saying?'

She glanced sideways, nodding and smiling towards a passing constable. When he'd gone, she lowered her voice further. 'You know what I'm saying.'

Archie took a breath and gulped.

'It's not like anyone's going to ask,' she added. 'We went to Middleton House on the off-chance Carl had returned – and he had. Nothing untoward there. We didn't know Donal was Carl's accomplice. How could we?'

It was true, of course – but that wouldn't change how it looked if it came out that she'd paid a suspect twenty quid. She wouldn't be able to prove what the money was for – it could have been to tell a lie that would implicate Brompton. They could both get off.

Archie nodded slowly. 'Did he call you?' he asked.

Jessica sank back into the hard-backed plastic chair. 'Bollocks – I forgot that.' She paused, thinking. Well... it shouldn't matter. We just have to find him.'

'What if he says you paid him?'

'Why would he?'

Archie shrugged. 'Why *wouldn't* he? If he's got any sense, it could get him off. His word against yours. I mean, people would probably believe you but...'

Jessica kicked the spare chair. '*Shit.*'

Archie didn't need to say it, but there would be big problems if Donal did get into an interview room and start saying how he'd been paid by a police officer to reveal Brompton's whereabouts. Regardless of whether it was in good faith, or if it was 'just' twenty quid, this was the sort of thing that ended careers.

Or worse.

Officers had gone to prison.

'I'm not going to say anything,' Archie said.

'We need to find Donal – like *seriously* find him. I'm supposed to be off and it's not like I can spend two days hanging around looking for him.'

'What are you asking?'

'If you get any sniff that he's been seen, text me. Make it something innocuous. Ask if I saw the United result, something like that. I'll know what it means.'

'Christ, Jess...'

'It's not as if no one's done it before. Tenner here, fiver there – ask someone to tip you off. We'd never find anyone if it wasn't for a bit of back-scratching now and again.'

'I know, but...' Archie suddenly clamped his lips closed as Izzy banged through the double doors and approached their table.

'I was wondering if you were still here,' she said.

'Did Carl get his chips?'

'I sent a constable off to Leo's especially. Got extra for the duty to shut him up.'

'Good.'

'There's something else,' Izzy said. 'It's about Samuel.'

Jessica was in Deborah Wareing's living room, peering out the window to the street beyond. There were parked cars, someone passing by, struggling with a bulging supermarket bag for life – not much else. So much for her days off.

'What did the man look like?' Jessica asked.

Deborah slotted in alongside Jessica at the window and peered both ways along the street. She had wet hair, probably not long out of the shower given the triangle of damp in the small of her back.

'I don't really know,' Deborah replied. She drifted across the room and found a spot on the sofa. 'Jeans, I guess; hoody.'

Jessica perched on the window sill and turned to face the other woman. 'What was he doing?'

'I know it sounds silly. I wasn't going to call, but then I thought of what happened to Evie and Samuel. I mean, you don't know, do you...?'

Jessica waited, not committing to a response.

'I suppose he wasn't really doing anything,' Deborah added. 'I just saw him a few times yesterday, walking back and forth. Then I saw him again this morning.'

'And you've never seen him before?'

'No. He was out there yesterday evening before it got dark. I thought he was taking photos.'

'You thought...?'

'He might have been on his phone...' She paused. 'I shouldn't have called. It sounds stupid when I say it out loud.'

'No, you did the right thing,' Jessica replied. 'I'm not sure there's an awful lot we can do – but it's definitely good to have it on record. We're going to make sure a patrol comes down here a couple of times each day just in case.'

'That's good.'

Deborah curled her legs underneath herself and yawned widely. 'Are you any closer to finding out what happened to Evie?'

'We're getting there. I can't say much.'

She yawned again, covering her mouth second time round. 'Samuel wants to go back to school,' she said. 'I spoke to his head teacher and form tutor and nobody seems sure what's best for him. They said that if he wants to come back, then perhaps that'd be beneficial.'

'What about you?'

Deborah blinked up to Jessica. 'You're the first person to ask me that. I was talking to my mum last night and she was asking how Samuel is, whether I've been looking after him, what plans *he* has...' She shook her head slightly. 'Sorry, it's not like I begrudge him anything, it's just...'

'...It'd be nice if someone asked about you once in a while?'

'Right.' Deborah uncurled her legs, squished her bottom deeper into the cushion. She glanced towards the door and then lowered her voice when she knew there was no one there. 'I spoke to a social worker yesterday. It's not like I want to send him away, it's just' – another glance to the empty doorway – 'I didn't ask for this.'

Jessica wasn't sure what to say. Neither Samuel nor

Deborah had asked for this. Samuel was fourteen, so hardly an infant. In less than two years, he'd get his national insurance number; he'd be old enough to marry; to work full-time. Deborah had her own life – a boyfriend? A girlfriend? Something that didn't involve having an unrelated teenager move in.

'What are you going to do?' Jessica asked.

Deborah first looked at Jessica and then stared past her towards the window. 'I honestly don't know.'

Jessica moved onto the second sofa. 'Can I ask you something?'

'Go on.'

'At Evie's house, there was a plug socket that was loose. Live wires were hanging out. The cold tap didn't work in the kitchen, either.'

Deborah frowned at Jessica and then apparently caught herself, turning towards the window. 'What are you asking?'

'It didn't feel right. Evie seemed responsible. When we first met, you said that you'd have to clean up your hallway because Samuel was here. Why would there be live wires exposed in a flat where there's someone who's blind?'

'I don't know.'

'Didn't she mention any of it?'

'Why would she?'

The reply snapped back with venom and then there was a moment of silence before Deborah apologised.

'Long week,' she added.

Jessica offered a flimsy smile, saying she understood. Deborah either didn't know the answer or had no interest in giving it. Jessica asked if she could see Samuel and Deborah pointed her up the stairs.

She found him in what was now an improvised bedroom. A camp bed was squeezed against a wall, with barely enough room for a rack of clothes on the other. His door was open and Jessica wondered if he'd heard anything of what they'd been talking about downstairs. She and Deborah had been whispering, but perhaps he'd developed some sort of super hearing. It wouldn't be any more implausible than teaching himself to see.

Jessica knocked and Samuel unleashed a flurry of clicks in her direction. 'Detective,' he said.

'How'd you know it was me?'

'I recognised you.'

Samuel was wearing a Spider-Man T-shirt this time. His white cane was on the bed next to him, his laptop resting on his knees. As she entered, Samuel moved his computer to the side and folded down the lid. She wished he hadn't – but Jessica couldn't help but shiver as he looked at her with the plain, milky eyes.

'Can I sit on the corner of the bed?' Jessica asked.

'Of course.'

She did and the bed sank slightly, creaking embarrassingly.

'Have you found the man with the leg?' Samuel asked.

'I'm afraid I can't talk too much about this, but... maybe.'

Samuel rocked on the bed. 'Did he drag his leg?'

'Sort of. He had one leg shorter than the other.'

'I told you,' he said.

'You did.' She paused, wondering how much she should say. She'd already screwed things up when it came to Carl and Donal. 'We wouldn't have found him without you,' she added.

Jessica wasn't sure she'd ever seen such a reluctant smile. Samuel had done something that by more or less any measure was extraordinary. Most witnesses who had eyes that worked couldn't remember anything with clarity – hair colour, clothes, height, even skin tone. If a dozen witnesses saw the same incident, there would be at least five different descriptions. Samuel was a blind boy under incredible stress and he'd still paid attention enough to help them get the right man.

'I need to ask you something,' Jessica said. 'At your house, we found a plug socket with the wires hanging out. Do you know anything about it?'

'Mum told me not to go near the cabinet in the living room. She was trying to get it fixed.'

'Do you know when it happened?'

'Maybe a day or two before. The tap in the kitchen was playing up, too. It was stressing her out.'

'Was there anything else?'

'She said there were lights that stopped working. The speakers under the telly were broken. She asked me if I used to move things.'

'Like what?'

'Her purse. Her bag. She'd say she left them in one place but they'd end up in another.'

'Did you move them?' Jessica bit her lip and then apologised.

Samuel shook his head. 'No. I think she just forgot.'

'How long was all this going on?'

'Maybe a couple of months?' He paused and then added: 'Why?'

Jessica tried to remember the layout of the apartment, trying to think if it mattered. Remembering how tidy Evie appeared. 'I don't know,' she said.

THIRTY-ONE

No messages.

Damn.

Jessica repocketed her phone, hoping Mark hadn't noticed her checking. She'd been looking at it on and off all day, hoping for a message from Archie. Anything to do with United was her cue.

Except she'd received nothing. Donal Doherty was still out there somewhere, waiting to be arrested and to explain how she'd paid him twenty quid for a tip. It was her second rest day and she could have spent it mooching the streets of Manchester hoping to spot him – but then how to explain it if she did? His story of her paying him would only gain more credibility. Her second day off had to *actually* be a day off – with a witness and everything.

She had to be elsewhere.

Elsewhere, yet still in the loop.

Except she *wasn't* in the loop because bloody Archie hadn't bloody texted.

'You all right?'

Jessica rolled down the hem of her coat, covering her

pocket once more. 'Fine,' she replied. 'Just wondering if I had reception.'

Mark laughed, held his hand out to indicate the vast expanse of green around them. 'Not much signal here,' he said.

He was right about that.

Mark was dressed for the occasion: combat trousers with an array of pockets for carrying useful stuff. Jessica was in jeans. He had heavy hiking boots with mud crusted to the sole. He'd probably been up the Himalayas or trekked the Amazon with those shoes. Jessica had a pair of battered steel-capped work boots that were good for the odd knacker kick, not so great for traipsing across dew-soaked fields. He was in some sort of super-light, fleecy utility top that would no doubt cost a fortune and have a label that carped on about its wicking properties. Whatever that meant. Jessica was wearing a woollen sweater that was far too hot the moment she started walking. She was sweating like Judas Iscariot as the cheese and cracker course arrived.

'I love it out here,' Mark added.

Jessica's natural instinct was a sceptical 'meh' – but it was hard to disagree. The Peak District sat to the east of Manchester, a vast expanse of England's green and pleasant land not even thirty miles from her house.

They were a little outside the hamlet of Castleton, following the line of a long, low dry-stone wall towards the greenest green Jessica had ever seen. Like a nature programme with the red and blue filters turned down – but for real. She'd lived in Manchester for half her life and yet she'd rarely ventured away from the red bricks and industrial remnants of the city. It was another world.

'How often do you come here?' Jessica asked.

She had the feeling that Mark had significantly reduced his pace to allow her to stay alongside him. She was far from a slow walker but there were times when he bounded ahead only to check himself and slow down.

'Once a week,' he replied.

'Doesn't your head get cold?'

He turned to look at her and Jessica flashed him a smile. He rubbed a hand across his smooth scalp. He sniggered before replying: 'That's why they invented hats.'

The road split at an enormous tree and they headed left, towards the vast steepling wall of emerald hill. The road was barely wide enough for two vehicles but they were on a gravelly path, heading steadily towards the gaping scar that nature had carved into the gorge.

Jessica wanted to enjoy it but she wanted even more for her phone to buzz.

'I can't believe you've never been here,' Mark said

'You always miss the stuff on your own doorstep. I've been abroad loads and spent time in other parts of the UK – but driving thirty miles seems too close for a holiday and then I have things to do on days off.'

Mark slowed once more, having got a couple of steps ahead. 'True.'

They walked in silence for a little while, reaching a small car park and a brick barn with a Union flag flying overhead.

'I feel like one of those people who get airlifted off mountains,' Jessica said.

'Why?'

'Wrong shoes. Wrong clothes.'

'You're not *that* bad. I've seen people wearing flip-flops before.'

'Up here?'

'All over. I was on Snowdon one time and there was a woman in heels trying to clamber over rocks, shouting at her kids because they'd dragged her out there. Just imagine that –

your kids point to a mountain and say, "Can we climb that?" What do you think the trail's going to be like?'

The road narrowed even further to a cattle grid and, after that, muddy grass covered the path as Jessica felt a squelch underfoot.

'This is Winnats Pass,' Mark said.

They stopped for a moment to take it in. The road curved steeply upwards, splicing through a gully that separated two cathedrals of grass and moss. An enormous triangular rock was sprouting from the earth on the right, with a lone tree clinging to the cliff high above.

Jessica suddenly felt very small.

There were no cars but a cyclist chugged past; legs pumping, chest heaving as he rose from the saddle to fight the brutal gradient.

'Rather him than me,' Jessica said.

Mark pointed to the path on their right that curved up and inexorably up. 'We can go over or through,' he said.

It wasn't much of a choice given how steep the other option was. Jessica took a couple of steps onto the path ahead. 'Through.'

They had only gone a short distance when Jessica realised how tight her chest felt. The angle of the climb was burning her calves – and the shoes weren't helping. Mark didn't say anything, but he knew what was going on, stopping and putting his hands on his hips as if it was his idea to rest. He offered her his water bottle and she guzzled down a couple of mouthfuls.

'I think I'm officially a city girl,' she said.

'Nothing wrong with that.'

Jessica was gasping as she set off once more, wanting to prove she wasn't as unfit as she felt. 'I never used to be,' she said.

'I assumed you were a Manc – what with being a police officer and all. You know the city well enough.'

'I grew up in the country – up Cumbria way. Moved here...' Jessica counted on her fingers. '...far too many years ago.' She paused, not just for breath but because she wondered if he'd open up without being asked. When he didn't, she added a quick, 'You?'

'Brighton.'

'How'd you get to Manchester?'

They continued for a few more steep steps. There was a series of small rocks embedded within the earth. Some were working as steps; others crumbling and threatening to take Jessica back down the hill with them.

'The ex-wife,' he said.

'Oh.'

'I, um... probably should've explained a bit better the other night when you were talking about your ex.'

'It's okay.'

Another pause. It was hard to tell if it was because of the exertion of hiking, or the awkwardness of him not filling the blanks.

'That doesn't really answer how you got to Manchester,' Jessica added.

'She left me,' Mark said. 'There wasn't much left for me at home. An old mate was up here running the company I work for and I asked if he had anything going. I'd say there's a long version, but that's pretty much it.'

Perhaps it was her police instincts but the word 'why?' was out of Jessica's mouth before she had the chance to shut herself up.

'Is this what you're like with a suspect?' Mark said with a laugh. A laugh with an edge, of course. Jessica knew that when she heard it. She did it enough times herself. 'I suppose

Manchester was as good as anywhere. Seemed like a decent place for a fresh start.'

'How old's your daughter?' Jessica asked.

'Nine. She's called Charlotte. I go down to visit, but it's not easy on her. My parents were separated and I used to hate having to make choices between them at the weekends. My ex and her bloke will say they're off to the zoo or something – and of course Charlotte wants to go there, too. But it'll be my weekend and so we'll be left doing something else. It's not easy on anyone.'

Jessica bit her lip to stop herself asking anything else. There'd be other chances... probably.

The road continued ever upwards, banking even more steeply to the right. The cyclist had long disappeared into the distance and good luck to him – walking it was plenty enough for Jessica. After the bend, the road and the path somehow became even steeper. Each step was a vicious yank of her hamstrings.

'Why police?' Mark asked, changing the subject.

'An accident. Something to do. One minute I was looking for jobs, the next I'd been accepted.'

'How long ago was that?'

'Too long.'

'But you've stuck with it?'

'I guess.'

'You don't sound so sure.'

Jessica lifted her knees high and pulled herself up over a rock. Her sweater was sticking to her shoulders and she could feel the beads of perspiration dribbling down her back, creeping through the gap at the back of her jeans.

'It's nice when things work out,' Jessica eventually managed.

Mark stopped again, passing over the water for her to drink once more. This time it took three large mouthfuls to help her catch her breath. It was only the scenery keeping her going, a pair of lush jade banks swooping upwards on either side, cupping the perfect blue of the sky.

'You do this every week?' she asked.

'Not *this* specifically – but something similar.' He pointed over the top of the hill. 'Mam Tor's over there and this whole area is full of climbs like this.'

'Bollocks to that.'

He laughed. 'Yeah, I used to think like that.'

Mark tugged on the smallest of the two hoops that were in his ear, pinching and scratching behind it.

Jessica set off once more. 'How much further is it?' she asked.

'Not far.'

'That's what they all say. Next thing you know, it's two hours later and you're stuck at the bottom of a valley as it starts to rain.'

He laughed again. 'It's *really* not that far.'

They'd only gone a few steps more when Mark asked if Jessica had children. It was all breezy, *nothing serious, y'know*, not quite the dagger it might have been.

Jessica told him she didn't. 'I do have a six-month old living in my house, though,' she added. 'With his mum, obviously.'

'Is that fun?'

'Depends on your definition. If you like the smell of vomit in the morning and think sleeping's for wimps, then it's very enjoyable.'

Mark sniggered the knowing laugh of a man who'd been through that himself, and then moments later, the road and path curved right. From nowhere, there was another cattle grid and a farmhouse. The path was no more, blending onto the road itself which – mercifully – flattened out so that it was only a gentle ridge.

Jessica stopped to sit on the wall and rest. She had some more water and took a moment to check her phone again.

Nothing – even though she had reception.

'Work?' Mark asked.

Jessica repocketed her phone, not bothering to deny it. 'Sorry,' she said. 'It's just...' She shrugged, not quite knowing the words.

'...It's hard to switch off,' Mark added.

'Right.'

She handed him back the water. 'What next?' she asked.

'Now we walk back down.'

'*Down?*'

'Back the way we came. We can go the long way round if you want?'

'I do not want.'

'Okay then...'

Jessica pushed herself up. 'Didn't the Grand Old Duke do this?' she asked.

'Yeah – but he had more men and, to be honest, I'm pretty sure he was more York-based.'

Jessica took Mark's hand and squeezed it. 'Good point.'

THIRTY-TWO

Jessica didn't hear a peep from Archie the entire day. She tried turning her phone's airplane mode on and off just in case there was some backlog in messages, then she switched the device itself off and on. The ol' classic. Rules one, two and three of IT support.

Afternoon became evening became night. Still nothing.

Donal Doherty remained out there.

The next morning, Jessica was on her way past Not-So-Fat Pat's reception counter, heading towards her office, when he called after her.

She turned but didn't get too close. 'You're not on a starve day, are you?' she asked, fearing the worst.

'Tomorrow – how kind of you to ask.'

She examined his face for sarcasm but it didn't appear to be there. Either that or it was harder to spot now he'd lost a couple of chins.

'Are you being nice to me?' she asked.

'Why wouldn't I be?'

'Because last year, you said I was the definition of everything that's wrong with the human race.'

He took half a step back. 'Did I?'

'More than once. You said I was the dictionary definition of evil.'

Pat placed a hand on his heart. 'Why would I say that?'

'Because I asked if you'd write down a phone number for me.'

He craned his neck backwards, eyes narrowing like some weird kind of cartoon bird. 'Are you sure it was me?'

'Definitely. After we shut down your favourite bakery because it was being funded by a gangster, you said there was a special place in hell for people like me.'

Pat was shaking his head. 'Sugar addiction. It does horrible things to people. I could show you some stats that would make you want to raze Bourneville to the ground. Praise be that I'm cured now.'

Jessica wasn't sure what to make of the new Pat. In many ways, she wanted the gossipy old version back. She was on board with that, she could handle him. She could do bitchy. An arse-shaking, Canal Street-frequenting, slimmed-down *nice* version was uncharted territory.

'What can I help you with?' she asked, politely.

Pat jabbed a thumb towards the waiting area on the other side of the counter that was just out of earshot. 'Someone reckons they might know who your missing bloke is.'

'What missing bloke?'

'The one you found in a ditch who'd had his head kicked in. *That* missing bloke.'

It took Jessica couple of moments to remember that the man with Chatresh Lodi's driving licence in his pocket still hadn't been identified. She'd been thinking only of Donal Doherty for the past two days.

'Oh,' she said.

Jessica craned her neck around Pat and peered out towards the waiting area. For the most part, the only people who actually visited police stations were those answering bail or looking to pick up someone who'd been banged up for a night after kicking off in the city centre. It was rare to get someone who didn't have a degree of nutter about them. Despite that, there was a relatively normal-looking woman sitting by herself. She had long, straight black hair and was in a smart business suit, knees together, back straight. If Jessica had to guess, she'd either a had a strict parent or attended a religion-based school at some point.

'What's her name?' Jessica asked.

'Marie.'

'Does she seem normal?'

'As normal as you or me.'

'I was worried about that.'

Jessica breezed back past Pat into the waiting area, hand outstretched. She introduced herself and the two women shook hands. Marie was nervous, stammering when she introduced herself and starting to stand, then sitting once more. Jessica asked why she was there and Marie wondered if there was somewhere private to talk.

She could have taken Marie to an interview room, perhaps even the meeting room, but it was early and Jessica figured the tape recorder and video cameras would make her even more nervous.

They ended up in Jessica's office, cup of machine coffee apiece. Jessica delved into her bottom drawer – the one she locked – and emerged with a packet of chocolate Hobnobs. It would partly make up for the coffee. Marie brightened slightly but waved her hand as a 'no' anyway.

'I saw the picture on the Internet,' Marie said. 'It looked like he'd been beaten up pretty badly.'

Jessica didn't particularly want to see it again herself but she loaded the photo onto her monitor and twisted it around for the other woman to see. 'That one?'

Marie peered at it, nodded, turned away. Jessica didn't blame her. The mystery victim was a pulpy mashed-up mess.

'You think you know him?' Jessica asked.

'Maybe.'

'He would have been missing for eight days at least.'

Marie nodded. 'Right.'

'So who do you think it might be?'

'It's sort of... complicated.'

'We do a lot of complicated around here.'

Jessica was smiling softly, trying to be understanding. Marie had made herself very small. Her posture had gone and she was hugging her knees to her chest, perching on the edge of the office chair.

Marie nodded at Jessica's monitor. 'Do you note down everything I say?'

'It depends on what you say. Not necessarily.'

'But I can talk, like, off the record...?'

'I want to say yes – but it really does depend. If you were to tell me you've committed some sort of crime, I can't then pretend you didn't.'

'It's nothing like that.'

Marie breathed in through her nose, hugged her knees a little tighter and stared off towards the bin in the corner of the room.

'I've been seeing someone,' she said quietly.

Jessica left it a few moments – but she was already sure of what was to come.

'And you think the person you're seeing might be the man we found...?'

'Right.'

A pause. Marie took another deep breath.

'But there's something else...?'

Marie wiped her nose with the side of her hand and then took the tissue Jessica was offering. 'He said he was single, but

I suppose I've always had a feeling he probably wasn't. Like when you think something's true but you don't want to ask just in case it's not.'

'What's his name?'

'Chris McMichael... or at least that's what he told me.'

Marie watched as Jessica wrote the name on a pad and then put the pen back down.

'He's not texted me for three weeks. I've tried calling, but his phone doesn't even ring. At first it told me to leave a message but now it does that thing where it says the number's not in service.'

She took a moment to blow her nose properly and then tucked the tissue into her sleeve.

'I know what you're thinking,' she said, looking up to catch Jessica's eye. 'I'd be thinking it, too. I'm just some silly woman who fell for a married man. Now he's dumped me.'

She clung to Jessica's gaze, wanting the condemnation.

'You can't choose who you fall for,' Jessica said.

Marie coughed a laugh. 'You sound like a self-help book.'

It could've come across as bitter, but it didn't. More an acknowledgement that she'd heard it all before. 'He used to go on business trips all the time,' Marie said. 'He said he sold office equipment, so he'd have to go to different countries, or different cities. He'd be gone for a week at a time and then we might get a couple of days together before he went again.'

'Did you believe him?'

'Maybe. He definitely travelled – but I wondered if he had a wife somewhere else. He told us both he was visiting somewhere when really he was spending a couple of days with her, a couple with me, and then doing his work in between.'

'Did you ever confront him to ask?'

'Once... sort of. Back in the summer. I asked why he couldn't get a job that didn't mean so much travelling. He said he loved his work. I asked if it was because he had another woman somewhere else. He asked if I loved him, if I trusted him... and what else could I say?'

'How long have you been together?'

'Three years. We met at a festival in Heaton Park. He had a flat in Salford. I'd been round a couple of times but we almost always met at mine because it was bigger. I went round there last week, but there was a mum and her kid living there. She said she'd never heard of a Chris – but that the man who lived there before her had moved out a year before. I've been phoning round Chris McMichaels in other areas of the country but no one's seen him – and most people aren't in the phone book nowadays.'

Marie was mid-thirties at the oldest, wearing the bleak features of a woman who knew this moment would probably come sooner or later. Jessica could picture her sitting at home by herself scrolling through the list of C McMichaels listed on 192.com, calling them one after the other.

'It's not that I don't mind being dumped,' Marie said, before correcting herself. 'Okay, I *do* mind being dumped. It's just it'd be nice to know. Maybe he *is* married and he decided to cut all ties – but maybe he's not and he got beaten up. Or he was hit by a car. Or his plane crashed. Or he drowned in a river. Or a hundred other things. I've been looking for men named Chris McMichael in the news, but then I realised it might not be his name at all. Three years and perhaps he's someone else? I've been thinking all this – and then I saw the photo and that explains it all. He's *not* married, he's *not* someone else. He *hasn't* lied. He just couldn't text or call because he's unconscious.'

Marie was contradicting herself, hanging onto the merest morsel of hope that, perhaps, she'd not lost three years of her life after all. In the end, she was like anyone else – she wanted an explanation so that the events of her life meant something.

'Does your, um, boyfriend have a tattoo?' Jessica asked.

'On his arm.'

That much had been in the news.

'What's it of?' Jessica asked.

'I don't know, not exactly. It's this sort of reptile, amphibian, lizard thing. It's green and black if that helps.'

Those specifics *hadn't* been in the news. The man who'd been found in the ditch did have some sort of lizard on his arm. One of the constables thought it was an iguana, but no one was quite sure. People got any old shite inked onto their bodies.

'Is that right?' Marie asked. 'Is it the same tattoo?'

'I wouldn't want to say for sure,' Jessica replied.

'But the other things match, don't they? Dark hair, he's the right height, the right shoe size. I saw that online. All that matches.'

'I can arrange for you to visit the hospital,' Jessica said, sounding as neutral as she could. It *did* sound promising – certainly more so than any other names they'd been offered to identify the mystery man.

'Oh, God,' Marie said. She smiled widely, dropping her legs to the floor and sitting back into her primped, proper posture. 'It really is him, isn't it? I've been worrying all this time, thinking who knows what – and it's not even his fault he's not texted. How long's he going to be in hospital? Do they know what's wrong with him? My poor little man.'

Jessica listened and gave answers where she could. She didn't want to remind Marie that, by her own admission, she hadn't heard from Chris for a good couple of weeks *before* the body had shown up. Still, it was always the hope that did for a person in the end.

THIRTY-THREE

By the time Jessica had finished dealing with Marie, the request had come for her to visit DCI Topper in his office. The financial expert, Tess, was already there, folders loaded onto Topper's desk.

'Are you here to do my self-assessment?' Jessica asked as they shook hands.

'The word "self" is your clue there.'

Topper nodded Jessica into a chair and then Tess started.

'Sorry about taking a couple of days,' she said. 'I've been on a case for Serious Crime and then trying to do this on the side. I do have an update, though.'

She unclipped an elastic band from the top file and spilled a sheaf of papers onto the desk, hunting through it and then passing a handful of pages each to Topper and Jessica. The first page was some sort of spreadsheet – columns and rows, numbers and colours, like a school project but much more impressive.

'Did you knock this up yourself?' Jessica asked.

'I had a free hour.'

'An *hour*?! I'd have needed a couple of days off for this.'

'I've found the money,' Tess said. 'Whether it was Robinson himself or the Evie woman you mentioned, they did a good job of hiding it to make the business seem legitimate. I'm not surprised he got it through HMRC.'

Tess directed them towards a column that was a light shade of blue on the spreadsheet.

'Owain Robinson bought about thirty per cent of his used cars from a series of companies in and around Grimsby,' she said. 'That's not in itself unusual. The port is used to import all sorts of vehicles from Europe. There are companies who bring in cars and vans from the continent and then sell on to other traders or to individuals. It would usually be *new* cars but new doesn't necessarily mean new.'

'What does it mean?' Topper asked.

'A car that's been on a forecourt for six months or one that's used for test drives might be classed as second-hand, even though it's not technically had an owner. There are all sorts of oddities that go on with car sales but for the sake of argument, let's say that Robinson wasn't doing anything particularly out-of-the-ordinary. It only becomes suspicious when you look at the wider picture. That's part two on your document.'

Jessica flipped the page and scanned down a list of companies. There were nine in total, all based somewhere in Lincolnshire, all with some sort of variance on the word 'auto' or 'car' in the name. They also each shared the same company director.

'Who's Iain Jennings?' Jessica asked.

'I don't know,' Tess replied, 'but I do know *what* he does. As well as the nine companies listed, he also runs Jennings Fishing Boats. Wanna guess what that does?'

'Fishing?' Jessica tried.

'Exactly.'

'But how does fishing relate to importing cars?'

'Precisely. Jennings Fishing Boats has been running for the best part of forty years. It'll be some sort of institution on the docks. The nine car importers were incorporated during a three-month period approximately two years ago.'

Jessica peered back to the document, flicking to the first page and then looking to Topper.

'Why would someone be buying cars from a man who runs a fishing company?' Jessica asked.

'You're going to have to answer that one,' Tess said. 'I think my work's done.'

Topper was looking a little too pleased with himself. The kind of look that meant Jessica's life was about to get a teensy bit more difficult.

'What?' Jessica asked.

'I knew you were busy downstairs,' he said, 'so Tess gave me a little preview of all this over an hour ago. We've already had the local plod go round to check out the offices of Jennings Fishing Boats.'

'And?'

'It's a small cabin on the Grimsby docks. They said it's been cleaned out. The boats are moored and there's no sign of life.'

'Does anyone know where Jennings lives?'

'Yep – someone knocked on his door, but there's no answer. I asked the chief inspector over there if he could spare me a couple of men, but, well, you can guess the reply.'

Jessica slumped back in her seat, knowing what was coming. 'I'm off to Grimsby again, aren't I?'

Topper smiled. 'Bring this old man back a stick of rock.'

THIRTY-FOUR

Grimsby still smelled of fish. If anything they were stinkier fish than the last time Jessica had been. It was the type of smell that quickly became a taste, perhaps even an entire essence of a place. It clawed at the back of a person's throat until everything else was completely overwhelmed.

Jessica was on the docks, not too far from the streets she'd walked with Archie when looking for Owain Robinson's invisible second garage. She had expected rows of boats, like Monaco, but without the sun or glamour. What she got was nothing of the sort. There was a handful of varying-sized boats moored against a sodden dock. They were riddled with scratched, chipped paintwork and battered cabins. The grim, grey nothingness overhead wasn't doing much for the atmosphere, nor were the seagulls who were busy squawking and kicking off with one another like drunken football fans arguing over who had the bigger dad.

And then there was the smell.

It was fair to say that, in almost every way imaginable, Grimsby was not Monaco.

The home of Jennings Fishing Boats could more or less be

called a shed. It was on the edge of the docks, a damp wooden shack with a scratched sign over the top of a door.

Although the 'local plod' – as Topper had called them – were too busy to help, they had managed to round up some of Jennings Fishing Boats' employees. Clichéd or not, they were identifiable by how bloody massive they were. Jessica wasn't entirely sure precisely what commercial fishing involved – though she doubted it was the rod, reel, flasher's mac and general weirdness possessed by any angling fan she'd ever met. What it definitely did involve was burly blokes with action-hero thighs and forearms. Unfortunately, the movie-star features didn't quite extend to facial or body hair – as, going by the specimens in front of her, being a fisherman apparently made men very hairy indeed.

Jessica called over the bloke who most looked like he knew what a razor was and they found a spot on the jetty, close to a row of small boats. 'Will' was a local – 'born and bred' with fishing 'in his blood'. It all sounded like quite the health hazard, but he was effortlessly charming. Early twenties, tall, well-built and a bit scraggy around the edges.

None of the men had been told what was going on – but they'd turned up for work that morning, only to find the office was locked. Nobody could get hold of Iain Jennings and so, for the first time in the three years since Will had started working for the company, everyone had gone home for the day. That was until the police had got onto them, asking them to come back. Nobody knew what was going on.

'This might sound like an odd question,' Jessica said, 'but do you ever bring in any cars on the boats?'

Will's reply was gruff, pure northern: 'What boats?'

'The boats you fish on.'

The man's eyebrows sank low. Not confusion as such, more bewilderment. He pointed over Jessica's shoulder to the harbour beyond. 'You have *seen* the boats, haven't you?'

Jessica had but she turned to look again. They were all small, enough for perhaps a dozen or so men with a little space to spare. Not much room for a car, let alone a ramp to get a vehicle onto the boat.

'Yeah, er... I was wondering if you had a bigger boat to bring in cars?'

'Why would we do that?'

He had her there. Cars might well be imported somewhere along the docks – but not on the small fishing boats Jennings used.

'What's Iain Jennings like as a boss?' Jessica asked, with a not-so-smooth change of subject.

'All right.'

Jessica waited to see if he'd add anything. When he didn't, she was forced to ask for a bit of elaboration.

'Pays well,' Will said.

'Anything else? Is he generally happy? Sad? Does he talk much about the business...?'

'I s'pose he's a bit mardy.'

Jessica figured that was as good as she was going to get. 'When did you last see him?' she asked.

'Day before yesterday.'

'Did anything untoward happen then?'

'Like what?'

'I don't know – that's what I'm asking you. Did he seem particularly upset? Was there any indication he might lock up the office?'

'He told us not to come in yesterday because the boats needed some work doing.'

'Is that normal?'

Will scratched his head, glanced past Jessica towards his workmates. 'Well...'

'How many times has that happened since you started working here?'

'Never, I suppose. There are two boats. If one needs work doing, we go out on t'other.'

'So yesterday was the first time you expected to be working but he gave you the day off...?'

'Right. Said he'd pay us and all that, so we weren't that bothered.'

'What about this morning?'

Will shrugged. 'T'were no one here. Usually t'boss opens up and out we go.'

'Any idea where he hangs about if he's not here and not at home?'

'He's always in t'Labour Club.' Will nodded past her once more. 'But Paddy checked and he ain't there.'

'Where is it?'

Will told her and then Jessica let him go. She spoke to a couple of the other lads – including Paddy – but no one had seen Iain Jennings since he'd sent them home two days before. Their biggest collective surprise was that he was neither at home, on the docks nor in the Labour Club. Or 't'Labour Club' as they called it. From what they said, he pretty much lived in one of the three places.

Jessica was on her way back to her car, chuntering about the local lot not being able to handle things, when she noticed the present she'd been left. One of Grimsby's own seagulls had clearly taken offence to her moaning and unleashed a torrent of white, grey and slimy black goo on her windscreen. It had dribbled along the glass, congealing unhelpfully on top of the wiper blade and then setting.

She reached for the tissues in her pocket, thinking murderous thoughts.

Walking into Grimsby's Labour Club was like walking back through time and emerging somewhere into the darkest recesses of Jessica's memory. It hadn't been a Labour Club when she was a child, it was the Conservative Club in her village. She remembered a stern man at the front door saying she wasn't allowed into the bar area. He fetched her an orange squash in exchange for a ten-pence piece. It was all ancient history now – from the bulldozed club to the man who used to carry around an umbrella in summer. Even the old-style ten-pence pieces were no more. A blink of memory.

This Labour Club still endured, though. The floor was cracked varnished wood, the bar was surrounded with fluorescent spiky cardboard stars for various drinks promotions, and there was a handwritten poster on one of the walls advertising a Shakin' Stevens tribute act for the coming weekend.

Mother of God.

As Jessica crossed the room, she could even see remnants of tape two-thirds along the floor. It stretched from one wall to the other. One side for the men, the other for women. It was almost gone now, just a few pesky sticky bits that hadn't been steam-cleaned. Along with the brown tar stains along the edges of the ceiling, it was a reminder of what these clubs used to be.

There were a handful of men off to one side, sitting around a bag of peanuts, watching darts on TV. Otherwise the place was empty.

The woman behind the bar had tattoos on her shoulders and she wore the pitbull face of a person who should not be messed with. It was all a little intimidating until she spoke, then the friendly northern, 'What can I do for ya, luv?' cracked through the mist of Jessica's past and she was back in the present.

'Do you know Iain Jennings?' Jessica asked.

'Know him? I practically have to chuck him out each night. What d'ya want him for?'

'I was wondering if you'd seen him?'

'Who's asking?'

Jessica used the flap of her jacket to conceal her warrant card from the group of men, not wanting to cause a scene.

The barmaid eyed it from a distance and then nodded. 'He all right?'

'If I could find him, I'd be able to tell you.'

She glanced towards the men and then back to Jessica, lowering her voice. 'Not seen him in a coupla days.'

'I was told he's in here a lot...'

'Right, well, he weren't in yesterday and I've not seen him today.'

'Did you hear him saying anything about if he might be going anywhere? Quick holiday? Few days away? Something like that?'

'Not me, luv. You tried his workmates – Paddy and that lot? That's who he's normally with.'

'They've not seen him either. Do you know if there's anywhere else he spends time?'

'Only the docks. I just work here.'

Jessica was going round in circles. This wasn't something with which she needed to be involved. The local chief inspector was playing silly buggers with Topper and she'd had to trek across the country for no particular reason.

She took her phone out as it started to ring. The barmaid glanced instinctively towards the 'no mobiles at the bar' sign that was pinned to a post, though she said nothing.

It was the station and Jessica started walking back to the door as she answered.

Not-So-Fat Pat sounded concerned: 'Where are you?' he asked.

'Grimsby.'

'Again?'

'My thoughts exactly. What are you after?'

'Your woman from this morning – Marie. She left a message for you, said it was urgent.'

'Go on.'

'The man at the hospital isn't her bloke. She says the tattoos don't match or something like that. Reckoned you'd know what that meant.'

Jessica pressed through the doors of the club and blinked into the grey. She rested against the pebble-dashed wall, remembering Marie's sudden burst of enthusiasm when she thought that, perhaps, her mystery bloke hadn't simply walked away. What would she be feeling now? Probably relief that her boyfriend wasn't in hospital, coupled with grief that she still didn't know what had happened to him.

Not knowing was the worst. Jessica knew that as well as anyone.

There was a beep as Pat continued to speak – a second caller trying to connect. Jessica didn't recognise the number, though it had a Manchester prefix. She thanked Pat for the update, shook her head at the overly polite, 'You're welcome', and then pressed to take the second call.

'Is that DI Daniel?' a woman's voice asked.

'Yes.'

'It's Deborah – Evie's friend.'

'Hi.'

'Can you come over? It's Samuel. He's missing.'

THIRTY-FIVE

It took Jessica nearly three hours to get back to Manchester. There was some accident on the motorway around Leeds, a convoy of lorries driving alongside each other near Huddersfield and a slowdown for no particular reason as she neared the M6o. The usual kind of British transport buffoonery.

By the time Jessica reached Deborah's house, Samuel had already been found. The panic had lasted for barely forty-five minutes before he'd click-clicked his way back into the house.

Deborah met Jessica in the hallway along with a family liaison officer. 'He was asking for you,' Deborah said blankly, as if it was as much a surprise to her as it was Jessica.

Samuel was sitting on the sofa in the living room, eating ice cream from a Ben & Jerry's tub and watching television. Or, at the very least, the television was on. It was showing a nature documentary: sharks and whales, that sort of thing. As Jessica entered the room, Samuel looked up towards her and started to click. He was wearing an X-Men T-shirt and his hair was ruffled and windswept. Otherwise, he seemed the same as when Jessica had seen him before.

'Hi,' he said.

'I hear you've been up to no good,' Jessica replied. She perched on the other end of the sofa, wondering if Samuel would know where she was facing. The expert at the university had explained that he'd know she was there but wouldn't be able to know in which direction her gaze might be directed.

She was looking at him anyway, forcing herself to focus on his milky white eyes.

'Do you want some ice cream?' he asked.

'What flavour is it?'

'Peanut butter cup.' He reached onto the table next to him, clicking twice and then deftly picking up a second spoon and offering it to her.

'I really shouldn't,' Jessica said.

'Because you're on duty...?'

'Because I'm nearly forty and I really don't want to have to start going running in the mornings.' She paused. 'You'll understand one day. It's all ice cream and cake until you hit about thirty and then your jeans start getting tight.'

Jessica bit her lip, wishing she had that voice in her head that would've said *shut up*. The voice that would've bellowed *shut up*, perhaps. The poor lad's mother had just been killed at a ridiculously young age – younger than Jessica – and now here she was, carping on to a teenager about getting old.

Samuel sat solemnly for a few moments. 'I think everyone should still be allowed peanut butter cup ice cream,' he said.

'In that case, you're a very smart young man.' Jessica waited, judging the mood.

Samuel had another mouthful of ice cream and licked the spoon clean. He put the tub on the side.

'Where were you this afternoon?' Jessica asked.

Despite the milkiness of his eyes, Jessica could've sworn she saw a sparkle. A glimmer of mischief. 'Up to no good,' he said.

'What's that? Climbing trees? Swimming across lakes? Fighting otters?'

Samuel laughed: 'What's an otter?'

'Um...' That was a really good question. Jessica stumbled over her words, trying to figure out how to describe to a blind person what an otter was. A sea-dog? Did that make sense? 'They're sort of like furry, weaselly sort-of dog-like things...'

Samuel interrupted by laughing again. 'I know what an otter is. I just wanted to hear you try to describe one.'

He pointed and laughed at her. *Literally* pointed and laughed.

His laugh was infectious and Jessica found herself joining in. She wondered if this was his thing, his way in with people. It was bloody good if it was.

'Where did you *actually* go?' Jessica asked.

'For a walk. I'm only blind – I still have legs. I can get myself around.'

'Why didn't you tell Deborah? Or anyone else? People were worried.'

Samuel shrugged and turned away, a proper teenager. He curled his legs up underneath himself and reached for the ice cream again. The dessert was the perfect mixture of solid and liquid, a gooey, peanut buttery king of creation.

'I wanted to be alone,' Samuel said quietly.

'Couldn't you have at least said you were going out?'

He shook his head. 'People worry.'

'I know, but—'

'When you're blind, people think you're alone, but the opposite is true. There's always someone around, asking if you need help. Mum used to say this thing about only under-standing other people when you see the world through their eyes – but *not* being able to see shows how nice some people are.' He paused. 'Sometimes, it's too much. You just want to sit in a corner without someone asking if you're all right, or if you need a hand. I went to the park to sit by the pond.' He stopped to lick his top row of teeth before adding: 'It was nice.'

Jessica didn't know what to say, largely because Samuel already knew. He spoke with such big-picture intelligence that he sounded more world-wise than she was.

'Do you know who killed my mum?'

In the space of a sentence, Samuel went from intelligent, street-smart fourteen-year-old to vulnerable, stricken teenager.

'We've got one of the men,' Jessica said. 'We know the name of the other. I would've visited you anyway. I'm sorry I didn't come earlier.'

'What'll happen to them?'

'They'll go to court and the judge will decide what to do with them short-term. In a few months there'll be a trial of some kind. If they admit what they did, that might happen sooner.'

'Will I be there?'

'Perhaps. It will probably be up to you.'

'What about me?'

Samuel put the ice cream tub down for a final time and twisted to face Jessica fully. His fingers were interlocked as if praying.

'I'm not sure what you mean.'

'With Deborah. I know she doesn't want me to stay...'

'I don't think that's true, Samuel.'

'It is. It's not her fault.'

Samuel looked sharply towards the door. It was closed, but Jessica wondered if Deborah was listening in on the other side. She'd not heard any shuffling herself, but then Samuel would have better hearing than she did.

'I can't give you an answer,' Jessica said. 'I'm really sorry.'

His lips were closed as he turned away from the door. He bowed his head slightly in acknowledgement. 'If you find the other man, will you let me know?'

'Of course.'

'Will you let me know quickly? Like as soon as you have him?'

'Assuming it's me, then yes. I can't promise. Somebody else might arrest him.'

Samuel bowed his head once more. 'I hope you find him soon.'

After leaving Deborah's house, Jessica drove around the corner and parked her car. She didn't have to scroll for long through her contacts until she found the name she was looking for. Andrew Hunter was an old... acquaintance. Probably not friend, definitely not an enemy. He was a private investigator for whom she'd done the odd favour in the time since they'd first met. He'd helped her, too.

He answered his phone with a laugh and a: 'What do you want now?'

For some friends or families, it was a running joke that they only contacted one another if they wanted something; with Andrew and Jessica, it was the undisputed truth.

'Are you busy?' Jessica asked.

'The usual. Ask no questions and I'll tell no lies.'

'Can you help me find someone?'

'Don't you have the entire resources of HOLMES to help with that? A massive, interconnected police network that you can use entirely to find someone?'

'It's not strictly police business. I was hoping it could sort of happen without the need for paperwork and the like.'

There was the shortest of understanding pauses. 'Aah,' Andrew replied, 'one of *those* searches. Just for my own peace of mind, can you at least tell me it's not anything illegal. No one's getting hurt, that sort of thing.'

'It's nothing like that. There's this bloke named Chris

McMichael – or something close to that. Perhaps Christopher, maybe his last name's just Michael. I'm not sure. He's got a tattoo on his right arm – some green and black lizard thing. He spends some time in Manchester, but I'm not sure if he lives here. He might work selling office equipment. Somewhere between late-twenties and forty or so.'

Jessica heard the tap of a computer keyboard.

'That's not much to go on,' Andrew said.

'I know. Sorry.'

'Is this a favour for someone?'

'Not really. It's complicated.'

Jessica wondered if she should tell him about Marie and how devastated the woman would be that the bloke she'd been seeing still hadn't shown up anywhere. It had come to something when she hoped he'd been beaten up just so she knew where he was. Chris McMichael – or whatever his name was – wasn't even an active police case and yet Marie had been stuck in Jessica's mind ever since Pat had called to say the man in the hospital was still unidentified.

There was a silence from the other end and Jessica wondered whether Andrew would push the issue. Ask for another name, or demand to know what was going on. In the past, they'd simply helped each other on the quiet. No questions asked, no lies told – as he'd said.

'What do I get?' Andrew asked.

'Eternal thanks.'

'Anything else?'

'You know those giant tins of Cadbury's Roses you get at Christmas? One of those.'

There was a pause.

'Is that it? They only cost a fiver.'

'I'll get you Quality Street if you prefer…?'

He laughed it off. 'Don't worry about it. I'll be in touch. Is there anything else?'

Jessica took a deep breath, checked her rear-view mirror for no reason. There was nobody there. 'It's just...'

She left a gap, not quite wanting to fill it herself but then realising she was going to ask anyway.

'There's a guy named Mark King,' she said. 'He works for a company named 'Appy Days in MediaCity. They design apps and that sort of thing. Could you...' Jessica stopped herself. It was too much. Bloody hell, she actually quite liked the bloke. Well, perhaps not 'liked', but she certainly didn't think he was a knob – and that counted for something. 'Forget it,' she added.

Jessica heard the tapping of the keyboard again.

'Sorry?' Andrew said.

'Forget that second name. Don't worry about it. Just Chris McMichael. Sorry for asking – I owe you one. Another one.'

Andrew waited, perhaps wondering if she'd change her mind once more. 'No worries,' he said. 'But I want that tin of Roses.'

THIRTY-SIX

Jessica's phone rang early the next morning. She was sitting at the kitchen counter with Caroline, halfway through a bowl of Rice Krispies, when DCI Topper's name popped up on her mobile. He didn't even bother to say, 'hello', leading straight in with: 'You'll never guess who just showed up.'

'Jesus?' Jessica replied. 'It's not the second coming, is it? There's no way the Rapture can happen now – I'm only halfway through *Game of Thrones* series two.'

'Iain Jennings,' Topper replied humourlessly. 'He walked into a police station in Grimsby, saying he's terrified after finding out that Owain Robinson had been killed in his own home. He's asking for protection and, in return, he'll tell us everything.'

'No,' Jessica replied.

'No, what?'

'I've been to Grimsby twice in the past week. I can't go again. This is cruel and unusual punishment. Can't we stick him in a van and bring him here?'

Topper didn't even try to sugar-coat it: 'Drive safely.'

. . .

'...Um, Scousers, I suppose. That's an obvious one. Then there's hairy fruit.' Archie was counting on his fingers. 'That's five,' he concluded.

Jessica glanced away from the road to Archie in the passenger seat. 'You hate hairy fruit more than the M62?'

'Who doesn't?'

'I've never heard anyone who's got a thing about fruit with hairs on.'

They were nearing the end of the journey, having spent forty-five minutes trying to get out of Manchester and then two more hours driving east towards the coast.

Archie was in his absolute worst 'are-we-there-yet?' mood and had taken to making a list of things he detested more than the local motorway network.

'What's wrong with hairy fruit?' Jessica added.

'I can't believe you're even asking that question. Food shouldn't have hairs on the outside. No one's ordering steak and chips and asking for extra hairs.'

'I like a good kiwi fruit.'

'Yeah, but you peel the hairy bit off.'

'What's wrong with a peach?'

'Have a nectarine. They're like peaches but without the hairs. Who'd take a peach over a nectarine? You'd have to be mentally unstable.'

'Is this what you wanted to talk about in the interview room the other day?'

Archie went quiet. Perhaps mercifully so. He shrank back into his seat slightly and pulled the seatbelt into a more comfortable position. 'Not now,' he said.

And that was all he said until they reached Grimsby's main police station.

The local officers welcomed the pair of them with a cup of tea apiece and a too-close-to-the-bone remark that Jessica might want to consider moving if she was going to spend so much time on the east coast.

Iain Jennings was a man in the same mould as the fisherman to whom Jessica had spoken the previous time she'd been in town. He had a prickly white beard, big shoulders and thick forearms. Like a tattooed Santa, if he worked out a bit and chose to dress like he slept rough.

Jennings didn't look as if he'd had a good night. He was a walking, talking embodiment of a yawn.

Jessica introduced herself and Archie as they settled in the interview room and Jennings nodded along, waiting for his moment.

'What happened to Robbo?' he asked when she was done.

'Do you mean Owain Robinson?'

'Aye.'

'We're still trying to figure out the specifics,' Jessica replied, 'but it sounds like you know the basics, else we wouldn't be here.'

Jennings pressed back in his seat, rubbing the peppery stubble on his chin. 'So it's true then?'

'How about you start by telling us how you and Mr Robinson know one another?'

'You know I want protection, don't you? They explained all that...?'

'We can only look after someone if we know who we're supposed to be protecting them from...'

Jennings nodded shortly, conceding the point. Considering he was in a police station, apparently hiding from someone who was after him, he didn't seem particularly on edge. He kept looking between Jessica and Archie, then glancing up towards the video camera that was filming everything.

'It was Robbo's idea,' he said. 'Supposed to be a small thing to clear a few debts. Guess it all got a bit out of hand.'

'Perhaps we should start over.' A pause and then: 'How did you and Mr Robinson meet?'

Jennings gulped and chewed his lips before apparently deciding it was better to cooperate. 'We met in a pub in Manchester a few years back. Got talking and stayed in contact. I bought a car from him, he put me in touch with a bloke who serviced boats. Nothing major. Just one of those things. One thing led to another.'

'And what *did* one thing lead to...?'

Jennings shot a glance towards the camera once more. He lowered his voice. 'Look, I need to know what's going to happen after this.'

'That depends on what you tell us.'

'But can you really, y'know... look after people?'

'You came to us, remember? You wanted our help.'

Jennings nodded slowly. 'Right... it's just...' He sighed. 'Okay, fine. Like I said, it was Robbo's idea. It was all him. Nowt to do with me. He was having a few money problems so he came to me saying he knew a guy in Rotterdam. He was hoping I could bring a few things over for him.'

'Things like...?'

'Shoes, clothes, boxes of fags – that sort of thing. At first it was a few things then it was a lot of things. I just pick them up.'

'You do a bit more than that, though, don't you?'

Jennings bit his lip, eyed the camera and then Jessica. He lowered his voice. 'Robbo said it'd have to look legit, so he sorted me out with these car businesses. Just a bit of paperwork. I signed a few documents and let him sort it. That was his thing, so I said it was fine.'

'*You're* the company director.'

'Yeah, well... what do you want me to say?'

They looked to each other but they both knew Owain

Robinson wasn't around to deny anything. Who better to blame everything on than the dead guy?

'Where do the shoes, clothes and cigarettes come from?' Jessica asked, knowing both Trading Standards and Customs would want their own chats with Jennings in the near future. He'd get the protection he wanted – largely because he'd spend the next few days in interview rooms repeating the same information over and over.

Jennings held his hands high, palms out. 'No idea. That's the God's honest truth. Some bloke in Africa, I think. I just do the Rotterdam pick-up. That's it.'

'What then?'

He shrugged. 'Hand it all over. Robbo collects and that's it. I don't know what happens after that.'

'Haven't you ever asked?'

Another shrug. 'Not my business, is it?'

'It literally is,' Jessica said. She paused a moment and then added: 'Who sells it on?'

'No idea. Robbo sorts that. Probably some dodgy clothes shop, innit?'

Jessica waited for more but it wasn't coming. 'You're telling me you don't know who you import from, you don't know who Robinson sells to – and all you do is sail a boat to Rotterdam and back?'

'Exactly.'

'Bit convenient, isn't it?'

'What?'

'Well, here you are asking for protection and yet it's all someone else's fault. All someone else's idea. You're some innocent bloke who's out to make a few quid.'

'What can I say? The truth's the truth.'

With no Robinson, there would only be one version of the truth – Jennings' – and he wasn't likely to give up too much more than he'd need to.

Jessica didn't need to nudge Archie. He was leaning forward, almost snarling. 'You, my friend, have given a new meaning to the phrase "load of old bollocks". You really think we're idiots, don't you?'

'No.'

Jennings didn't seem particularly intimidated, possibly because he towered over Archie by at least a foot.

Archie half turned to Jessica. 'I say send him packing.'

'Let him go?' Jessica replied.

'Aye. Give Trading Standards his name and address and tell them he's full o' shite. Let them deal with him. We've got better things to do.'

That did the trick. Jessica was only halfway out of her seat when Jennings lunged across the table. 'Hey, hang on—'

'What?' Jessica asked.

'You said you'd protect me?'

'Only if you told us the truth, not a bunch of old nonsense.'

'I *am* telling you the truth. It was Robbo's idea.'

'Sure it was. You bring in all these goods for Robinson, he sells them on and gives you a cut. You filter it through the books of some fake car import businesses to make it look legit. At no point do you think to ask who he's buying from, who he's selling to – nothing. I don't believe a word of it.'

'Honestly, I don't know who Robbo deals with in Manchester. I really don't. If I knew that, I wouldn't be here.'

'So why *are* you here?'

Jennings took a deep breath, scratched at his stubble. 'Something's obviously gone wrong, hasn't it? Robbo pissed someone off along the chain – and now they're coming for me.'

'Why'd you say that?'

'Because someone broke into my house the night before last. They set off the silent alarm. I hid in the wardrobe.'

Jessica left it a moment, wondering if Jennings would

finally crack. His voice had wavered but he wasn't quite there yet. She nudged Archie with her elbow.

'You got a silent alarm, Constable?'

'Nope.'

'Me either. I mean, why would a pair of law-abiding everyday citizens need silent alarms on their houses?'

Jennings wiped the sweat from his forehead. 'All right, fine. It doesn't mean I knew who Robbo's contacts were – but it's not like I thought they were nice guys, is it?'

'So you took precautions?'

'If you like.'

'What happened while you were hiding in the wardrobe?'

'Well... nothing, I suppose.'

'So someone broke in – and then broke out again?'

'Pretty much.'

Jessica exchanged a somewhat sceptical glance with Archie. '*Why?*'

'I dunno – you tell me. Robbo's killed in his own home, I guess they were coming for me.'

'*Who* was coming for you?'

Jennings thumped a hand onto his chair, raising his voice though not quite shouting. 'That's what I keep telling you – I don't know. I didn't recognise the fella.'

'What do you mean you didn't recognise the person? I thought you were in the wardrobe?'

'I was – but I've got security cameras. I recorded the whole thing. He had a gun.'

Jessica was finally interested. She bit her tongue, holding onto the immediate enthusiasm, making Jennings wait for it.

'Where's the footage?'

'On a pen drive. I left everything with the guy on the front desk when I got here. It's an MP4 – just stick it in any computer. I've got it on my phone, too.'

Jessica spoke far more calmly than she felt. She stood,

telling Jennings to follow her so that he could retrieve the pen drive. It wasn't long before he was back waiting in the interview room while Jessica was sitting in a room across the corridor with a borrowed laptop on the desk. It might need to be verified, but the video file was dated and timed, with the camera pointing directly at what was presumably the back door of Jennings' house. Jessica wasn't sure what she was expecting, but she jumped as a man suddenly burst in. It wasn't even clear how he'd got through – but the door sprang inwards and then he appeared in a porchway.

Jessica and Archie watched it twice and then she rewound it once more before pausing at the moment the man peered up to the camera, pistol hanging limply at his side. The still shot was a little grainy and the footage was in black and white – but that didn't stop it being clear enough to make out the intruder's features.

'Well,' she said to Archie, 'isn't that a familiar face?'

THIRTY-SEVEN

Jessica knocked loudly with her fist on the front door. It had already been a long day of driving to Grimsby and back – and she really wasn't in the mood for yet more arseing around.

'I don't think he's in,' Archie said.

'He better bloody be.'

Jessica thumped the door once more and then kicked it for good measure.

No answer.

Jessica marched to the side gate, rattling it back and forth to ensure it was locked. 'Right, that's it – give me a bunk up.'

'You can't just break in.'

'I'm not breaking in – I'm going for a look round the back.'

'It's sort of the same thing.'

'In what way is climbing over a gate considered breaking in?'

'In the way that the gate is locked – and you're, well, tres-passing...'

Jessica frowned. She'd seen Archie do things on duty that were far worse than climbing over a gate. 'You're lecturing *me*?' she said, only realising too late that she had a hand on her hip like a scolding teacher. 'He might be hiding in a shed or something.'

'Let's just go,' Archie replied, nodding back towards the car. 'We'll get tactical entry on the case.'

'We sodding well won't. Not yet, anyway.'

'They can't wait to get the battering rams out – it'll give them something to do.'

Jessica stopped, one hand on the gate. 'What is going on with you recently? It wasn't that long ago you'd be over the gate yourself.'

'Nothing's going on.'

Jessica hoisted her left leg. 'So what's the problem? Give us a bunk.'

Archie sighed and then cupped his hands to hoist her up and over the gate. Jessica dropped down onto a paved path and then unlatched it for him to follow. He mooched after her like a downtrodden kitten following its mother.

He was right, of course. There was nobody hiding in the garden. The back door was locked and neither of them could see anyone through the windows. The house was either empty, or its main inhabitant was doing a bang-up job of keeping his head down.

Jessica and Archie made their way back to the car, resting against the bonnet and eyeing the house suspiciously.

'What do you want to do?' Archie asked.

Jessica was fuming silently. Part of it was the whole running around to Grimsby thing, mostly it was because she worried that every moment she wasn't finding Donal Doherty, somebody else might be.

'I don't know why any of us believed Chatresh's bullshit story about having his wallet nicked,' Jessica said.

'He *did* have his wallet nicked,' Archie replied. 'Happens all the time. How could we know he'd break into some bloke's house on the other side of the country? We didn't even know who Iain Jennings was back then.'

He was right – again – but that didn't make her feel much better.

'Chatresh has a brother,' Jessica said, remembering the conversation they'd had. 'He said someone named Rajiv was covering the market stall for him. I'll call it in and get someone to find an address for Rajiv Lodi and check it out in case Chatresh is there. Then I'll get onto someone to find out if either Chatresh or Rajiv has left the country. You can drive.'

Jessica under-armed Archie the keys and he caught them one-handed. 'Drive where?'

'Wythenshawe market.'

Jessica and Archie headed up and down the row of stalls. It was the usual rainbow of tat. Faded phone cases, knock-off charger cables that would set someone's house on fire, ill-fitting cheap clothes, some bloke with a giant wall of electrical tape. Nothing unexpected.

They completed a loop but didn't notice Chatresh. Jessica didn't know what Rajiv looked like – but the market's most unassuming stall was manned by a woman selling children's clothes. Jessica hovered across the way until there were no customers and then she headed across quickly.

She'd barely finished her question before the woman answered it. She knew Chatresh and Rajiv, pointing to a space a little further down the rank of stalls. There were metal poles and a cream canvas cover across the top. No Chatresh, no Rajiv – and no merchandise.

'That's their pitch,' the stallholder said.

'The empty one?' Jessica asked.

'Right. They're usually here. I guess they're on holiday or something.'

The woman was wearing a big mumsy woolly jumper. She didn't seem the type who roughed it out rain or shine on a market stall each day.

'How often are you here?' Jessica asked.

That was enough for her to ask who Jessica was. The warrant card got a wide-eyed show of surprise.

'I'd appreciate it if you could keep this between us,' Jessica said.

'They're not in trouble, are they?' the woman said. 'They always seemed so nice. Used to go on coffee runs each morning. Neither of them minded getting me a soya milk latte. Some people are funny about that.'

Jessica continued her thin-lipped awkward smile. The answer-the-question look.

'I'm only here twice a week,' the woman said, cottoning on. 'I've got a toddler, so I fit it around his nursery.'

'But either Chatresh or Rajiv is usually here on the days you are...?'

'One of them is always here. I was quite surprised when I was setting up this morning and they weren't around. They were here a few days ago.'

'What do they sell?'

'Clothes, shoes – that sort of thing. I got a pair of boots from them. They gave us trader rates.'

Jessica felt Archie tense. 'What type of clothes and shoes?' she asked.

'Designer stuff. Either genuine and cheap or a really good fake. I don't mind either way.' She put a hand to her mouth. 'Oh, I probably shouldn't say that to you, should I?'

Jessica thanked the woman for her time and scuttled off towards the empty market stall. An electrical socket was hanging from a wire fixed to one of the metal posts – but there was little else to see.

'I bet that's what was in all those boxes at Chatresh's

house,' Archie said. 'We've been running around trying to chase all the knock-off clothes Jennings was bringing in for Robinson – but they were there the whole time. Chatresh and his brother have been selling on the dodgy goods through the market stall. He probably runs a couple.'

'You're not helping,' Jessica said.

Archie went quiet. All he was doing was reminding her that she'd been standing right next to the bloody merchandise they were after and failed to notice. It still didn't explain properly why Chatresh had broken into Jennings' house. Jennings clearly thought it was with murderous intent given what had happened to Robinson, but why would Chatresh want to kill one or both of them? And why had his driving licence shown up on some unidentified bloke just days before?

Someone would want answers to all those questions – and Jessica had no idea what to say.

The trader opposite confirmed that he'd not seen either of Chatresh or Rajiv for three days – 'really unlike them,' he added – which also wasn't that helpful.

Jessica and Archie were back at the car when the information came through on the radio that there was no sign of life at Rajiv Lodi's house. A couple of officers had knocked on the front door and checked with the neighbours. There was no car on the drive and a small pile of mail visible through the letter box.

Nobody had seen Rajiv in days.

The drive back to the station was a grim, quiet one. Jessica hadn't just been inside the house of a man now prime suspect for the killing of Owain Robinson, she'd shown him his driving licence, passed it onto the labs for fingerprinting, given him a bit of advice about contacting the DVLA.

They'd spent days wondering how Robinson was shifting all the dodgy merchandise – and she'd practically leant on the boxes containing it all. Of course, there were mitigating circumstances – but those were the simple facts – and that was before the issue of Donal Doherty came up. He'd been one of the men who'd broken into Evie Briers' house, causing her death – purposefully or not – and Jessica had paid him to tip her off about his mate.

This was really, *really* bad.

Archie didn't speak until they were almost back at the station. 'Do you remember the photos of all those planes?' Archie asked.

'Where?'

'On Chatresh's wall. He had those models, too. He said he part-owned a Cessna in Lancashire.'

Jessica didn't reply at first. With all the thoughts of dodgy market gear, the planes had slipped her mind.

'Good thinking,' she said quietly as she pulled into the car park.

Archie nodded in acknowledgement, but it wasn't the time for praise.

There was only marginally better news as Jessica got to her desk. The Lodis had not been tracked leaving the country at any port. Given the state of Britain's immigration control, that didn't necessarily mean much, but, at least officially, Chatresh and Rajiv were still in the country.

Jessica had one more thing to check before she handed the mess over to the night crew. After a bit of searching on the Internet, she ended up speaking to a pleasant-sounding woman who ran a microlight airfield close to Garstang in Lancashire. She knew Chatresh and, mercifully, confirmed that the small plane he co-owned was sitting a little off the grass runway in full view of her window. She was concerned to know the police was calling – but promised to get in contact if Chatresh turned up.

With that, Jessica was done for the day.

THIRTY-EIGHT

The house smelled of rich tomatoey pasta sauce once more as Jessica got through her front door.

Caroline and her bloody vegetables!

Shoe number one was sent spinning into the stairs with a satisfying amount of force, while number two thudded noisily into the wall. There might have even been a crumble or two of plaster – which would have been *really* rewarding.

Unfortunately, Jessica's dreams of spaghetti, fleecy pyjamas and an evening with trashy television were quickly destroyed.

Mark was sitting in the kitchen, gently rocking Russell back and forth in his crib, while merrily chatting away to Caroline, who was at the stove. They both turned to greet her, but Jessica's poker face had deserted her.

'You forgot you'd invited me over, didn't you?' Mark said.

'No...'

'It's fine,' Caroline replied, talking over them both. 'I made enough for everyone!'

There was an awkward moment where Mark stood and

Jessica wasn't sure whether they should hug, kiss cheeks, kiss mouths, shake hands or just sort of nod to one another.

In the end, he took her right hand in his left and they half shook, half embraced. It was wholly unsatisfying either way. She really *had* forgotten she'd invited him over. In her initial thoughts, it had been an excuse to not have to leave the house. They could stream some god-awful movie and chat about the god-awful people they knew. Of course, with everything that had happened at work, it had completely slipped her mind. Now here she was, barefooted, outnumbered and off guard in her own kitchen.

'I said you're often late,' Caroline chirped up, not being helpful at all.

'I'm not *often* late,' Jessica replied, 'I'm *occasionally* held up due to unforeseen circumstances.'

She was going to elaborate, but then a yawn overpowered her like a heavyweight taking on a bantamweight. Even a flapping hand wasn't enough to send it back from where it had come.

Mark was half biting his lip, half grinning, while Russell was busy burbling.

'Caroline's been telling me all sorts of interesting tales...' Mark said.

Jessica felt a sinking feeling in her stomach. That could mean literally anything. They'd been friends for so long that they each knew where the other had buried the bodies. 'It's all lies,' Jessica said, mind racing. 'Lies, damned lies and more lies again.'

Mark laughed. 'Oh, I'm sure it is.'

After another vegetable, rubbery-shoe-based tea, Caroline disappeared upstairs under the guise of 'settling Russell down for the night'. Her conspiratorial wink said far more than her words.

Jessica and Mark were on the sofa, a strategically placed cushion acting as a Berlin Wall between them. Jessica was busy being afflicted by another attack of the yawns as Mark watched on, small crinkles around his mouth failing to conceal his amusement. He'd made something of an effort, with smart tight trousers and a shirt. Not too over the top, not too casual. He didn't have to bother with his hair and, for the first time, Jessica could really understand the bald appeal. She was still in her work clothes. Again. Aside from the ramble through the Peak District, he'd only ever seen her in work clothes.

'I actually did forget you were coming over,' Jessica said.

'I know. It's okay.'

'Things have been really busy at work.'

'You don't have to explain. I probably should've texted this morning to remind you and check times.'

Jessica's gaze faltered, slipping from Mark towards the television, more specifically the photo that was a little off to the side. She hadn't meant to, it had just happened. There she was in Vegas wearing a pair of oversized glasses with LEDs around the edge. Adam was at her side, tongue out, arm outstretched to take the photo. The snapshot was unlike them, not really in either of their personalities, which was probably why Jessica liked the photo so much.

'Is that him?' Mark asked.

'Yes.'

'How long ago was it taken?'

'A few years.' Jessica tried to count in her head, but they all blended into one. She'd been living in Caroline's flat at the time. Things had changed completely.

Mark rocked back and delved into his pocket, pulling out his wallet. He flipped open the front and offered it towards her. 'That's my daughter,' he said.

The girl in the photo had long blonde hair. She was kicking a football around, wearing a red and white kit.

'She looks older than nine.'

Mark smiled. 'I know. It's a cliché, but they really do grow up ridiculously fast. She's into sports and *Star Wars* – not like me at all, nor her mother. I don't know where she gets it from.'

'Does that mean you'd have blonde hair if you weren't so... y'know... bald?'

'Ha! I used to be sort of gingery.'

Jessica pointed to the door. 'Get out!'

Mark laughed again. He didn't move. 'You're not a ginger-ist are you?'

'I have many friends who are ginger.'

Jessica grinned and so did Mark. They both relaxed slightly onto the sofa as Mark put his wallet away.

'How's the, er, app business?' Jessica asked, not really knowing what to say. Small talk wasn't her speciality.

'Ticking along. How's the arresting-people business?'

'Ticking along.'

The silence was awkward, the smiles forced. Mark leaned forward, ignoring the cushion wall and basically making a move on West Germany. He was bloody Stalin! A distinctly non-dictatory hand crept around Jessica's neck, cupping her far shoulder as he hovered close enough that she could see the stubbly bits on his chin.

'Is this okay?' he asked.

Mark didn't wait for an answer, pressing gently forward. At the same time, Jessica edged gently backwards.

The invading hand was instantly away from her shoulder, the wall back in place.

'Sorry,' she said.

'Sorry,' he said.

'Sorry,' they both said together.

Mark started to stumble over his words as he backed away. 'I, um...'

'It's just that Caroline's upstairs,' Jessica said, pressing a hand onto the top of his. 'It's a bit weird.'

'I get it.'

'I had a really good time with you in the Peaks, despite the hills. This evening was probably a mistake – *my* mistake – I didn't realise how busy I'd be at work. Then it's mayhem here with Russell and everything—'

'It's fine. You really don't have to—'

In a flash, Jessica lunged forward and pressed her lips to his. It was a good job her aim was on target, else she might have nutted him. Mark pulled backwards at first, probably avoiding the headbutt, but then he leaned into her, resting one hand on her elbow, another on her thigh.

The kiss only lasted a few seconds and then Jessica angled away once more, returning to the corner of the sofa. It wasn't all church bells, spine-tingles and cupid with a sodding harp, but neither was it all saliva with a lip up her nose.

She wasn't sixteen any longer.

'I didn't expect that,' Mark said.

'I'm not sure I did.'

'Wanna try again?'

Jessica didn't need to think second time around. 'Okay.'

THIRTY-NINE

Jessica's yawning was really getting out of hand. She was halfway through a sentence when the urge overcame her and she found herself flashing her tonsils.

'Sorry,' she said.

'Late night?' Izzy asked.

'Russell,' Jessica said. 'Sometimes he sleeps through, other nights he's a whiny little you-know-what.'

Izzy nodded along in agreement. She well knew those nights. They were in Jessica's office, working out who was going to do what that day. Plus having a natter and a moan, of course.

'The guv's on one,' Jessica continued. 'Another jogger was mugged at knifepoint last night – out by the uni, apparently. Victim was the son of a local councillor, so the guv's been getting it in the neck from the super. Wants to know why we haven't caught the guy after last week's attack.'

'How about because there are no cameras where the mugging took place, the victim said it was an Asian guy in a beanie hat but couldn't describe anything more than that, and there were no witnesses? It's not like we've been doing nothing all week.'

Jessica raised her coffee cup. 'I know. *He* knows. But he's copped a load of shite and that only dribbles downwards. Franks is off this week, too – and there's nobody to take over his workload. Then there's the whole Chatresh-driving-licence-stolen-goods-disappearing-act debacle.'

Izzy sipped her own drink. 'I've been accepted,' she said by way of nothing.

'The convent?'

'The PGCE course. I can start in January. One year and then I'd be a full-time teacher. I also got an offer to start as a teaching assistant in the new year if I want.'

Jessica spoke instinctively. Trying to be funny was better than the truth. 'Deserter,' she said. 'This would get you shot in some cultures.'

Izzy cocked her head, smiled with half her mouth. 'Sorry.'

Jessica bit her lip. She wasn't sure what to say. 'No, I'm sorry. I *am* pleased for you – it's just...' She held both hands up to indicate the office... the job in general.

'I'm not definitely going,' Izzy said. 'It's not as much money, plus Mal wants another child. We're talking over options. I might carry on here as if nothing's happened.'

'Why would you do that?'

'I don't know... imagine being a teacher. All day with kids. *All day!* It's bad enough when Amber's in a strop. Imagine ten of them at a time – or twenty.'

'Can't be any worse than half the constables.'

'True.'

They spent a few moments saying nothing, listening to the gentle hum of the station on the other side of the door. Someone was clumping past in a pair of heavy boots, heading to the canteen.

'Would you miss it?' Izzy asked.

'The job?'

'All of it: the people, the warrant card, the buzz when something happens, the mornings you're woken up because something important has gone on...?'

Jessica needed time to think because she didn't know the answer.

'It's not that simple,' she said eventually.

'I think I'd miss it,' Izzy said, 'but you miss all sorts of things, don't you? Like an old boyfriend. Even when you've done the dumping, there's a time where you think of all the good bits. Then, after a while, you move on and find someone else.'

The phone on Jessica's desk started to ring and they both turned to look at it. It didn't feel like the conversation was done – but fate had decided it was over anyway. Jessica answered but the message didn't take long to be passed on.

'It's our mystery man who had his head kicked in,' she said. 'He's woken up.'

Given the fact he'd been in a coma for ten days, the mystery man was in relatively good shape. His face was thin and stubbly, with his eyes drawn back into his skull, leaving dark circles around the sockets. He groaned when he spoke, and the sore in the corner of his desert-dry lips wasn't helping – but Jessica had seen worse sights when she'd been in uniform patrolling Deansgate Locks, having to deal with the weekend stag parties. Dragging men out of the gutter who'd puked up a night of alcohol along with half a lung really was a tough gig. Even more so when they started drooling on a plucky constable's neck, slurring that she was 'bloody gorgeous' and wondering why the compliment wasn't returned.

The mystery man, on the other hand, looked almost refreshed from a week-long kip, so much so that Jessica felt a pang of jealousy. She could probably do without the whole being-kicked-into-a-coma-thing, but the sleep…

Jessica was sitting at his bedside, the man plumped up on a pillow. There were tubes and machines, beeps and buzzes – but then hospitals really were really becoming her thing.

'Your name's Thomas?' Jessica asked him.

'Tomasz,' the man said, pausing to cough slightly. 'With a zed.'

Much of the bruising around his face had subsided but, according to the nurse, his ribs were still in a bad way. There was a gentle wheeze every time Tomasz with a zed breathed in.

'Do you remember how you got here?' Jessica asked.

Tomasz frowned and it looked painful. The crinkles in his forehead mashed with the scars. 'A plane…?'

They looked to one another, each confused until Jessica realised what he was on about. 'I meant to the hospital,' she said, 'not to England.'

'Oh.'

'Are you Polish?'

He dipped his eyes slightly: a nod but not as painful.

'How long have you been in Britain?'

'How long was I asleep?'

'A bit over a week.'

Tomasz almost smiled. Or, at least, he started to and then pulled out because of the pain. 'Five years,' he said. 'I stay for the weather.'

This time he did smile, even though he winced at the same time.

Jessica laughed. 'You definitely count as a local if you want to talk about the weather. Anyway – do you know how you ended up in hospital?'

Tomasz inhaled a wheezy breath, then rocked his head from side to side.

'What's the last thing you remember?'

He moaned slightly and shifted himself upwards in the bed. 'I have bruises on my bruises,' he said. 'The nurse says it makes me more rugged, hey?'

Despite his condition, there was a twinkle in Tomasz's eye. A right ol' charmer. Jessica waited for the proper reply.

'I was riding home from work,' Tomasz said. 'Riding home and then... here.'

'You were on a bike?'

'Right.'

Jessica's first thought was that Tomasz had been hit by a car. It wouldn't be the first time some motorist ploughed into the back of a cyclist and then drove off. Except no bike had been found anywhere near the scene. The medical reports hadn't mentioned anything to do with a car or a van, it had pointed out the bruises on Tomasz's torso and neck that were consistent with feet. He'd been kicked, not run over.

'Where do you live?' Jessica asked.

'Near the graves.'

'A cemetery? Which one?'

'Swinton.'

Jessica couldn't prevent the surprise from creeping onto her face. It wasn't that far from where she lived, perhaps a mile from where Tomasz had been discovered in the gutter.

'We've put out pictures of you,' she said. 'No one's come forward to say they recognised you – or the tattoo on your arm. Is there family we should call? Friends?'

'My sister's still in Polska. She has husband. He, how you say here... bell-end.'

Jessica smiled. Tomasz was far more conditioned to the British vocabulary than he might give himself credit for. Given the creeping grin on his face, he was also something of a flirt. So much so that Jessica dreaded the next question.

'Do you have a wife?' she asked. 'Girlfriend...?'

'Not yet...'

It might have been a twitch, but Jessica was almost certain Tomasz tried to wink at her. In someone else, it could have been creepy – but he was so pathetic, his smile so genuine, that it simply made her laugh.

'All right, Romeo,' Jessica replied. 'I think you're going to be out of the game for a few weeks yet. Some girls do go for the beaten-up look, throw in a few scars here and there, so perhaps you'll be in with someone.'

'Who is Romeo?'

'Never you mind. Anyway, we can get in contact with your sister and let her know you're safe. Is there anyone else?'

'Only my boss.'

'Where do you work?'

'Market.'

The tingling, creeping *oh-no* sensation was back. Of course he worked on a bloody market. Of course it was all connected. This was perhaps the only way in which things could have been worse than they already were.

'Which market?' Jessica asked, knowing the answer.

'It's hard to say. Harder to spell.' He coughed, delaying the inevitable. 'Withy... Within—'

'Wythenshawe?'

'Yeah.'

'Who's your boss?'

Jessica didn't need to ask. The answer was obvious – it had been the entire time: it had been in Tomasz's pocket the day they'd found him.

'Chat,' Tomasz said. 'Chat and Raj. They sell clothes.'

FORTY

'Fake?' Tomasz said after Jessica told him about the clothes and shoes he'd been selling.

'Counterfeit,' Jessica said. 'Dodgy, bogus, copied, forged.'

'Oh.' Tomasz screwed up his mouth and then flinched, remembering he was injured. 'I didn't know. Am I in trouble?'

Jessica shook her head. 'Probably not.'

'Chat and Raj?'

'In more ways than you can imagine.'

For the first time since she entered his ward, Tomasz seemed shaken. He'd been fine flirting and pretending he wasn't injured, now he sank back onto the pillow and the battering he'd taken suddenly seemed more apparent. He grunted as he shifted his weight from one side to the other.

'This might sound like a silly question, but have you made any enemies?' Jessica asked.

'Enemies?'

'Someone gave you a kicking and left you in a ditch. You're either incredibly unlucky to have been in the wrong place at the wrong time, or someone doesn't like you very much.'

Tomasz nodded softly, taking it in. 'I don't know many people.'

'Do you live alone?'

Another nod.

'By yourself?'

'I had a flatmate but he moved back to Polska. Left me with rent.'

'No one else?'

Tomasz turned slightly to the side, avoiding her gaze. The bravado was an act – he was a lonely man trying to make enough money so that he could take it home at some point. Either that, or waiting until he met a girl who fell for his front.

'Did Chat or Raj ever mention anything about where the clothes and shoes came from?'

Tomasz's Eastern European accent was becoming thicker as he spoke more slowly. 'I never ask.'

'Were there any other employees?'

'I only help out on certain days if busy. They call in the morning to say come in.'

'How were you paid?'

Tomasz's brow rippled: 'With money...?'

'Cash?'

He didn't answer – but that was confirmation in itself. No paperwork, no contract – just a phone call on the mornings he was needed and then cash-in-hand in the afternoon. No wonder there was no formal connection from the Lodi brothers to Tomasz. It also explained why the woman selling children's clothes at the market hadn't mentioned an employee – she was only there a couple of times a week and likely hadn't seen Tomasz. Plus, if he had no friends of note, that was why nobody had phoned them to confirm Tomasz's ID. Chatresh would've known when Jessica returned his driving licence but had remained tight-lipped.

'How did you get the job?' Jessica asked.

'I asked.'

'You walked around the market asking for a job?'

'I walked around a lot of places. Chat and Raj said they needed help sometimes. Took my number.'

'Do you have any idea who might have harmed you? Had you fallen out with either of the brothers? Had someone come to the stall who was angry with them?'

'No – nothing like that. They are kind to me. Give me job.'

Jessica pressed away from the bed, leaning against the back of the chair. It was like having the pieces to a puzzle yet not knowing how they all went together. She knew something Tomasz didn't but wasn't sure whether she should share...

'Chat and Raj are missing,' she said, letting it hang.

'Missing?'

'For at least three days. Their houses are empty, the market stall packed up, no sign of either of them. Raj has a wife and kids – and they're gone, too.'

'Gone where?'

'If we knew that, they wouldn't be missing. We think they're still in Britain.'

'Oh... right.'

'If they're not at home and not at the market, do you know where they might be?'

'I only work for them.'

'But have they ever mentioned anywhere they spend time? A friend, perhaps? Another part of the country?'

Tomasz wrestled with the covers, trying to free a hand. He grunted as he lifted his arm, scratching the corner of his eye. 'Have you tried the lock-up?'

'What lock-up?'

FORTY-ONE

The full tactical entry team of ninjas and big battering-ram-wielding burly blokes had assembled around the corner from a set of garages not far from Stockport centre. It was only a couple of miles from Wythenshawe market and apparently where the Lodi brothers kept their stock. It had also been rented in the name 'John Smith', which was quite the piss-take. The owner had apparently met neither brother and was happy to rent to more or less anyone who had the money.

As the tactical entry lot massed near a set of police vans, Jessica was with Archie watching from a nearby car.

'What's taking so long?' Jessica asked.

'They're probably ip-dipping over who gets to use the battering ram,' Archie replied.

'Ip-dipping?'

'Didn't you ever do that at school? Ip dip sky blue, who's it, not you. Keep going until you only have one left. I used to cheat big time.'

'How'd you cheat at ip-dipping?'

'Count the syllables. As long as you know who to start on, you can make sure you're always last.'

Jessica took a breath and continued watching the officers near the vans. 'I really don't think they're ip-dipping,' she said.

'I'd bloody love to go on a tactical entry course,' Archie replied. 'Bit of splintered wood in the morning, some broken glass. Nothing quite like a smashed-up plastic door frame to get rid of the cobwebs after a late night. The course was full the last time I put in. I'd quite like a crack at tactical firearms, too.'

'I wouldn't trust you to set off the pepper spray without getting yourself.'

'Haven't you ever put in? I would've thought smacking in a few doors would be right up your alley.'

Jessica twisted to face him. 'What are you trying to say?'

Archie's eyes widened and then he slunk back into his seat. 'Nothing...' He nodded towards the van, conveniently able to change the subject. 'Looks like it's about to kick off.'

He was right. Half a dozen officers were clumping their way towards one of the garages. Jessica was too far away to see the detail, but she hoped someone knew what they were doing. The garages were numbered, but it wouldn't be the first time the wrong door had been smashed in.

Jessica clicked open her car door and crossed the road, Archie in tow, heading towards the opening between two streets and police vans beyond. The garages were in a square with a common patch of tarmac in front. A couple of houses were able to overlook the area, but it was otherwise free from prying eyes. Given they were expecting a lock-up full of clothes and shoes, the tactical entry team was probably overkill – but then both Lodi brothers had disappeared and Chatresh had, at the absolute least, broken into Iain Jennings' house with a gun.

No chances were being taken. Not this time.

Everyone was in place. Three-two-one: *WALLOP!* The garage door offered little resistance as the team blasted their way through. A couple of officers disappeared through the gap, leaving Jessica with a nervous few moments to wonder about what might be inside. It was probably clothes... *probably*... but she'd seen so many things over the previous years. Could Chatresh or his brother know how to booby-trap a door? Would they have reason to? Would everything go bang...?

No.

The pair of officers emerged from the garage not long after they'd gone in. They spoke to the supervising officer, who waved Jessica across.

'All yours,' he told her.

The now mangled garage doors were wrenched higher, allowing light to flow into the cramped space. Jessica had to weave around a stack of boxes to find herself in what felt like the smallest clothes store ever. The jumble sales at TK Maxx had nothing on the Lodis' store. Rack upon rack was filled with jackets, tops and bottoms – with everything crammed together so that there was barely any space to move. One entire wall was filled with shoeboxes, each covered with the logos of various sporting manufacturers. The other wall was stacked with cartons of cigarettes and cigars, plus boxes of booze. Trading Standards were going to have a field day when they got their mitts on the place. It would be Christmas bonuses all round. Jessica couldn't even guess at the street value of everything being stored. Definitely tens of thousands, probably hundreds. Perhaps more.

Archie had slotted in at Jessica's side. He whistled long and low. 'The guv's gotta be happy with this lot,' he said.

'I bloody hope so.'

Archie picked up a loose pair of trainers that had been on top of the boxes, flipping them around in his hand and sniffing the inside. 'If these are fake, someone's done a bang-up job.'

Jessica's phone started to ring, which would likely mean

one thing. 'Herogram from the guv,' Jessica told Archie as she pressed the answer button confidently.

'Where are you?' DCI Topper asked.

'Raiding that garage. There's all sorts here – Trading Standards are going to be singing our praises when we give them this lot.'

'Right.'

Topper's tone didn't sound too congratulatory. In fact, he was distinctly un-herogram-like.

'What's wrong?' Jessica asked.

'That Doherty bloke you were looking for – we think he's shown up.'

A short stabbing sensation in Jessica's chest filled the momentary pause. Donal Doherty had finally reappeared – and with him the tiny little matter of the twenty quid she'd handed him.

'You "think"...?'

'We're waiting for confirmation. Some dog walker found a body down an alley close to Middleton House.'

'He's dead?'

'Either that or he's playing a really good game of sleeping lions.'

FORTY-TWO

Dog walkers: it was always the dog walkers. Adrian was in his early twenties, fresh-faced and so bloody young, with a little black and white Boston terrier named George. George seemed content enough to sit around the edge of the alley, occasionally toddling off to the end of his lead to sniff at whatever interested him. Usually someone's shoes, a lamp-post or the possibility of another dog's backside.

Adrian wasn't in such a good way, constantly repeating himself and staring towards the opposite end of the alley where a white tent had been set up.

'I've never seen a body before,' he said. 'You see it on TV and that, but this bloke's skin was just so... I dunno. Like wax. Like Tussauds at Blackpool. You ever been?'

Jessica shook her head.

'It's shit. I wouldn't bother.'

It was better than most TripAdvisor reviews.

The hedge that ringed Middleton House was across the road, barely steps away from where the body had been found. If it was Donal Doherty, then they'd been searching much too far afield for him. He'd probably been sleeping in the gardens, hiding out, knowing the police would be coming for him sooner or later.

Cars were slowing on the adjacent roads, with rubber-neckers trying to get a glimpse of whatever was going on. A nice juicy body would make some cracking teatime gossip.

'My fiancée's pregnant,' Adrian said. 'Five months. She wanted a fruit 'n' nut, so I'd taken George out for a wander. Thought I'd take a shortcut to the shop. Wish I hadn't bothered.'

'What did you actually see?' Jessica asked.

'I thought it was some bloke sleeping. You know what it's like round here. There's always the odd homeless having a kip. I thought I'd check he was all right. I figured he'd roll over and tell me to piss off, or whatever. Didn't think he'd actually be... y'know...'

Adrian dug into his pocket and fished out an e-cigarette. It flared a purply-blue and he sucked hard on it before spewing a fruity-smelling puff of smoke into the air.

'I've never phoned 999 before,' he added. 'I didn't know what counts as an emergency. You see all those stories about people who call the police because their missus won't hand over the remote and that. I thought I'd get a bollocking for calling the wrong number – but I couldn't remember the non-emergency one.'

'A dead body definitely counts as an emergency.'

'Right, well, I guess I know now.'

He sucked the plastic stick again as George sauntered across the paving slabs to sniff Jessica's shoes. He looked up with pricked ears, big bright eyes wide and alert.

'He's hungry,' Adrian said. 'Eats better than I do.'

Jessica crouched and ruffled the dog's ears. He nestled into her hand, tongue lolling from the corner of his mouth.

'You did the right thing,' Jessica said. 'Not everyone would've stopped to check – and I'm pretty sure that some would've kept walking even if they knew it was a dead body.'

Adrian nodded meekly. 'What happens now?'

'First we find out who it is, then we tell the person's family.'

'Right.' Adrian eyed the e-cigarette but repocketed it instead of having another puff. 'Do I have to do anything else?' he asked.

'Probably get that fruit 'n' nut for your other half…?' Jessica rubbed George's head once more and then stood. 'Probably feed the dog as well.'

'I can do that.'

Jessica told him someone would be in touch if they needed to check anything else – but that he'd already done plenty. After that, she headed across to the crime scene protection officer, who was busy guarding the scene-of-crime tent – and, perhaps predictably, chatting to Archie about football. Jessica only caught the tail end of the conversation, but it was enough.

'…You can't play four in the middle in this day and age,' Archie was saying as the other officer nodded along.

'Stone-age stuff,' the man agreed.

They both quietened as Jessica stepped into the conversation. 'I'd go three in the middle with a pair of wide men,' Jessica said.

Archie craned his neck backwards. 'What?'

'I'd play the three-five-er… how many is it again? Three?'

He cracked into a smile. 'You had me going then. I thought I'd finally got you into United.'

'I was only copying something you were banging on about the other week. Three in the middle, five in the middle, I don't know what you're on about.'

Archie bobbed high on his heels. 'You have defence, midfield and—'

Jessica snorted: 'I wasn't asking, Arch.' She nodded

towards the tent, turning slightly towards the protection officer. 'Am I allowed a look?'

'You can check with the SOCO. Not my call.'

Jessica stood off to the side, waiting for the Scene of Crime officer to emerge from the tent. When she did, it was a vaguely familiar face. With a dwindling budget and too few SOCOs, it was inevitable the same people would stumble across each other. If Jessica had ever known the woman's name, then she'd certainly forgotten it.

'Can I have a look?' Jessica asked.

'I'm just finishing up.'

'I might know him. Perhaps save a bit of time with the ID – even if it's informal...?'

The officer sized her up and then nodded, sending Jessica over to the car, where she changed into an ill-fitting paper suit with hairnet. Milan chic it was not.

Jessica headed into the tent with the other officer a little behind. The body was curled up with an olive green coat at the side. The jacket was enough, but Jessica scooched around until she could see the face clearly. The stubble was longer, the hair grungier – but there was no doubt about the identity of the man.

'It's him,' Jessica said quietly as she exited the tent and removed the hairnet. No point in prolonging the grim experience.

She stood with the Scene of Crime officer a little away from the tent. Someone would be along to collect the body soon enough and then the autopsy would give an official cause of death.

'Did you see the track lines on his arm?' the officer asked.

'I only looked at the face – didn't pay too much attention to the rest.'

'You sure it's your man?'

'Unless Donal Doherty's got a twin, then it's him. I've

arrested him a couple of times – plus I've been staring at his picture all week.' Jessica paused, glanced towards the tent and then Archie, who was still chatting to the protection officer. 'What do you reckon?' she asked.

'There's vomit on the pavement, around his mouth and on the inside of his coat. He probably choked to death. I wouldn't want to say for sure – not with the track marks. He might've overdosed. I don't think it was very nice either way.'

Jessica wondered if her twenty quid had gone up Donal's arms. There was the tiniest part of her, somewhere deep down, that couldn't help but feel relief that he wouldn't be able to expose her.

Her worry was that that part of her wasn't that tiny after all.

She was about to head back to the car to strip off the paper suit when Archie caught Jessica's eye. He was at the far end of the alley now, where Adrian and George had been waiting. He was hardly subtle at the best of times, but it almost looked like he had a facial tic given the way he was motioning to her.

Jessica smiled her way back past the protection officer and headed across to Archie.

'You having some sort of panic attack?' she asked.

Archie angled his gaze downwards and Jessica followed until she noticed the small polythene bag nestled into the shadows close to where George had been sniffing. She started to crouch, but Archie hissed an urgent 'no'. He was smiling over her shoulder towards the other officers, hands in pockets, casual as you like.

'What?' Jessica asked.

'It's full of brown stuff.'

'Tea?'

'Not bloody tea. *Brown*. I couldn't see any needles or foil.'

Jessica glanced down to the bag again. It was much bigger than she'd first thought. Way more than twenty quid's worth.

Archie nodded towards the tent and Donal's body. 'You reckon it's his?'

'Probably.'

'What do you want to do?'

Jessica could feel the protection officer watching them, wondering what was going on. She was still in the paper suit. 'I'll go chat to him and you get rid of it,' she said.

'"Get rid of it"?'

'What good's going to come if we check it in? It's not going to bring Donal back to life, is it? We'll put it through the system, there'll be an order to destroy it – and then it'll be gone anyway. One way has us filling in a stack of paperwork, the other sees it disappearing down a drain. It's the same outcome.'

Archie chewed on his lip. 'There might be fingerprints on the bag,' he said.

'Which will prove what? Donal was a druggie? We already know that.'

He seemed reluctant, but Archie nodded. 'You head over there and I'll flush it down the bog later,' he said.

Jessica smiled her way over to the protection officer, joking about how sexy the paper suit looked. He smiled along, attention on her, not looking in Archie's direction at all. At least the bag of whatever-was-inside was one fewer thing she'd have to deal with.

That and there was less chance of her bribe to Donal being exposed...

FORTY-THREE

Carl Brompton had been remanded to Manchester Prison – or Strangeways as everyone still called it. Jessica was semi-familiar with the place, although she didn't recognise any of the security staff as she passed through the gates.

Police officer or not, it was the same level of checks for everyone. With her pockets unloaded and phone left behind, Jessica passed through a second set of security until she was in the main corridors of the prison. The tight walls, echoing foot-steps and distant hubbub was all a reminder of her previous visits. Old names echoed through her mind, Donald McKenna for one. It had been years since she'd been here to interview him after his DNA was found at various crime scenes, despite the fact he was locked up. It was a lifetime ago, but the more things changed, the more they stayed the same – and it wasn't long before she found herself at the room in which she'd spoken to McKenna when she was a different person.

It was empty as the guard showed Jessica inside. He offered a friendly smile and said he'd be right back. Without a phone with which to waste time, Jessica was left pacing around the small room. There was a clock high on the wall close to the door but the minute hand didn't seem to be moving, not quickly enough anyway. It hung and stuck, leaving her nothing to do until the double knock finally came.

Brompton thumped and slid his way into the room, reminding Jessica that he had one leg shorter than the other. He was looking marginally better than the previous time she'd seen him, though not having a face full of snot and tears definitely contributed to that. He'd had a shave at some point since being remanded, perhaps combed his hair, too. It was still hanging behind his ears but looked a lot less like damp silly string.

'Oh,' he said as he was led in.

Jessica explained to him that he was entitled to a solicitor and under the same sort of caution as at the station. Everything he said was to be recorded. Brompton nodded along to say he understood. He didn't want a solicitor.

'Do you remember what you said the last time we spoke?' Jessica asked. 'About the person you said you were with at Evie's house?'

Brompton squirmed, not answering.

'It was recorded,' Jessica added. 'I can request the footage if you want and play it back to you.'

'No.'

'Who did you say you were with?'

A pause. Brompton was staring at the table, cupping his chin with his thumbs and rubbing his temples with his middle fingers. 'Donal.'

He spoke very quietly, emphasising the 'Doh' and then allowing the second syllable to drift into nothingness.

'Donal Doherty?' Jessica asked.

Brompton nodded.

'I want you to say it,' Jessica said. 'Who were you with at Evie's house on the night she died?'

'Donal. Donal Doherty.'

'Around three hours ago, Donal Doherty was found dead in an alleyway close to Middleton House. There's no official cause of death yet, but chances are he choked on his own vomit. He died alone, wrapped up in that green coat of his.'

Brompton peered up from the table between them, staring into Jessica's eyes until he knew it wasn't a trick.

His voice was a quiet croak. 'He's dead?'

'Dead.'

Jessica waited to see if Carl would add anything, but all he did was turn his attention back to the table.

'The question is,' Jessica said, 'was it an accident?'

Brompton looked up once more: 'You said—'

'I said he probably choked on his own vomit. *Probably*. But that doesn't mean he wasn't given a helping hand. He's an addict and someone's been supplying him. Either that or whoever it was who paid the pair of you to give Evie a scare really didn't want Donal to talk...'

Jessica left it hanging. It was a bit of a jump in thinking – but without the name of the person who'd paid them to frighten Evie, anything was on the table. Chances were, Donal *had* overdosed and then choked to death – no one was likely to miss a junkie who spent much of his time begging at cash machines – but Brompton wasn't to know that.

'Like it or not,' she continued, 'prison is probably a safe place for you. If someone did get to Donal, then it's going to be a lot harder for them to get to you. One thing is for sure though: if you don't tell me who it was, then there's not a lot anyone can do to ensure you stay safe...'

Brompton was nodding along, following her logic.

'Who paid you to scare Evie Briers?' she asked.

He looked up, biting his lip, scratching his cheek so hard that flecks of dry skin flaked to the ground. 'I don't know,' he said.

'You don't know what? You don't know anything? You don't know the name?'

'It was his idea.'

'Well, Donal's not really around to dispute that, is he?'

'She gave him the money.'

A pause. She was finally getting somewhere – all it had taken was a string of dead bodies. 'Who's "she", Carl?'

'I don't know her name. Donal knew her. I don't know how – I was just there.'

'Where?'

'The cash machine.'

Jessica let out a low breath. It was almost too simple. Donal Doherty had been picked up so many times for begging next to cash machines.

'Which one?' Jessica asked.

'Near the uni. Donal's spot.'

That definitely sounded plausible. It didn't mean it was true, but there was a ring of legitimacy about it. Jessica had herself arrested Donal at that very spot years before.

'To be clear, you were at the uni with Donal begging for money near a cash machine?' Jessica asked.

'Right.'

'What happened then?'

'There was this woman. She knew him. She called him over to this doorway and gave him money.'

'You saw her giving him money?'

'Yes.'

'How much?'

'I don't know – he said it was for a small job, that I could help. He said he'd give me a hundred quid.'

Brompton pressed back into his seat and lifted his knees to his chest, hugging them close. His breathing had become shorter and shallower and it sounded like he was near to an asthma attack.

'How did they know each other?' Jessica asked.

'She knew his name. I think he might have done jobs for her before.'

'Did he talk about any of them?'

'No.'

'Did he say her name?'

'No.'

'Describe her. Tell me what she was wearing.'

It took a few minutes of garbled descriptions, but Brompton eventually got there – and then, from nowhere, Jessica finally understood what the hell had been going on with Evie and her apartment.

FORTY-FOUR

One of the lashes stuck to the headlights of Sally Nugent's brand-new car had started to peel away. Coupled with a few muddy marks across the wings and it was looking a bit women's-toilets-at-the-end-of-a-night-out. The false eyelashes were becoming unstuck, mascara smeared, a nail was lost, phone left somewhere unknown, tears streaming. That was Sally Nugent's car in its current state.

Jessica was walking around it when Sally appeared in the doorway still wearing her baby pink towelling tracksuit. She was still chewing as well.

'Oh, it's you,' Sally said.

It was morning and Sally was wearing a pair of fluffy Uggs. Her hair was in a set of rollers and she didn't seem like she'd been expecting anyone.

'I thought you were the nosy cow from over the road,' Sally continued. 'Was just about to come out and tell you to piss off.'

'Have you got a few minutes?' Jessica asked.

'Is it about Evie?'

'In a way.'

Sally angled back towards the house. 'I'm kinda busy with... stuff.'

'Do you think the stuff could maybe wait ten minutes?'

The two women eyed each other and then Sally knew the game was up. She didn't say anything, she simply nodded towards the house and headed inside. Jessica followed, closing the front door and finding herself in a living room that looked like a pink bomb had gone off. The sofa was pink, the cushions were pink, the rug was pink. Even the walls had a soft pink hue. Sally's tracksuit almost had her camouflaged into the background.

'How's Samuel?' she asked, curling onto the sofa and not meeting Jessica's gaze.

'He's okay – about as well as you'd think, what with his mother dying and everything.'

'Right... of course.' She glanced towards the door. 'I did kinda tell you everything I know. I'm not sure how else I can help...'

'I think you know why I'm here,' Jessica said.

Sally shrugged but her body language couldn't have been any guiltier if she'd tried. She'd shrunk down within herself, making her shoulders and elbows pointy. She'd gone from no eye contact to way too much, refusing to allow Jessica to look away.

'I've been to that Ford dealership where you bought your car,' Jessica said.

'Oh.'

'You paid for the whole car in one go. No loans, no finance. That's a lot of money to pay at once. You must've been saving up for a long time...?'

Another shrug, but Sally was actually sweating. Small beads of liquid were forming around her temples and she wiped them away before catching herself. 'What of it?'

'Where'd you get that much money?'

'I had it lying around – savings accounts, y'know...'

'You know we can check that, don't you? I can come back this afternoon with proof, one way or the other.'

Sally gulped. 'Yeah, um...'

'How much did Shaun and Julie Viceroy pay you to move out?'

'I, er...' Sally looked up, caught Jessica's eye and then looked away again. 'Am I in trouble?'

'For what?'

'I don't know...'

'As far as I can tell, you've not done anything wrong. They paid you to move out – and you moved out. It would have *really* helped if you'd told me that the last time I was here.'

Sally threw up both hands. 'They told me not to. They made me sign this paper to say I wouldn't tell anyone.'

'A contract?'

'I guess.'

'Do you have a copy?'

'No – they said it was for their records. I had to move out within seventy-two hours and then I'd get the money. I went into a hotel for a week or so until I got this place.' She covered her mouth with her hand. 'Oh my God! Have I broken the contract by talking to you? I don't have to give the money back, do I? I've spent it. Am I going to end up on *Judge Judy*? They can't make me pay back what I don't have, can they?'

Jessica left it a few moments, if only to watch Sally squirm. So much of what had happened could've been avoided if she'd told her all this days ago.

'You won't have to go on *Judge Judy*,' Jessica said.

'Oh, my Lord.'

'Who made you sign the agreement?'

'The landlord?'

'Shaun Viceroy?'

'No – his missus, Julie.'

Which is precisely what Jessica had suspected. Shaun and Julie had sat in their house and denied knowing anything about what had been going on with Evie. Both had lied.

'Did they tell you why?' Jessica asked.

'Why what?'

'Why they were giving you so much money?'

'Something to do with trying to sell the house. I didn't really ask. I figured it was free money. I was looking to leave anyway – but it's not like I was going to tell them that.'

'Is there anything else?'

'Like what?'

'I don't know,' Jessica said, 'you waited all this time to come out with this. I really don't want to come back again, so if there's anything else to say, you should probably do it now.'

Sally shook her head slowly. 'Are you saying I can keep the money?'

Jessica stood, eyeing the wall of pink. 'Something like that,' she said.

Jessica was sitting in her car outside Evie's apartment. It had been a few days since the crime scene had been closed and the property handed back for Shaun and Julie to deal with.

It hadn't taken them long.

Nailed to the front gate post was an estate agent's board with 'SOLD' in big capital letters. As quickly as that.

Jessica got out of the car and crossed to the board. She took a photo of it with her phone in case she needed to contact the agents at some point. She was wondering what to do next when the radio buzzed and one of the handlers asked for her by number.

She was wanted at the airport.

FORTY-FIVE

Jessica looked from the passport photo to the man in front of her. She held the document at arm's length so she could compare the two properly.

'You've really done yourself down here, Raj,' Jessica said. 'The bloke in this passport has a good twenty years on you. Probably a couple of stone as well. Few more greys, different-shaped nose... is this *really* the best you could do?'

Rajiv Lodi seemed a broken man. He was sitting with his legs splayed, head drooped low to his knees, hands in his dark hair. By all accounts, it had been a shoddy attempt to get through security with a passport in the name of 'Ranjiv Lodhi'. After being pulled to one side by Border Force, he'd struggled to confirm his identity – and then someone had spotted his name, picture and details on the watch list.

It was a bad enough situation as it was – and that's if he hadn't been with his wife and three kids.

'Whose passport is it?' Jessica asked.

'Does it matter?'

'Probably not to me – but the border lot will have another go at you in a bit and I think they'll want a proper answer.'

'I'm not saying anything until I know where my family is.'

'They're in a different room down the hallway,' Jessica said. 'Your son's happily playing with his *Star Wars* figures, your daughters are colouring in and your wife... well, I think she probably wants this all to be over and done with.'

'Can I see them?'

'Not yet. I don't think you're really in a position to be making demands.'

Rajiv finally sat back. Given his predicament, he was actually in quite a comfortable seat. It was soft and foamy, a staffroom special complete with coffee stains on the blue canvas. He was a good-looking guy, with swept-back thick hair and dark eyes. Unfortunately, that was offset by even darker rings around his eyes. He seemed even more tired than she felt.

'You've killed me, y'know.' His accent was local but with the merest hint of subcontinent heritage.

'Who's killed you?'

'You lot.'

'How'd you work that out?'

'My kids, too. My wife. You've killed us all. You don't even know what you've done.'

He glared up with furious fire in his eyes.

'You're going to have to help me out here, Rajiv.'

Rajiv pointed towards the door. 'How about you let my wife and family get back on the plane. As soon as they're gone, I'll tell you everything.'

Jessica left it a moment, letting him think it was an option.

'The problem with making demands is that you actually need to offer something in return. If you don't want to tell us anything, then don't. I'll leave it to Border Force and you can go to prison for ten years for using someone else's passport. That's before we even talk about all the knock-off gear we found in your lock-up. Trading Standards will want a word about that, too.' She started to stand. 'I'll just get off, shall I? Got things to do anyway.'

Rajiv reached forward, not quite pulling her back but motioning to.

'No,' he said.

'As far as I can tell, your wife and children haven't done anything wrong. They're using their own passports. Theoretically, the only thing stopping them being allowed to fly to Bangladesh is you.'

'What do you mean?'

'You're under suspicion of committing more than one crime. You were due to fly on the same ticket, so they're being held here because of that. If you were to cooperate, I can't make any promises, but the border authorities are far more likely to let them go. They know it's you we wanted.'

'I want to know for certain.'

Jessica stood this time, taking a step away from the seats. They were in a small interview room in the restricted area of Manchester Airport's Terminal One. The distant hubbub of passengers was a constant and every few moments the building would tremble with the merest hint of an earthquake as another plane soared into the sky.

'Certain doesn't exist,' Jessica said. 'You don't have anything to bargain with. Not only that, but this involves too many agencies. Even if I wanted to tell you your family would be put on the next flight to Dhaka, I can't make that happen. All you can do is cooperate and hope for the best. If you really think your family's lives are in danger, I don't know what other option you have.'

She'd reached the door by the time Rajiv called her back this time.

'What do you want to know?' he asked, sounding defeated.

Jessica waited at the door, one hand ready to press down on the handle. She was never really going to leave, but he didn't know that.

'Why have you been trying to disappear?'

'How'd you mean?'

'Your house has been empty for at least three days, the market stall's been shut down, the mail's building up, the Sky Plus series links are getting out of hand – now you show up at the airport. Doesn't take a genius to work out you've been keeping your head down.'

Rajiv scratched hard at a spot behind his ear. He eyed the door longingly, knowing his family was a little way down the corridor.

'It's not me,' he said.

'So who is it?'

'Chat... my brother. He owes money – but they say it's *our* debt, not *his* debt.'

'Who says?'

Rajiv opened his mouth and, for a moment, Jessica felt sure he was about to say a name. She felt herself edge forward half a step, willing it out of him, but then he shook his head ever so slightly. It wasn't much, but it was plenty enough to put an end to that line of questioning... at least for now.

'What happens if the debt's not paid?' Jessica asked.

'What do you think?'

'I don't know... some bloke takes your telly?'

Rajiv snorted through his nose. Not a laugh, not really, more wishful thinking.

'I don't suppose these mystery people you owe money to happened to find Tomasz Kotula, did they?' Jessica asked.

Rajiv nodded. 'That was the message.'

'Leaving Chatresh's driving licence on Tomasz was a message?'

'I suppose. We didn't realise it was serious until then.'

If nothing else, that was the mystery of Tomasz cleared up. He likely didn't even know why he'd been attacked – but it was little to do with him, more to tell the Lodi brothers that whomever they owed money to meant business.

'Tomasz has a sister in Poland,' Jessica said. 'She'd not heard from him in over a week. You could have at least let us know who he was. He's been lying in hospital all this time with nobody knowing who he was.'

'It's not like we wanted this.'

'Where did they get Chat's driving licence?'

'A fake.'

Not entirely surprising – but it *was* a good fake. It wasn't as if Jessica had inspected every microscopic millimetre of it, but she'd noticed nothing untoward. Chatresh was smarter than she'd given him credit for. His wallet *had* been stolen and he'd thought quickly enough on his feet to let them think his driving licence had gone with it. All the time, he probably had the real one. They'd only found the fake in Tomasz's pocket. Aside from being fingerprinted, it had never been inspected properly. Why would it be?

'We've been to your lock-up,' Jessica said. 'Quite the haul.'

Rajiv sighed long and loud. He was wearing a pair of Adidas training bottoms, with a light navy T-shirt. Probably some of his own knock-off gear. The unscuffed white trainers looked smart and new.

'It started small,' Rajiv said. 'Chat's idea. We sold a few pairs of trainers, then it was perfumes – have you seen the mark-up on that stuff? It's not like anyone was getting hurt. These companies make millions and then pay their workers nothing. It's all greed. People want the goods but don't have the money, so we were helping them out, making Christmas better, y'know. They didn't need big money to buy the bags they wanted...'

He made it sound like a public service and spoke so

assuredly that even Jessica felt a twang of agreement. But that wasn't really the point – and the Lodi brothers were hardly altruistic charitable types. They were raking it in, too.

Jessica let it go. There were bigger questions to ask.

'Where did the fakes come from, Raj?'

From keeping tight-lipped, Rajiv was suddenly singing like a tone-deaf idiot in the shower. He sat up straighter, gesticulating wildly with his hands. Jessica wondered if he was thinking of his family a short distance away, or if he was finally relieved to get it all out.

'Chat knew this guy,' he said, 'a garage owner – Robbo. He bought a car from him and they got talking or something like that. I wasn't there. Anyway, Chat said that he had a market stall and Robbo asked if he sold shoes and clothes, that sort of thing. We sold a few pairs of trainers we got off him and it built from that. Compared to our other dealers, we paid less for the stuff Robbo had and could sell it for more.'

'You started with some trainers? How long ago was that?'

'Eighteen months or so? I don't know for sure, but definitely before Christmas last year. We'd sell things within a day or two of getting them in, so Chat wanted to go bigger. He'd buy huge stock from Robbo, but we didn't have anywhere to keep it, so we got the lock-up. Even that wasn't enough. There were boxes all over his house. I wanted to keep it small, just the stall, but Chat wanted another market pitch, perhaps even a shop. He kept saying bigger, while I was saying smaller.' Rajiv looked up to Jessica, making eye contact. 'I didn't want *this*.'

'Did you fall out?'

'We argued. That's when I found out he was selling other things...'

'Like what?'

'Passports, IDs, documents. It was fine before that, with just the clothes – but he couldn't let it be. He always wanted more, more, more.'

That was news to Jessica. It perhaps explained the fake driving licence in Chatresh's name that had been found on Tomasz. It also gave an indication of where Rajiv's dodgy passport had come from – but she hadn't heard from anywhere that Chat and Raj were actually selling fake documents. It wasn't her field of expertise, more something the Serious Crime Division would be involved with, but it was a very murky world. Counterfeit passports weren't likely to be produced by the friendly grandmother down the road.

'Why did you say we've killed you?' Jessica asked.

Rajiv looked up, looked down, hung his head and then shook it.

Jessica waited, giving him the chance to say the name. A minute passed until she spoke again.

'I'm not sure what you expect to happen if you won't tell me who's threatening you,' she said. 'If you and your family are in danger, we might actually be able to help. There's not a lot anyone can do if you say nothing.'

'You've seen what they do.'

'Tomasz...?'

'Right... You could let us go, let us get on the plane.'

'You know that can't happen, Raj.'

He bobbed his head, staring at the floor. 'Is Chat safe?'

'Your brother?'

Rajiv peered up through veiny eyes. 'Who else?'

'I thought you knew where he was?'

'The last time I spoke to him was the day one of your lot showed up at his front door with his driving licence and a photo of Tomasz. He called and told me to get out of the city.'

'You both went into hiding separately?'

'He said it was safer. If they found him, he wouldn't be able to say where I was. It'd be the same if they found me.'

'If *who* found you?'

This was the moment. If Rajiv continued to shake his head

and say nothing, then he was on his own. He'd given up a few pieces of the puzzle and some of the others would start to slot into place regardless of his help.

'Do you know the Cork brothers?' he asked quietly.

The name rang a bell from various briefings over the years. Something to do with gangs around the city, more the SCD's thing.

'I know *of* them,' she replied.

'I wish I didn't know them at all.'

'But they know you?'

'They know Chat – and I'm his brother, so yes. I guess that's their way, the debt belongs to the family.'

'Are you saying Chatresh owes money to the Cork brothers?'

'Lots.'

'How much?'

'I don't know. More than we have.'

There was a set of clumping footsteps from outside and, for a moment, Jessica thought someone was going to come barging into the room. It wasn't an exaggeration that other agencies were lining up to talk to Rajiv. Regardless of how cooperative he was, he'd be a busy boy for a long while. They both turned as whoever it was boomed past the door and continued along the corridor. There was the sound of another door opening and then quiet.

'I don't understand,' Jessica said. 'A few minutes ago, you said you paid less for Robinson's goods and sold everything for more. Surely you were making lots of money?'

'After those first few pairs of trainers, Chat said Robbo wanted to sell in bulk. He was getting in big shipments and didn't want to split it up between all sorts of traders. It was too much hassle, too much chance of you lot getting involved. He said Chat could only be involved if he wanted to buy the lot.'

'And so Chatresh borrowed money from the Cork brothers to buy everything Robinson had in stock...?'

'I didn't know that then. I would've said no, would've stopped him. It's probably why he didn't involve me. Chatresh wanted to buy a Ferrari. It was always his thing. He had a little toy car when we were kids and he'd race it around the back yard. He kept saying how he wanted a real one. He liked his suits and sunglasses. I was happy at home.'

There was no bitterness in what he said, just an acceptance that it was probably always going to come down to something like this.

'If you made enough from selling these things on your stall, why do you still owe money?' Jessica asked.

A shrug. 'Chat.'

Rajiv still couldn't quite put the boot into his brother entirely. The implication was there – Chatresh hadn't paid back the money because he'd spent it. At best it was on more stock, at worst it was on the expensive things he liked. He did part-own a small plane, after all. He probably thought he could sweet-talk the Cork brothers – and then Tomasz had been kicked half to death and it was suddenly serious.

'Do you know Evie Briers?' Jessica asked.

He looked up, met her eyes. 'Who?'

'You'd know the name.'

'I don't know who that is. Should I?'

It was Jessica's turn to shake her head. 'Perhaps not.'

There was an interwoven web there – but Evie was probably just doing small accounting jobs for Owain Robinson on the side. Everything else in regards to her apartment and the timing of what had happened was an awful, awful coincidence. There was, unfortunately, still one more thing Jessica knew that Rajiv didn't.

'You said that Chatresh called you after I'd been round with his driving licence.'

'Right.'

'And he told you to leave the house...?'

'Yes.'

'What exactly did he say?'

Rajiv rubbed his temples, trying to scratch the memory out. 'That Tomasz had been beaten up and that it was a message for us. He said he owed lots of money and that we wouldn't be safe until he paid it back. He said he was going to find somewhere to keep his head down and that we should do the same.'

'What did you say?'

'What do you think? Called him a few names, then realised he wasn't joking around. There wasn't much point in arguing and fighting, not if we were genuinely in danger. We went off to Bradford for a few days – paid cash to stay in a hotel. I figured the safest thing was to get out of the country until it was all sorted.'

'You've definitely not seen your brother since that day?'

'Honestly? I don't think it's a good idea for us to see each other right now.'

There was silent, seething fury there. Rajiv knew he was in trouble, yet Jessica believed him when he said much of it stemmed from his brother's actions. Whatever Chatresh had done had put Rajiv's wife and children in extreme danger and that was hardly likely to be forgotten over a sibling lunch.

'Do you know anything about Robbo?' Jessica asked.

'Not really. I'd never met him. Don't even know his first name.'

'He was shot in his own home a few nights ago during what looks like a burglary gone wrong.'

Rajiv stared at her, processing the words.

'Someone went after Robinson's supplier, too. A man named Iain Jennings. Someone broke into Jennings' home in Grimsby. This person had a gun – possibly the same weapon that was used to shoot Owain Robinson. Iain Jennings got away unharmed, but it's all on his security camera.'

'Who?'

'It was Chatresh. He broke into Jennings' house – and he's the man we think shot Owain Robinson.'

FORTY-SIX

DCI Topper had his most serious face on. The one where his eyebrows arched downwards in the middle and it looked like he'd swallowed a wasp. At times, there were chinks in his demeanour. He might tell her to do one thing, but there was a hint that, perhaps, the instructions weren't airtight. Other times he was deliberately vague.

On this, he was not messing around.

'You are not to go anywhere near the Cork brothers,' he said.

'I get it,' Jessica replied. His office suddenly felt very small and she was trapped in the chair across the desk from him.

'Do you?' he asked. 'Do you *actually* get it? Because this isn't me telling you to leave them be, this comes from so far on high that I'm not even sure who's giving the orders.'

'Santa?'

That got a crinkle of a smile, but only for a moment. 'I'm not joking, Inspector – and this isn't funny. This is above Serious Crime. We're talking Interpol or the bloody Home Office. I don't even know – what I *do* know is that we are not to interfere in any way whatsoever with the Cork brothers. Do you understand?'

'Yes,' Jessica replied. 'It's not like I know who they are or where they live. I wasn't going to turn up on their doorstep with a pecan pie and a "welcome to the area" card.'

'Not funny.'

'Sorry, sir.' Jessica paused, wondering if she could try her luck. 'Can you at least give me something?' she added. 'For my own peace of mind. They're brothers, obviously, their last name is Cork – hence the whole "Cork brothers" thing – but you must know something else...?'

Topper examined her for a moment and then his features softened. 'Fraser and Fergus Cork moved down from Scotland,' he said. 'Each served a prison sentence up there for various things. Not even the usual: assaults, possession of weapons – proper nasty stuff. They came down here as a pair once they were released. As far as I know, things were quiet for a while. Police Scotland were glad to see the back of them. That was a couple of years ago. They're running a pub out Warrington way. Cheshire Police got a tip-off about drugs being dealt over the bar but didn't have enough proof to go in. That's all I have – and, believe me, that's more than I want to know. They don't even live in Greater Manchester, so it's someone else's problem. I do *not* want this to become our problem in any way whatsoever. Got it?'

'Yes, sir.'

'Good.' He took a breath, apparently relieved. If she was honest, Jessica didn't blame him. 'There is something you should be doing...' he added.

'Go on.'

'If everything Rajiv Lodi said is true, you should probably make an extra-special effort to find his brother before Fraser and Fergus do.'

'It's not like I've been sitting around signing off expense forms all day.'

Topper held up a hand to stop her as his phone rang. She wriggled in her seat as he ummed his way through a conversation before hanging up.

'Do you believe Rajiv?' he asked as if the interruption had never happened.

'I believe he wants to protect his wife and kids. We only met Chatresh once and it looked like he had an eye for smart suits. He said he part-owned a plane. I can see how he might have got himself far deeper into something than he intended.'

'It's a bit of a jump from that to shooting someone in their own home.'

'True – but we don't know he definitely planned to shoot Owain Robinson, assuming it *was* him. He might've gone to Robinson's garage looking to find money to pay off the Corks but come away with nothing. Then he went to Robinson's house getting increasingly desperate – and things escalated. If he still couldn't find anything there, it'd give a reason why he ended up at Iain Jennings' house. Perhaps Robinson gave up his mate? It sounds like the Corks put Tomasz in intensive care just to send a message, so who knows how far they'd go if they got hold of Chatresh or Rajiv?'

Topper nodded along. After a murky week in which there had been barely anything more than confusion, it was actually starting to come together. 'Do you think Rajiv Lodi really is in the dark about his brother?'

'I think Raj is steaming that Chat put him in this position. I can't see him making up stories about his brother when he knows how much danger his wife and kids are in. All he wants is for them to get out of the country.'

'So much so that he'd make up a story about his brother...?'

Jessica stopped to think, picturing the way Rajiv had

spoken to her. The urgency in his voice, the insistence at wanting their safety for his story.

'Maybe,' she said, 'but I think he was telling the truth.'

'In that case, what I said before stands – get out there and find Chatresh Lodi before anyone else does.'

FORTY-SEVEN

DCI Topper's instructions were all well and good – but he made it sound as if finding Chatresh was as easy as popping out to the nearest Tesco. He'd not offered to ask neighbouring stations for extra officers, neither had he authorised any more overtime.

Besides, what did 'find Chatresh Lodi' mean? Stop any males on the street with remotely brown skin in case he was disguised? Knock on every door in the city in case he was there? They'd been doing the usual things – looking for any properties to which he might have a connection, checking with known friends and associates, monitoring to see whether any of his bank or credit cards were used. If his own brother had no idea where he was hiding out, then it wasn't as if they could magically come up with a location. As for having the public help out, his photo was already up on their social media feeds – but no sane person was trawling those in the hope of actually helping. Finding a person who didn't want to be found only ever came down to two things: stupidity on the missing person's part, or luck on theirs.

Chatresh was clearly stupid when it came to money but

Jessica doubted he was thick enough to present himself anywhere that Fraser and Fergus Cork might get their hands on him. As for Lady Luck, well, she'd pissed off long ago.

Jessica had briefed her team and then headed back to her office for a few minutes of peace and almost quiet. She did wonder how Rajiv was getting on. As days went, he'd gone from hoping to get onto a plane, to facing a mini inquisition. Someone always had it worse than she did.

Before long, Jessica's thoughts had wandered to one of her other concerns. She found herself searching the website of the estate agency that was named on the board outside the house where Evie lived. She scrolled through listing after listing, reading the same language tropes over and over. 'Cosy' meant minuscule; 'brimming with character' meant some artsy type had turned the place into a new-age wreck; 'walking distance' meant miles away; 'ideal for first-time buyers' meant small and shit; 'unofficial terrace' meant hole in the roof; 'popular area' meant surrounded by dickheads, yummy mummies and pricks in 4x4s.

It was all the usual nonsense – but the house owned by Shaun and Julie Viceroy wasn't listed anywhere – not even under the sold section. Jessica googled the address instead. At first she tried the house itself, then the road name and number. It was only when she stopped searching for houses sold and instead looked for the road itself that she stumbled across what she was looking for.

The plot of land on which Shaun and Julie Viceroy's house lay, the place where Evie Briers had lived, had sold for £4.15million to a development firm barely days before. The house itself wasn't mentioned – simply the plot of land. It was bigger than Jessica would have suspected from being in Evie's flat, but she hadn't gone into the back yard.

The article said the development firm also owned a patch of land at the back of the road and were going to build an entertainment complex. They had planning permission that was going to run out at the end of the year.

Jessica stared at the figure and then wrote it out with all the zeroes.

£4,150,000.

Whew.

No wonder Shaun and Julie Viceroy didn't have a problem in giving Sally Nugent enough go-away money to buy a car. The others would have got something, too. Peter and Veronica Haversmith, whom Jessica had never met, were off on a cruise according to their neighbour – and it was a good bet where that money had come from.

What was a few thousand here and there when there was four million to come down the line? It was an insane amount of money. Archie had been blathering on about gentrification and there it was. Half the street was being knocked down to make way for an entertainment complex.

If she could stop him from talking about football, he might be worth listening to.

Jessica was about to head back to the main floor when her phone started to ring. The number was unknown, which usually meant call centre. Against her better judgement, she answered anyway.

A man's voice: 'Jess?'

'Who's this?'

'Andrew Hunter.'

'What's going on with your number?' she asked.

'I'm at a payphone.'

'A payphone? Do they even still have those?'

'I figured you might not want *my* number on your phone bill too often. I have a burner phone but I don't really use that.'

'Good point.'

Andrew cleared his throat, he sounded hesitant. 'Sorry,' he said, 'this phone box smells funny.'

'Of course it does – everyone's got a mobile nowadays. More people use phone boxes as urinals than they do for making calls.'

'That's very nice to know. Thanks for that.'

'You're welcome.'

'What were you supposed to be buying me? A tin of Roses?'

'It's not Christmas yet – they're not in the shops. It's all Hallowe'en. I'll sort it. Are you calling in your favour?'

'Not yet – but I have news.'

Jessica settled back into her seat. She'd completely forgotten about poor old Marie and her missing man, who may or may not have been having affair.

'You wanted a Chris McMichael,' Andrew said.

'Right.'

'I've found you a Michael Christopher. He has a big tattoo of a gecko on his arm. I've got the pictures.'

'A gecko?'

'Lizardy, reptiley-thing. Sort of sticks to stuff. You find them in all types of places. They like New Zealand, apparently – and they can lick their own eyeballs.'

'I know what a gecko is – I was expressing surprise that someone would choose to have one tattooed on their arm.'

'I can't help you with that.'

Jessica was doodling on her pad. Chris McMichael and Michael Christopher.

'He really didn't make much effort in concealing his name, did he?' she said. 'It's like me calling myself Daniel Jessica to go trolling on message boards.'

'He works as a bank teller,' Andrew said. 'I've got a Facebook page for him, plus he's on Tinder. Don't ask me how I know that.'

Jessica laughed. 'Please tell me you spent an afternoon

swiping through images of semi-naked men...? Did you get any matches?'

'Do you want the info or not? I'm not even getting paid for this!'

Jessica apologised but it didn't sound like he was serious anyway. Then she asked what was perhaps the key question: 'Is he married?'

'Yep – four kids, including twins: Ava, Bella, Charlotte and Daisy. A-B-C and D. The next one will probably be Emily or Ella. He lives in Bolton.'

Jessica didn't know what she'd expected. Assuming it was the right man, Chris McMichael – or Michael Christopher – had spun Marie quite the barrel of bull. He'd spoken of business trips and time abroad. Jessica thought he might live in a big city, but there he was, a few miles up the road in Lancashire. It was all a fantasy.

'Can you email me the details?' Jessica asked. 'I'll give you my personal account.'

'Is it encrypted?'

'What do you think?'

'All right – I'll give you a website link and a password. You can log on and look at whatever you want. It's better that way.'

It all sounded a bit over the top, but who was Jessica to argue. 'Thanks,' she said. 'Again. I owe you one.'

'More than one.'

'Yeah, that too.'

Jessica sat outside the three-bedroom house and stared up at the normality of it all. There was a plastic lightsaber resting against one of the upstairs windows, with *Frozen* curtains in the other. The front garden was small and more for show – but she could see along the side of the house to a trampoline at the rear. The house was on a row of similar properties, all with midsize nearly new cars on the driveways. A typical two-point-four children estate: mums and dads, daughters and sons. Mornings would see kids being driven to school and parents heading off to work; evenings would be arguments over Wi-Fi and whether dinner had to be eaten at the table.

She got out of the car and went for a walk, slipping between the cut-throughs and weaving her way around the estate. It was perhaps a decade old, with the grime of everyday life beginning to cling to the brickwork.

A normal estate for a normal man with a normal family.

Except normal could be boring. For some, it definitely was.

Jessica found herself back at the car just as the sun was starting to dip below the houses. She was off-shift but this wasn't a job for being at work. Caroline would have cooked and it would be getting cold but Jessica had never asked for that. She was beginning to feel like a lodger in her own house.

Four kids.

Bloody hell. She wasn't even sure what she felt about Michael Christopher. The immediate reaction was obvious. What a scumbag: cheating on his wife, potentially breaking up a family with four young girls, leading along another woman...

And then Jessica looked up to the normalcy around her. Red bricks, three bedrooms, a trampoline in the back garden. Drive to work, drive home. Drive to work, drive home. No wonder he created a fantasy life for himself.

He was still a scumbag, though.

Jessica checked the photograph on her phone, imprinting it to her memory as much as she could to ensure she remembered him. He was decent-looking as a package, the sort who worked on his body because the face had little to offer. Andrew had passed on a Facebook picture in which Michael was on holiday. He was shirtless, toned and athletic, hoisting his twin daughters onto his shoulders and showing off the distinctive green and black gecko tattoo. He had freckly, pimply skin more often seen on someone who spent a day in front of a deep fat fryer, but his daughters must have got their mother's looks as they were angelic.

When she was sure she'd recognise him, Jessica set off for the front door. She knocked twice and it was quickly answered by one of the twins. She was seven or eight but brimming with confidence as she stared up at Jessica.

'Hello,' she said.

'Is your daddy in?'

'He's watching television.'

'Can you get him?'

There was a loud male shout of 'who is it?' from the inside and then the little girl smiled sweetly before disappearing inside. It wasn't long before Michael Christopher strolled along the hallway. Jessica had some big story planned out – she was a TV producer in the area making a show about tattoos and someone local had pointed her towards him – but as it was, he was wearing a vest, shorts and flip-flops anyway.

'All right?' he said, approaching the door.

Jessica eyed his pimply face and then the tattoo. It was precisely as Marie had described, exactly what was in the photos: a long black lizard along his forearm with green streaks across the back.

'I think I've got the wrong house,' Jessica said, taking a step back.

'Who are you looking for?'

'Someone named Chris.'

His eyes narrowed. 'Not here.'

Jessica apologised once more and then spun on her heels, striding back to the car. She clambered in and started the engine without turning around, but, as she headed into the distance, Michael's unmoving silhouette in her rear-view mirror was clear enough.

. . .

Marie blinked as she opened her front door. She took an involuntary step back.

'Oh,' she said, 'I can't remember your name.'

Jessica didn't bother to remind her. She dug into her pocket and pulled out what had been the photograph of Michael with his daughters. She'd folded and ripped it down until it showed only the arm.

'Do you recognise the tattoo?' she asked.

Marie's eyes widened as she reached forward and took the scrap of photo. She squinted and then started to nod enthusiastically. 'You've found him?!'

'He's alive,' Jessica said.

'Where is he? Did he say anything about me? When can I see him?'

Jessica took the photo back and screwed it into her pocket. She stepped backwards but Marie reached out and gripped her arm.

'What did he say?'

'You're asking questions I can't answer. You said he'd stopped contacting you, that you were worried he'd died and you couldn't face not knowing. I'm telling you the truth: he's alive. That's it. I can't help any more than that.'

'But—' Marie stopped herself and removed her hand. 'You're right,' she said.

Jessica hovered for a moment, thinking about passing on some sort of helpful advice: 'Find yourself a proper man', all that clichéd nonsense. As if Marie couldn't figure it out for herself. Instead she gave a thin smile and turned back towards the car.

'Thank you,' Marie said.

FORTY-EIGHT

Shaun Viceroy was full of gruff Scottishness as he opened the door. He mumbled something to himself and then went to fetch his wife. Julie was surprised to see Archie and Jessica and clearly reluctant to let them inside. She mentioned something about having 'loads of paperwork' to get on with and that they were 'expecting visitors'. Jessica smiled through it all, saying they only needed a few minutes.

With a huff and puff, Julie stepped aside and let them inside. They ended up back in the living room with the computer. This time, Julie took a seat on the sofa, sitting with a straight back and crossing her knees. Shaun was at the back of the room using the computer. There was no offer of tea and biscuits this time round. She was dressed smartly in a prim chocolate brown suit, her heart necklace still high on her neck.

Archie hovered in the door, bobbing from foot to foot. 'Do you mind if I use your toilet?' he asked.

Shaun examined him for a moment and then grunted: 'Upstairs, right ahead of you.'

Archie said thank you and then disappeared out of the room.

'I almost brought champagne,' Jessica said.

'What are you talking about?' Julie replied.

'I hear congratulations are in order?'

Julie glanced past Jessica towards her husband at the other side of the room. 'Congratulations?'

'A little birdy told me you're in the money – four point one five million. It must be party time…?'

It was a curious look that Julie sported. There was a hint of a defiant snarl with the curl to her lip, but the short, sharp peep towards her husband and the way she slipped towards the edge of the sofa and leant forward showed her nerves.

'Is this really the best use of police resources and taxpayers' money?' she said. 'I understand you were here because of what happened – but what does a private sale have to do with anything…?'

The old classic: 'taxpayers' money'. Jessica wondered why people used it. Whether it was the drunken credit-to-society-types stumbling along at three in morning complaining about 'harassment' or too-thick drivers who couldn't get their heads around a speed limit, people always arrived at the 'taxpayers' money' argument.

What did they think would happen? That a traffic officer would have a sudden change of mind? That after clocking someone doing forty-five past a primary school, the ticket would be ripped up because the officer decided that, yes, taxpayers' money could be assigned in a different way? Aside from out-and-out pig impressions, there were few things that made a police officer more inclined to deliberately piss someone off.

'Bit convenient, isn't it?' Jessica said.

'What is?'

'That Evie, your one remaining tenant, left the property a few weeks before the end of the year. Planning permission takes a bit of getting your head around, but, from what I understand, the company that paid you so much money would've had to reapply in the new year. That's more money, more time, more risk it could be denied. Might've cost you four million quid if this had dragged on. Tenants' rights can be a pesky thing.' She paused. 'Probably not so convenient that she died...'

Julie was frozen for a moment before her gaze flickered towards her husband once more. She pursed her lips and then spoke slowly and deliberately: 'What are you implying?'

With that, the sound of a flushing toilet echoed through the house. Archie's footsteps clumped down the stairs and then he appeared in the doorway, peering between the three of them. 'Did I miss much?' he asked.

Nobody answered as he took a seat next to Jessica, wiping his hands on his trousers.

'I'm not implying anything,' Jessica said. 'I'm simply pointing out the convenience.'

'I hardly think a young woman's death is convenient.'

'Me either. It's just that very interesting things have been happening with the other tenants of that house.'

'Like what?'

'Peter and Veronica are away on a cruise at the moment. Sounds nice – bit expensive, though. Sally's got a brand-new car. Not my kind of thing – bit too much pink going on – but each to their own. I do wonder where the money came from, though. Both went from a one-bedroom flat in one of your properties to living in bigger houses and being able to afford cars and cruises. In the meantime, you were happy to leave those rooms unoccupied, even though empty rooms are usually the worst nightmare for most landlords.'

'How is it our concern what our tenants do *after* they move out?'

'None, I guess. There are no laws about paying tenants to move out – but I bet you were confused about why Evie wouldn't simply take your money and go.'

Julie started to answer and then closed her mouth. She stared defiantly back to Jessica, almost daring her to continue.

'That flat was set up perfectly for Evie's blind son,' Jessica said. 'Why would she move? She'd spent all that time making it Samuel-proof that it would take something special for her to want to start again – especially as he's fourteen. It might have been different if he was a toddler. She didn't need the money, either. She had her own source of income...'

Jessica wondered if Julie would ask. She'd obviously be curious – but had no way of knowing about the way Owain Robinson was stumping up the money for Evie to do his books. Shaun and Julie would've seen Evie as an easy touch – an agency cleaner with a blind son. Of course she'd take the money.

Except she hadn't.

'Whose idea was the harassment?' Jessica asked. She pressed higher on the armchair, turning to look at Shaun behind her and then Julie in front. Shaun was staring unwaveringly at the computer monitor; Julie was glaring daggers at Jessica.

'I have no idea what you're talking about,' she said.

'Of course not. Strangers making noise, setting fires in the front yard... how odd that only happened outside Evie's place when all the other houses on the street were unaffected. Even that didn't put her off, though. She was determined to stay, despite the noise and trouble outside. She needed to be pushed further, an actual home invasion, two druggies bleating about money. Who wants that sort of thing around their blind son? I'd probably leave after that if it was me. Shame that Evie never got the opportunity...'

Julie swallowed, her façade beginning to slip as she fidgeted on the spot, uncrossing and recrossing her knees.

'How did you meet Donal Doherty?' Jessica asked.

There was a momentary spark in Julie's gaze, perhaps a

flinch. Nothing too extreme but a realisation that she wasn't as clever as she thought she was.

'Who?' she said.

'I'm guessing it was innocent enough,' Jessica said. 'You were probably taking out money from a cash machine and he asked if you had anything to spare. You probably said no and then had a thought – what if he wanted to make some real money? Real money to him, anyway. Twenty quid here or there – and then a hundred quid for a big job...?'

Julie wasn't even bothering to reply any longer. She was twiddling the heart necklace between her index finger and thumb.

'Interesting necklace,' Jessica added.

'Huh?'

'Donal Doherty died a couple of nights ago,' Jessica said. 'He probably choked on his own vomit after finding himself with something he shouldn't. The thing with junkies is that they always talk eventually. Donal obviously can't – but his friend could. I asked him about the person who'd paid them to give Evie a scare – and he described a necklace just like that...'

Julie let go of the necklace immediately and there was a flicker of fear across her face. Jessica had seen fear, she'd lived it herself – and Julie was riddled with it. Her bottom lip bobbed, her head rocked back, her chest rose with the deep intake of breath. She was trying to maintain eye contact, to keep up the intimidating glare, but there was little force to it any longer. She sucked hard on her lips and then spoke very slowly and deliberately.

'I have no idea who this Doherty man is – but even if anything you're saying was true, who would believe the word of some *junkie*?'

Jessica didn't reply. She sat still, looking between the photographs on the wall. There was Julie and Shaun on holiday somewhere sunny; Julie and Shaun on ski slopes; Julie and Shaun next to a lake.

'Don't you have something smart to say?' Julie was spitting poison, trembling with a mix of fear and anger.

'I think I'm done,' Jessica said.

Shaun's thick Scottish voice broke the impasse with a growl from the back of the room: 'I think it's time for you to go.'

'I was thinking that exact same thing.'

Jessica rose to her feet. Archie followed and they headed through the house and unlocked the front door. Neither Shaun nor Julie moved to see them out.

They didn't speak until they were back in the car and on the way back to the station.

'What was that all about?' Jessica asked.

'What?' Archie replied.

'The toilet break?'

'I needed a wee.' Archie paused and then added: 'I can't believe they're going to get away with it.'

'*Technically* they've not done anything wrong – certainly nothing that could be proven. Some homeless druggie mentions something about a heart necklace? We'd be laughed at. The bank's CCTV is long gone – and that's assuming Carl could give us a definitive day. He could ID her – but so what? Even if we had concrete evidence of Julie handing over money to Donal Doherty, she could say she was giving money to a beggar. What a kind act. She didn't know he'd break into Evie's apartment, nor that he'd spend whatever else on drugs. We've got nothing.'

'We could ask the other tenants to testify that they were paid to leave.'

'True – but Shaun and Julie wouldn't have to deny they offered Evie money. They could say they did but she turned it down. That's the end of that. The only thing that really matters is that Carl and Donal were in the apartment when

Evie died. Perhaps Julie gave Donal a key – but even that can't be proved because he's not here. That front door sticks, so they could've walked in, knocked on her apartment door and then barged in. Once they were inside, we don't even know if she slipped and hit her head, or if she was pushed. Samuel *couldn't* see it and Carl says he *didn't* see it. Everyone else is dead.'

Archie sighed. 'Assuming she gave him the money for the brown stuff, do you think Julie knew Donal would end up dead?'

Jessica stopped at a set of traffic lights and pulled up the handbrake. 'I doubt it,' she said. 'It was likely shut-up-and-go-away money, but who knows? She'll have a few days of worrying and then realise there's not much anyone can do to her. The four million will soften the blow. If Julie or Shaun are really worried, they'll get a solicitor – but the moment he or she looks at anything, it'll be obvious it's all coincidence and circumstantial.'

Archie bumped his head against the rest as he pressed back into the passenger seat. It looked like he'd done it on purpose.

'What?' Jessica asked.

'Nothing, just... that blind kid loses his mum and they get four million scot-free. It's bollocks, isn't it?'

Jessica didn't disagree. 'Not much we can do, Arch. Put the shits up them for a few days and hope they forget to get their car taxed in the future. I doubt they'll be around for much longer anyway. With four million in the bank, they'll be off to Alderley Edge or a town house in France.'

Archie sank lower in his seat and mumbled something Jessica didn't catch. Either way, she felt exactly the same.

FORTY-NINE

Jessica had parked the pool car outside Chatresh's house. Archie had been dropped back at the station to make a start on the paperwork – he was in a funny mood anyway. Jessica had work of her own to get on with, but she couldn't face it quite yet. She clambered out of the car and headed to the house once more. It had only been a week and a half previously that she'd been there clutching Chatresh's fake driving licence. If she'd asked the right questions then, Owain Robinson might still be alive.

Might.

Jessica didn't even know if it was Chatresh who'd gone after him. All they knew was that he'd turned up in Grimsby with a gun. He'd not been seen since.

She rang the doorbell and waited, tried banging the glass with her fist. It wasn't a surprise when nobody answered. She tried next door, finding a friendly old woman with a yappy little dog. The woman said the police had been round twice previously looking for Chatresh but that she couldn't help. She'd not seen him in a week or so and had rarely spoken to him anyway.

'It's such a shame,' she added. 'I try to get on with everyone on the street.'

'Are you saying he's not very friendly?' Jessica asked.

'I think he's just busy, love. You should see him rushing around all the time. Then he's carrying boxes in and out all day long. It's such a shame. When some of the neighbours go on holiday, I pull their curtains and turn the lights on and off for them. You can't be too careful nowadays.'

Jessica thanked the woman for her time and then mooched her way along the street, knocking on doors and generally asking questions that had already been asked and answered. Nobody knew where he was. She was on her way back to the car when she remembered how close the butty shop was. Past the 'for auction' house, down the alley and there it was.

Her stomach grumbled greedily at the thought of a bacon and sausage doorstop special. Heartburn be damned.

She was on her way past the auction house when she stopped to look at it properly. It was on the row opposite Chatresh's but a few doors down. The styles were exactly the same along the entire street, but this particular one had installed a set of rounded bay windows at the front to add a few thousand to the value. Jessica and Archie had walked past the house to get their lunch the first time she'd visited and thought nothing of it.

Jessica unlatched the creaky gate and headed along the path. She ignored the front door, heading for the window and cupping her hands over her eyes to peer inside. There were no curtains and the view was clear: a wide-open, empty living room with wallpaper peeling from the side walls. There was a bricked-up fireplace but little else to see.

She turned, facing Chatresh's house and the perfect view the house offered. From any of the front windows, whoever was inside would have an unobstructed view of Chatresh's place.

Jessica crossed to the front door of the empty house, checked over both shoulders for onlookers and then softly *squeezed* down the handle.

It didn't give.

The door was locked.

Jessica continued around to the side of the house, using a window frame to lever herself up to get over the gate. She dropped down on the other side and found herself in a garden that was beginning to look rough around the edges. The grass was growing into the soil flower beds, with mulchy leaves covering much of the rest of the area. She followed the path to the windows at the back of the living room and then pressed herself to the glass, peering all the way through the empty space to the garden at the front. She tried the handle of the back door, first pulling it gently and then much harder.

That door was locked, too.

Jessica inched backwards away from the house, moving onto the grass. Chatresh's passport hadn't left the country. He might have used a fake or found a way to smuggle himself out, but it didn't feel right. He had too much going on in the UK – plus, his brother had been arrested the day before. His only other family links were in Bangladesh, so where could he have gone? Rajiv had paid cash to stay in a hotel and Chatresh might be doing the same – except he'd need to stay in touch with what was going on in the area.

Her jacket pockets were a haven for rubbish and Jessica fumbled through them, sorting out various receipts and memos until she found the Post-it note Chatresh had given her with his number on. She took out her phone and dialled it, peering up at the house and listening for a ringtone. Her phone rang but there were no sounds from the house. It rang and rang and then went silent.

'It's Chat. I'm busy, so leave a message.'

Jessica hung up. Anyone sensible had their phone on

vibrate anyway. There were definitely a few points on the psychopath scale for those who left the sound up.

She tried the back door again but only got the same result. The entire house was locked. She could ask the estate agent to let her in, but what would be the point? If she couldn't get in, then who could?

Except...

Jessica levered herself back over the gate again, crossing the road and knocking on the little old lady's door. Her yapping dog was scratching at the door from the other side, barking its little head off until the door was opened.

'You're back,' the woman said.

'When I was here just now, you said you used to close curtains and switch lights on and off for neighbours who went on holiday,' Jessica said.

'Oh, I do, love.' She nodded towards the dog. It was some fluffy white breed that Jessica didn't know. 'I take Pipkin for a walk anyway, so it's my pleasure.'

Jessica pointed towards the empty house opposite. 'Did you know whoever lived there?'

'Of course. They were a lovely couple – Joanna and...' she clicked her fingers. 'Whatshisname...' She continued clicking and then shook her head. 'They're off to Australia. He got a job out there.'

'Did you look after their place when they went away?'

'I did, you know.'

'I don't suppose you still have the key, do you?'

The woman's smile slipped. 'Um... why would you want it?'

Jessica's warrant card was on a lanyard around her neck and she made certain it was showing. She angled her body to ensure the woman could see the parked police car. 'I thought I saw someone snooping around,' she said. 'I just want to double-check. I'll bring the key right back... assuming you have it...?'

'I might...'

She disappeared back along the hallway, leaving her dog to give Jessica the sideways stinkeye that she probably deserved. A few minutes later, the woman toddled back with a pair of keys.

'It's one of these,' she said, passing both over. 'Should I call someone?'

Jessica shook her head. 'It's fine – I'm sure it's nothing. I'll be back in a minute.'

Her heart was thumping as she headed over the road. She'd crossed a few lines in her time, but lying to an innocent old lady was a new one.

The first of the keys slipped straight into the front door and Jessica pushed her way inside. The smell of stale, dusty carpets immediately hit her, something old and discarded. Jessica pulled the door closed, feeling the old woman watching from the house opposite.

'Hello?' Jessica called. 'Chat?'

Her voice echoed up the stairs, through the empty house, reverberating back to her. It sounded shakier than she expected. Was she actually nervous?

Jessica moved past the stairs into the kitchen. There was a gap where the washing machine would have been, another where there was once a tall fridge-freezer. She checked a floor-to-ceiling cupboard, but it was empty except for an abandoned mop.

The stairs creaked as she made her way up; the banister wobbled. Onto the landing and it was still quiet. The first room was bare, not even a bed or carpet, so was the second. Into the bathroom, which was similarly untouched. Even the cupboards were left hanging open to expose the empty interior. Jessica was about to turn back to leave when she noticed the splashes of water around the sink bowl. It could have been a leaky tap... except the tap wasn't dripping.

The hairs on the back of her neck prickled.

She stepped back onto the landing. One more door to go. She'd left it until last because it was at the front, facing the street.

The door screeched loudly as she pushed it open and took a step back. She craned her neck, trying to peer inside. This room wasn't completely empty. There was a single bed. No sheets or covers, simply a mattress on a frame.

'Hello...?' she said.

Nothing.

Jessica paused as a floorboard squeaked under her foot. She eyed it suspiciously and then took a step forward, poking her head but not her body into the room.

It was empty.

She crouched, peeped under the bed.

Nothing.

Jessica finally breathed out and moved into the bedroom. She crossed to the window with a few quick steps and stared out towards the old woman's house.

She was in the living room window, glasses on, staring nervously across the road. When she spotted Jessica, she waved, so Jessica returned it with a dainty little crease of her fingers. Practising a royal wave in case she should ever get the big job of monarch and supreme leader.

It was unlikely.

She spun back, ready to return to the car – and that was when she bumped into Chatresh Lodi.

FIFTY

He had appeared from behind the door, knowing that there was no way he could go unseen once Jessica had turned.

Jessica leapt back, feeling the window sill pressing into her back. Chatresh stepped away, too – but he was between her and the door. He was a far cry from the photo of the man on the driving licence. His beard was long and ragged and he'd lost weight – even on his face. It didn't look like he'd eaten much in the past week and a half. The suit that would have once been designer smart was now hanging from him and there was a slice along one of the arms. It looked like he'd had it on for a while.

He held up his phone. 'You rang?'

Jessica pushed herself away from the window, making Chatresh take a step back. She stood tall and confident, unworried and definitely not a woman whose heart was thundering as quickly as a racehorse's hooves. 'Surely this place isn't as comfortable as your own house?' she asked.

He stared at her curiously. 'No...'

'How'd you get in? Key under a plant pot and you locked up behind you?'

'Something like that.'

She tried to take another half-step but this time Chatresh didn't shift and all she did was move closer to him.

'Did you kill Owain Robinson?' Jessica asked.

Chatresh stood firm, eyes narrow.

'We arrested Raj at the airport,' she added. 'We're waiting to find out if his wife and children are allowed to continue onto Bangladesh, but there's no decision through yet. Raj was travelling on a false passport, so he's not going anywhere soon.'

Chatresh flinched, shoulders drooping slightly. It was news to him.

'We also know about the Cork Brothers,' Jessica said. 'We know about the money. We know about Iain Jennings and the gun you had when you broke into his house – we have that on video. We know about the market stall, the debt – we know it all.'

His shoulders wobbled once more and then he crumpled slightly. He still stood tall over Jessica but there was no pretence of using it to bully her.

'It was all a mistake,' he said quietly.

'What was?'

'I need you to protect me,' he said.

'We can probably do that... but you must know how much trouble you're in...?'

A slight nod. 'It wasn't meant to happen like this. I said I'd get the money but they wanted it right away. I'm just a normal bloke. You see these sorts of things on TV, but I thought they'd be reasonable. I mean, they're going to get their money either way, aren't they? They just had to wait a while.'

It sounded like an argument he'd been having with himself for days, perhaps even weeks. It also didn't sound like he'd done any research on the people from whom he'd borrowed money.

'What did you do?' Jessica asked.

'It was just a few thousand.'

'How much is a few?'

'Twelve... well, at first. Then another twenty-five, then another forty. Seed money.'

A quick bit of mental arithmetic. Seventy-seven grand. No wonder the Corks wanted their money back. Chatresh must've been out of his mind.

'Didn't you make enough money to pay them back?' Jessica asked.

'It takes money to make money. Everybody knows that. That's what I tried to tell them. If they could just wait a bit, there'd be millions down the line.'

'Let me guess, the interest rates were a little higher than you expected.'

Chatresh threw his hands up, making Jessica step back. He didn't seem to notice. 'Exactly! I tried paying back the original twelve but they said I owed more like twenty. One thing led to another and then...'

'...And then Tomasz was kicked into a coma.'

Chatresh crept backwards, moving towards the door, his gaze not leaving Jessica's. 'I didn't know that was going to happen.'

'You could've told me when I knocked on your door.'

He sighed and ran a hand through his hair. 'Bit late now...'

'What did Owain Robinson say when you asked him for money?'

It was a bit of a jump but Jessica knew Chatresh felt the weight of what she was asking. He was in deep and would cop it for any number of things. Owain Robinson's death hadn't yet been linked to him.

'We found hairs,' she said. 'Black hairs.'

It wasn't true, not completely. Hairs *had* been found at the scene but no one had been identified because of them. Chatresh hadn't ever been arrested, so he wasn't in the DNA database. Even if there were hairs at the scene that belonged to him, no match would show up.

Chatresh was nodding slowly. 'It was Robbo's gun,' he said. 'He pulled it on me, said he didn't have the money to give me even if he wanted to. Told me to get out.'

'That sounds reasonable. People will believe you. *I* believe you.'

'I'd never seen a gun before, not a real one. I didn't know what to do.' His nose was twitching, bottom lip starting to go. 'I bet you've seen loads of guns, haven't you?' he added.

'Not really.'

'Has anyone ever pulled a gun on you?'

Jessica nodded, remembering the moment. It was hard to forget the booming thunder when the shotgun had gone off, the painful ringing in her ears, the disorientation of not actually knowing whether she'd been shot.

'Yes,' she said.

Chatresh seemed surprised. 'Oh... I wouldn't have thought...' He tailed off and then added, even more quietly: 'It's scary, isn't it?'

'At the time, it was the most frightening thing I'd ever faced.'

Despite the situation, there was a moment of solemn understanding between the two of them. Chatresh wasn't lying. Stories could be invented but the emotion couldn't.

'I thought he was going to shoot,' Chatresh said. 'He raised it and pointed it at my chest, said if he ever saw me again he'd shoot without thinking. I was trying to apologise. All I'd done was ask for money and then he'd pulled the gun. Said he'd seen rats like me before. That's the word he used.'

There was a tremble to his voice, a very real recollection.

'He said he'd put me down and then, well, I sort of went for him.'

'In what way?'

A shrug. 'Just kinda threw myself at him, I suppose. Figured if he was going to shoot anyway, I may as well go down fighting.'

'But he didn't shoot?'

'I don't know. We were fighting, just rolling around and then...'

Bang.

Chatresh didn't say it. He didn't need to.

'I swear it wasn't even me,' he added. 'I wasn't holding it. I've never shot a gun – not ever.'

'You did take it, though...'

'I figured if Fergus was going to come after me, I'd be able to make him see sense.'

'But instead you took it to Grimsby...?'

Chatresh must've wondered how exactly she knew. It was clear from the camera footage that he hadn't noticed he was being filmed. His left eye flickered with nerves, his right hadn't left her.

'Before he pulled the gun, Robbo said he bought the goods from a bloke who ran a fishing company in Grimsby named Jennings. He said that was where the money had gone. I just wanted to ask if he could lend me the money, but he wasn't even there when I went.'

'You were caught on camera,' Jessica said.

He nodded, surely knowing the game was up.

'If you work with us – you and Raj – we can make sure his wife and children are safe. We can take statements and look into the people you borrowed money from. It's all up to you. We can go now if you want? You can probably talk to Raj later...'

Jessica took a small step forward, hoping Chatresh would lead the way out of the bedroom. He was nodding as if agreeing but he hadn't moved.

'I like your vest,' he said.

Jessica peered down to her outfit. She was wearing a regular constabulary vest with all the bells, whistles, radio and pepper spray. The type of thing a uniformed officer would routinely wear on patrols. It was only there to make herself look more police-like while going up and down the street. Better than the regular suit jacket by itself.

'Is it bulletproof?' he added.

Jessica was far too slow. Chatresh reached into the waist-band at the back of his trousers and pulled out the gun. Whether it was Owain Robinson's didn't really matter – because it was being pointed at her. Jessica backed away, hands up, until the window sill was pressing into her back once more.

Chatresh gripped the weapon hard with both hands. His knuckles were white and his whole body was trembling.

'Chat—'

'All the bullets are still in there,' he said. 'All except one.'

He raised the gun, so it was pointing at her head. The handle was rattling against a ring on his finger as he continued to shake. His voice was a wobbly mess, but none of that mattered because he was so close that even a badly aimed shot would hit her.

'You don't have to do this, Chat. We can go downstairs and forget all about it.'

'No.'

'You can leave me here. Take my phone and my radio – and just go.'

She motioned to reach for her phone, but he screeched something that wasn't even a word. Whatever it was made her freeze, hand at her side.

'You're going to drive me,' he said.

'Where to?'

'I know an airfield in Lancashire. You're going to drive me there in your police car and then I'm going to fly myself out of here.'

FIFTY-ONE

Jessica did as she was told and walked calmly out of the house. The old woman from across the road was no longer in the window, which was just about typical.

Chatresh followed a short distance behind. Jessica didn't bother to look to see whether he still had the gun in sight. Even if he didn't, it would be close at hand and she could never get to him before he could pull it out.

She climbed into the driver's seat of the police car and clipped her seatbelt in. When Chatresh took his place next to her, he did the same and it was almost like they were off for a quiet cruise around the countryside. As soon as the door was closed, Jessica could see the weapon pointing sideways at her, sandwiched between his elbow and torso and hidden by his folded right arm. He was holding the gun in his left hand, index finger uncomfortably twitchy on the trigger. A rogue speed bump and it could all be over.

'You need to get on the M6,' he said. 'Follow it all the way to the final Preston junction and then get off and head towards Barton. It's all signposted. Can you do that?'

It didn't sound much like he was asking politely, especially when Jessica glanced sideways to see the muzzle of the gun still pointing at her.

Jessica started the car and checked her mirrors, doing everything normally. She pulled away slowly and stopped at the T-junction before edging into the traffic that was heading for the main road. It would be at least fifteen minutes before they got anywhere near the motorway, let alone the M6 itself. Fifteen minutes of stop-start, traffic-light-filled time for her to think.

'I'm not stupid, you know,' Chatresh said. He was stuttering.

'I never thought you were.'

'I want you to drive me straight up to the plane. No funny stuff. I've got the gun.'

'I can do that.'

Jessica wondered what his plan would be after that. Even if he managed to get the microlight into the air, it was hardly a fully fuelled jumbo jet. At best, she figured he might get to France or Ireland – but that was a guess. She had no idea how long those things could stay in the air for. She had to assume he knew more than her and that it was a viable option. He might have even thought it through far more than she gave him credit for. Perhaps there was a boat waiting for him on the Isle of Man? A second plane somewhere in the Highlands of Scotland?

Chatresh remained quiet as Jessica negotiated the Manchester traffic. She slowed for an amber light and stopped before it turned red, but he didn't tut angrily. With or without the gun, he was a better front-seat driver than Archie.

Jessica reached the M60 ring road after exactly quarter of an hour. She followed it towards the M62 westward link road, all while Chatresh sat low in his seat mumbling to himself but not to her.

'I'm on the M62 now,' Jessica said. 'We'll be on the M6 in about fifteen minutes.'

'I know.'

'Will the airfield know you're coming?'

'What?'

'I don't know how it works. Is your plane already there? Can you just get in it and go as if it's a car?'

'Don't worry about it. Just drive.'

Jessica did as she was told – at least for another minute.

'What's the name of the airfield?' she asked.

'What?'

'What's the airfield called?'

'Barton, I think. You can't miss it. Just drive.'

'How long will it take? I don't often drive up this way.'

Jessica didn't turn but she felt Chatresh glance to a watch, or perhaps his phone. 'Forty minutes.'

That was all Jessica needed to say. It was only a short while later and they were on the M6, heading north. The city of Manchester was quickly gone as they passed Haydock Racecourse and headed towards Wigan. Jessica slotted into the inside lane, got her speed up to sixty-five and then sat tight. A few miles passed, a few minutes – and then Chatresh noticed. Jessica had wondered whether he would.

'The road's really quiet,' he said.

'Is it? I don't usually drive during the day. I wouldn't know.'

He sat up straighter and she could feel him staring at her.

'What's going on?' he asked.

'What do you mean?'

The gun pressed into Jessica's ribs from the side, digging hard into a gap between the bones. 'What did you do?'

No point in lying about it now – he'd find out soon enough anyway. 'All these cars have trackers inside,' Jessica said. 'I couldn't have turned it off even if I wanted to.'

'But how would they know where you were going?'

The gun pushed even harder into her and Jessica yelped involuntarily.

'My radio,' she said.

Chatresh reached across and plucked the radio from her vest. 'This?!'

'It's broadcasting.'

'How long?'

'Since I got into the car.'

There was a gasp – this time from Chatresh as he realised why she'd been giving a running commentary of getting onto each motorway. He started to fumble around the front panel of the car and then the window hummed down, first hers – then his. Before she could say or do anything more, her radio was sent spinning through the passenger-side window and then both sheets of glass hummed back into place.

'Not broadcasting now, is it?' Chatresh snarled.

Jessica didn't trust herself to speak. She focused on the empty road ahead, keeping to the inside lane, her speed a constant sixty-five.

'If you stop the car, I'll shoot,' he said.

'Okay.'

'If anyone else tries to stop the car, I'll shoot.'

'Okay.'

'At the airfield, you're coming with me. If anyone tries to stop me taking the plane or does anything I don't like the look of, I'll shoot.'

He rammed the gun into her side to prove his point and Jessica squirmed with pain. She could feel the metal grinding against her ribs. The car drifted into the second lane and then she hauled it back into the first.

'Do you get it?'

'Yes.'

'DO YOU GET IT?!'

Chatresh was shouting, far angrier than Jessica had seen him before. The earnest moment of understanding between them from the bedroom was gone. There was a sign off to the left mentioning the upcoming services and then, in the distance, a concrete bridge that crossed from one side of the motorway to the other.

Jessica squeezed her foot onto the accelerator and the engine roared. Up to seventy-five.

'What are you doing?' Chatresh said. The gun had been away from her ribs momentarily but he pushed it into her.

Jessica didn't reply. She simply eased harder onto the accelerator, trying to inch away from the gun. The car swerved into the second lane.

Eighty-five.

'What are you doing?' he repeated.

'You can't shoot me,' Jessica said. She was shouting over the groaning wheeze of the engine.

'I will.'

'Shoot me at this speed and what happens then? I'm driving the car, remember.'

Chatresh pressed away and then, from nowhere, the gun was at her temple. She could almost see it in her peripheral vision but not quite. She squeezed the accelerator harder with her foot and felt the car vibrate through the pedal. Up to ninety. Halfway between the second and third lanes of the empty motorway.

'I'll shoot,' he said.

The fields on the side of the road were whipping past, one big blur of green.

'Do it. I don't have any kids. I'm not leaving anyone behind. What do you think will happen to you when I lose control at ninety miles an hour?'

The gun was gone.

Chatresh rocked into the passenger door and, for a

moment, Jessica thought he might try to open it and leap out. The carriageway was clear and she wondered where the tyre stinger and roadblock would be. It couldn't be far – perhaps another mile or two. Somewhere safely away from other people, other roads, more traffic. She was surprised they'd managed to set something up so quickly. She'd thought they'd be off the motorway and on the way to the actual airfield before she saw any signs of activity. Somebody had done some serious finger pulling out.

'Slow down.'

The gun wasn't touching Jessica but she could feel its presence somewhere close to her head. She said nothing.

'Slow *down!*'

Chatresh was far more forceful this time, but Jessica still didn't ease her foot away from the pedal. Even though the windows were closed, she could feel the rush of the earth, the pressure of the speed through the vehicle to her body. It felt as if her seat was vibrating. It might have been – but there was every chance she was trembling, too. She'd told Chatresh that having a gun pointed at her once before was the scariest thing she'd ever faced. It was true – but only up until that point in her life. She'd got past that and been even more frightened since. But this... this was something else. The speed, the adrenalin, even the gun, perhaps.

The engine whined its way up towards a hundred miles an hour.

'Slow—'

Chatresh didn't get to finish whatever he was going to say. The bridge was approaching at a dazzling speed, so fast that it almost felt like slow motion. Jessica could see the scene with crystal clarity. With her left hand, she reached into the well between the seats – and with her right, in a perfect piece of symmetry, she wrenched the steering wheel hard to the right.

She closed her eyes. She was going to die anyway, right? At least she could do it on her own terms.

Glass shattered, metal twisted, tyres screeched: an almighty, dizzying crescendo of machine and concrete.

The car hadn't slowed as it hurtled unwaveringly into the bridge's central pillar. Jessica thought she heard glass smashing, but it was hard to know. Perhaps she'd passed out before then. Perhaps it was only the final thoughts before the blackness arrived.

Then there was silence.

FIFTY-TWO

Jessica was sitting on a low wall. The harsh corners of the bricks were digging into her backside – but she barely registered that pain.

Izzy pointed to Jessica's shoulder. 'Does it hurt there?'
'Yeah.'

Her other shoulder. 'What about there?'
'Can you just assume it hurts everywhere?'

Izzy patted her own breastbone. 'What about there?'
'I'm officially ignoring you.'

Izzy swung her legs and climbed off the wall, spinning around to get a proper look at Jessica. 'What's the damage?'

'Minor bruising, minor scratches, sore arse, sore boobs from the seatbelt, mild case of sarcasm, large dose of boredom from spending thirty hours in the same bed.'

'Is that it?'

Jessica's left arm was in a sling but her right was free. 'I poked myself in the eye when I was trying to get my top over my head.'

'Came off a bit better than Chatresh, though...'

Izzy plonked herself back down on the wall and took out her phone. She checked something and then repocketed it.

'How long until your taxi gets here?' she asked.

'I don't know, it's a taxi – he said ten minutes so it'll probably be about an hour.'

'The guv doesn't know I'm here. I said I had a witness to interview for that community centre break-in.'

Jessica rested her head on Izzy's shoulder for a moment and then groaned her way back into a sitting position. 'That hurt,' she said.

'I can take you home if you want. Sod the taxi off, tuck you up in bed. I'm sure Caroline will put some tea on for you.'

'I've got to go to Moston Vale.'

Izzy didn't say anything at first, she simply kicked her feet out in front of her as if she was on a swing. 'Could Professional Standards not give it a few days?' She nodded to the building behind them. 'You've only just got out of hospital. I mean *literally* just got out. You've not even been home yet.'

'I told them I'd go,' Jessica replied firmly. She hadn't actually thought they'd say yes, but then Professional Standards were an absolute bunch of bastards, so it wasn't a complete surprise.

'You know what they're like,' Jessica continued. 'If you're not dead, they want a report.'

'What did the guv say?'

Jessica stared ahead, focusing on a tree and refusing to look anywhere else. Some kid was trying to climb it but wasn't having a lot of luck. He was clinging to the lowest branch with all four limbs.

'Not much. What can you do when your passenger jabs you in the ribs with a gun? The car swerved. I don't even remember hitting the bridge. He should've been wearing a seatbelt.'

Izzy said something in reply but Jessica missed it. The kid

had hauled himself up onto the lowest branch and was reaching for the one above him. His friends were at the base, egging him higher.

'Sorry,' Jessica said, 'I didn't hear any of that.'

'I tried to talk to you last night,' Izzy said, 'but you were smacked off your face on whatever painkillers they gave you. Shaun and Julie Viceroy's house was raided. I thought you should know.'

Jessica turned to Izzy, assuming it was some kind of weird joke, or that she'd misheard. 'Raided? Why? I was only there two days ago.' She paused. 'It *is* two days, isn't it?'

'Anonymous tip,' Izzy said. 'The person said they were dealing class-A drugs. Gave very specific information, so the warrant was issued.'

'Class-A drugs? What are you on about? They just got four million from selling a house.'

'I don't know – but, lo and behold, the boys came out with a giant bag of brown stuff that was hidden in the toilet cistern. They're denying all knowledge, got some hotshot solicitor on the case, but whaddyaknow? The search team was in there all night ripping up the floorboards.'

Jessica stared at Izzy, aware her mouth was hanging open but unable to do anything about it.

'How many drugs are *you* on?' Izzy asked. 'I've don't think I've ever seen you lost for words.'

'I don't know what to say.'

Izzy dug into her pocket and pulled out her phone. 'I'm going to have to record this. No one will ever believe me.'

Jessica batted her away and went back to staring at the kid climbing the tree. He was even higher now, scampering upwards like a baby orang-utan.

'That's for you,' Izzy said. She lifted herself off the wall and Jessica turned to see a taxi pulling in. 'Are you all right?' Izzy added. 'You've gone white. I can take you back inside...'

Jessica cut her off with an overly sharp 'I'm fine', for which she immediately apologised.

She was in the back of the taxi when she finally managed to blink back into something close to reality. She'd been given her possessions in a box when leaving the hospital and, somehow, her phone had survived the crash.

She turned it on. The battery was dwindling but there was enough to scroll through the contacts and hover over Archie's name.

FIFTY-THREE

'What did you do?'

Jessica and Archie were sitting on a bench in Moorside Park. It was a short walk from her house, not too much further from where Tomasz had been found two life-changing weeks ago.

It *felt* like a lifetime.

Despite the 'minor' bruising – *minor, my arse* – Jessica's neck was burning with pain. She could barely turn from one side to the other.

The bench was in the middle of the park, away from prying eyes and curious ears. Away from anyone. It was dusk and beginning to get cold. Anyone sensible was inside.

'How'd it go at Pro Standards?' Archie asked.

'Don't change the subject – what did you do?'

'What do you mean?'

'I heard about Shaun and Julie, the anonymous tip-off and the bag of' – she lowered her voice and hissed the words – '*you-know-what* in their toilet cistern.'

'Oh,' he said, 'that.'

'Tell me it wasn't that bag we found near Donal's body.'

Jessica couldn't turn to look at him even if she wanted to – which she most definitely did not. She'd been waiting for him to get off work, unable to walk much further.

Archie didn't reply. He was fidgeting on the bench, perhaps plucking up the courage.

'Well?' she demanded.

'It's not as simple as that.'

'Not as simple as what? I told you to chuck it down a drain or flush it down the toilet, not hide it down the back of someone's toilet.' She paused, corrected herself. '*Plant* it,' she said. '*Plant* it down the back of someone's toilet.'

Archie was silent.

'I've just spent an afternoon with Professional Standards,' Jessica said. 'I'm back there tomorrow if I can heave myself out of bed. Going over minute by minute how I stumbled across Chatresh without telling anyone. How I turned around and he was bloody there. Telling them about the gun and the car. I do all that and, meanwhile, you've gone and done this.'

She wanted to clap her hands together to make her point but the sling was still in place.

'You know I have to report this, don't you?' she added. 'It's too much.'

Jessica expected a swift reply. Perhaps anger, more likely an explanation. She didn't get any of that. Archie had frozen on the spot and she forced herself to twist around until she could see him. Arcs of pain jolted through her neck as she got into a position where she could see side on. Archie was resting against the back of the bench, arms crossed.

'You can't,' he said quietly.

'I really can.'

'You can't.'

He spoke with such solid authority that Jessica felt like giving him a damned good whack to remind him he was a constable. A sodding constable!

'Why not?' she asked.

Archie was biting his lip, not looking at her and not speaking.

'Look,' Jessica said, trying something a little more conciliatory, 'I know they were going to get away with it but—'

'What happened to Chat's seatbelt?'

Jessica closed her mouth and the two of them stared at each other. He was sometimes hard to read – especially recently when it felt like he had a split personality – but there was no doubt now. This was the real Archie. The Manchester estate kid who deep down was only ever a step or two away from working on the other side of the law.

The *wrong* side.

He was snarling, ready for a ruck.

She could see the way he'd fought his way through various schools – the little lad being picked on who had to show his classmates that he could look after himself.

The lad about town, the cheeky chappie, the football nut.

He was none of that, not really. He would always be the miniature brick shithouse from a broken home in broken Britain.

'What do you mean?' Jessica replied. She heard her own voice waver.

'Simple question: what happened to Chatresh's seatbelt?'

'He wasn't wearing one.'

'It was half around his arm when he went through the windscreen.'

'I don't know what you're talking about, Arch. He jabbed the gun into my ribs. I can show you the bruises if you want.'

Jessica motioned to do just that, but her top snagged on her sling and she couldn't get her arm that high anyway.

'What about that money you gave Donal Doherty?' Archie said. 'Got him to call it in when his mate turned up – then it turned out he was the one we were after all that time.'

Archie was talking with a cocky growl. Like United had given City a four–nil pasting and he couldn't contain himself.

'I didn't know. It's hardly the same as what you did.'

Archie was nodding along, tongue in the corner of his mouth. 'I know... it's just... you don't even realise...'

'Realise what? You think I wanted that?'

'They were going to get away with it. I thought' He stopped and took a breath. 'Do you know how many times I've nearly told you? How often I wanted five minutes of your time but you were too busy? Or when we were alone but it wasn't right?'

'What are you talking about?'

Archie was on his feet in a flash, standing in front of her and then pacing back and forth. He was taking long, deep breaths; fists balled as if building himself up for a boxing entrance.

'Arch—'

'You know when I was brought back from suspension?'

'After the collision?'

He stopped, stared at her. 'It wasn't a collision, Jess. I killed a man. Ran the poor bastard over.'

'It wasn't your fault. You know that.'

Archie shook his head. 'You know I was brought back after that, but it was all a bit quick.'

'There was a bomb scare – we needed bodies.'

Another shake of the head. 'Professional Standards wanted me to do something for them. I said no. I kept saying no, but they kept going and going. Told me my career was over. Over before it began. Do you know what that's like? What I gave up to do this? The friends I left? The mates I grew up with who won't even look at me, let alone talk? Do you know what that's like?'

He was back to pacing and it sounded like he was pleading

with her. Jessica saw tears in his eyes. He'd never been like this before.

'Arch—'

'I told them I'd do it, Jess. I walked out of the room back on the job but knowing I was done.'

Incy-wincy spider crept along Jessica's back and she could do nothing but shiver. Her shoulder jolted and she bit her lip to send away the pain.

'What did they ask you to do?'

Archie stopped pacing, looked at her, said nothing and then started again. He couldn't say. He'd never been able to.

'*Me?*' Jessica whispered.

Archie stopped.

'They want *me*?' she said.

From nowhere, Jessica's head was flooded with everything she'd done in her career. A shed she'd broken into, the illegal boxing match she was at, the breaking and entering that had led her to a kidnap victim.

Scott Dewhurst.

A line that had been crossed and could never be uncrossed.

The end justified the means in all those cases and yet... DCI Cole had chosen to resign rather than work with her.

He'd been right – because look at what was happening now.

'Is this why you asked me about the money in Evie's apartment?' Jessica asked.

Archie nodded, tears still forming underneath his eyes. 'I'm sorry,' he whispered as he dropped back onto the bench next to her, head in his hands.

They sat for a couple of minutes, maybe more, staring towards the darkest edges of the park as the sun disappeared for the day. There was a gentle hum of traffic, but that was it.

'What now?' Jessica eventually said.

'What do you mean?'

'I mean just that – what now?'

'I thought you'd be angry. You'd never want to talk to me again and all that. Call me a Judas, a traitor.'

Jessica closed her eyes and allowed her neck to roll backwards until she was staring up. It was almost comfortable. 'I think it's been a long time coming, Arch. Do they want me to resign or do they want me in prison?'

Archie snivelled a sob up through his nose. 'Honestly? I really don't know.'

FIFTY-FOUR

'So out of the two of us,' Samuel said, 'I'm the blind one and yet *you've* got your arm in a sling?'

Jessica rubbed at her wrist. Caroline had helped replace the bandage that morning but it was itching badly. 'That is pretty much it,' she replied.

Professional Standards had finally finished their second day of waterboarding her and then packed her off home in a taxi. She'd given the driver Deborah's address.

'What did you do to it?' he asked.

'I was in a car accident.'

'My mum used to say people were always driving too fast. "In a rush with no time to flush," she said – although I think that was because she was a cleaner.'

'I was probably going too fast,' Jessica replied.

'Does it hurt?'

'No more than I deserve.'

Samuel didn't seem to know what to make of that. He smiled at her, probably thinking she'd made a joke and he should laugh. If she was honest, his milky eyes had made her feel a little creeped out at first, but now she thought they suited him. It made him mysterious – which worked with his personality. Even now, even after everything he'd been through, there was a mischievous, adventurous streak. She wondered if he'd ever tried to climb a tree. She was certain he could manage it.

Samuel turned towards the door and fired off a quick pair of clicks. Jessica spun but then remembered how much pain she was in. There was no one there anyway.

'I know I promised I'd let you know when we found the second man who was in your apartment that night,' Jessica said, 'but it's been a surreal time.'

'The crash?'

'Right... and other things.'

It felt like Samuel was staring through her, as if those eyes were some sort of lie detector. 'Who is he?' Samuel asked.

'He was called Donal, a drug addict. He was found dead in an alley a few days ago.'

'But you're sure it was him?'

'We're sure.'

Samuel nodded acceptingly. 'And the other man will be in court?'

'He will.'

'Did either of them say sorry?'

Jessica couldn't look at Samuel any longer. It wasn't anything to do with his appearance, it was her. All her. She should lie and say 'yes', but, in truth, it was a question she'd never asked. Was Carl Doherty sorry? She didn't know.

'No,' she replied.

Samuel nodded once more and then reached to the side of the sofa. His fingers fumbled and then grasped his laptop.

'Do you mind if I play my game now?' he asked.

Jessica stood, saying she didn't mind at all. She had one final look at the boy and then headed into the kitchen, quietly and deliberately clicking the door closed behind her.

Deborah was there, on her knees, scrubbing the back of the oven. She turned to see Jessica, but then twisted back to the oven and continued. She was wearing pink rubber gloves and there was a slim stream of sudsy water around her knees.

'Thanks for coming by,' she said. 'Do you need showing out?'

Jessica perched on a stool and didn't reply. After a few more energetic scrubs, Deborah turned to look at her. She dropped the wiry sponge in a bowl and then sat back on her knees.

'I'm thinking of applying for adoption,' she said. 'It's not a common thing because he's nearly fifteen. He'll be a full adult soon enough. I'm not sure what to do, but it's not like I can leave him by himself.'

Jessica tried to wriggle her shoulder into a more comfortable position but her body wasn't having it. *Minor* bruising. *Minor*. What on earth counted as major nowadays? Did she actually have to have her arm amputated?

'How did you spend the money?' she asked softly.

Deborah was silent.

'I didn't clock it right away,' Jessica said. 'Perhaps it was the car crash that gave my brain the jolt.'

It was a long time before Deborah spoke, but Jessica wasn't about to stand up and walk out. 'How'd you know?' she whispered.

'Those little things around Evie's house. The tap that was broken, those sockets with the loose screws. The light that didn't work. S*mall* things. I didn't know Evie – but one thing I do know is that she was very safety-conscious. She would've had those things fixed – which means they kept happening, almost as if the house was falling apart around her...'

Deborah's head dipped. She pulled off one of the gloves and then the other, pressing back against the open oven and leaving herself sitting in the pool of mucky water.

'How much did Julie Viceroy pay you?' Jessica asked.

She wasn't sure if she expected an answer but it came straight away anyway. A sad, sincere confession. 'Five hundred.'

Jessica left it to linger. How much had Evie's life been worth? A couple of hundred quid or so to Carl and Donal, five hundred to her best friend.

'They were offering Evie thousands to move out,' Deborah said with a glance to the doorway. 'She wouldn't take it. Said she was happy where she was because Samuel felt safe there. I couldn't believe it. I was telling her to take the money but she said she didn't need it. That's when I started wondering about her second job. She never told me what it was, I swear.'

Jessica believed her. Not that it mattered.

'I was on my way out one day when this woman was pulling up. I didn't know her but she said she was Evie's land-lady. We had this little joke, "I can't believe she's turning down all this money" and that. Nothing serious. I asked why she wanted Evie out and she said it wasn't like that. They were trying to get out of the letting business and it was easier to sell an empty house than one with tenants. It sounded fair enough.'

'That's when she offered you five hundred quid?'

Deborah wriggled and Jessica could hear the squelch.

'She said she'd give me five hundred quid to change Evie's mind. I couldn't see the harm. Evie would still get her money and I'd get a bit, too. I tried talking her round, saying Samuel would be happier in a bigger place, that she'd be able to protect him wherever they moved. She kept saying she liked it there, that it was close to Samuel's school and all that. She wouldn't listen!'

Deborah almost shouted the last sentence. She eyed the door to the living room and waited.

Samuel did not appear.

'So you started fiddling with things in the flat?' Jessica said.

'Not big things...' Deborah pushed herself to her feet. 'You're not going to tell him, are you?'

'Samuel?'

'Everything I said about adoption is true. I didn't know all this would happen...'

'You knew the landlords wanted Evie out and that they'd go as far as to offer her best friend money. When someone broke into her flat, what did you think had happened?'

'I don't know.'

'You could've told me this two weeks ago.'

'I know! I wish I had. It's just...' She gazed towards the door.

Samuel.

'What are you going to do?' she asked.

Jessica eased herself off the stool, bit her lip to stop herself wincing at the pain in her shoulder.

'*Please*,' Evie said. 'Please don't tell him. I didn't mean for this to happen. I really want him to stay. He needs someone. He needs—'

'A mother.'

Deborah bowed her head. 'Let me make it up to him. Please.'

FIFTY-FIVE

Jessica was sitting on the toilet when her phone rang. The caller was unknown, but after the week she'd had, that meant she should probably answer it.

It was a man's voice: 'Jessica?'

'If you're calling in your favour,' Jessica replied, 'you should probably know that I'm off on the sick. I'm a drain on society.'

'Oh,' Andrew Hunter said. 'I did *not* know that. Are you okay?'

'It's nothing really. *Minor* bruising. Bloody minor bruising? Can you believe that? *Minor?*'

Andrew laughed: 'You sound as if you've taken it well. Are you definitely all right?'

'I'm alive and, for now, I'll take that.'

He sniggered awkwardly, unsure if it was a joke.

'I really can't do you a favour right now,' Jessica added. 'I'm not being funny, I'm just not at work.'

'I'm not after a favour.'

'Oh...'

'Do you remember that you asked me to look into someone named Mark King?'

Jessica sat up straighter, forgetting her knickers were around her ankles. 'Give me a minute,' she said.

It took the full minute as well. The sling had been discarded the night before but that didn't mean Jessica's shoulder and arm were working properly. She struggled to get her pants back up and then lowered the toilet seat to use it as a chair. She was naked aside from her underwear. That left her shivering – which only made the pain in her shoulder worse. She really needed better painkillers. Co-codamol wasn't hacking it. If things hadn't been such a rush the night before, she'd have brought a change of clothes. Still, that would've spoiled the spontaneous, illicit thrill of it all.

It had been a long time. A *really* long time.

Jessica picked her phone back up and apologised. 'Didn't I say to forget that name?' she snapped.

'You did,' Andrew replied. He hadn't picked up on her tone. 'It's just, well... I suppose my interest was piqued. I figured I'd do a quick job, ditch the results, no harm done. Practice, if nothing else.'

Those tingles were back once more. Jessica peered to the unfamiliar door in the unfamiliar bathroom. It was far larger than the one in her house, much neater as well. Full of man things, of course – but then it was a man's bathroom.

'What did you find out?' she asked.

Andrew cleared his throat. 'Here's the thing, were you asking for personal or professional reasons?'

'Why?'

'It's just... if it's personal, sometimes it's better not to know the truth.'

Oh, God.

'Truth about what?'

'I need to ask you a really important question,' Andrew replied. 'Perhaps we should do this in person?'

'No!' Jessica had spoken too loudly. She leapt off the toilet to make sure the door was locked. It was. 'Tell me now,' she hissed.

'Are you sure you want to know? You can't un-remember something.'

Before Jessica could answer, there was a knock on the door and a man's voice called through to her: 'Jess?'

Jessica clamped a hand over the bottom of her mobile. 'Just a minute,' she replied, trying to sound chirpy and happy.

'I thought I heard you talking to someone.'

'Just, er, talking to myself I guess.'

'Right.' A pause. 'Are you coming back to bed?'

He sounded playful and it was no wonder after what they'd been up doing most of the night, dodgy arm or no dodgy arm.

'Jess?'

'I'll be there in a minute.'

Jessica heard Mark's footsteps padding along the corridor. She waited until she was certain he was back in the bedroom and then she turned back to her phone. She held it to her ear and listened.

'Jess?' Andrew's voice asked. His tinny voice clamoured from the small speaker. 'Are you still there?' A pause. 'Jess?'

THE GIRL WHO CAME BACK

Thirteen years ago Olivia Adams went missing. Now she's back... or is she?

When six-year-old **Olivia Adams** disappeared from her back garden, the small community of Stoneridge was thrown into turmoil. How could a child vanish in the middle of a cosy English village?

Thirteen years on and Olivia is back. Her mother is convinced it's her but not everyone is sure. If this is the missing girl, then where has she been - and what happened to her on that sunny afternoon?

If she's an imposter, then who would be bold enough to try to fool a child's own mother – and why?

Then there are those who would rather Olivia stayed missing. The past is the past and some secrets *must* remain buried.

THE WIFE'S SECRET

Charley Willis was thirteen years old when her parents were killed in their family home and she was found hiding in a cupboard upstairs.

Fifteen years later, Charley is marrying Seth Chambers. It should be the happiest day of their lives, a chance for Charley to put her past behind her, but just hours after the ceremony, she is missing.

No one saw her leave. No one knows where she is.

One thing is for certain... Seth is about to discover he doesn't really know the woman he just married. And his nightmare is only just beginning.

Printed in Great Britain
by Amazon

61341242R00203